FASTENED TO THE MARSH

A SAVANNAH SAGA

fastened to the marsh
a savannah saga

jan durham

BONAVENTTURE
books
SAVANNAH

To Joan!
A sister in
the faith and
the fiction.
Fondly,
Jan.
2/12/08

Cover photo by Bryan Stovall

Author photo by Lorna Cross

Library of Congress Cataloging-in-Publication Data

Durham, Jan, 1943-
   Fastened to the marsh : a Savannah saga / Jan Durham. -- 1st ed.
      p. cm.
   ISBN-13: 978-0-9724224-7-5 (alk. paper)
   ISBN-10: 0-9724224-7-1 (alk. paper)
1. Savannah (Ga.)--Fiction. 2. Domestic fiction. I. Title.

PS3604.U734F37 2008
813'.6--dc22

                                    2007046636

First Edition, Jan 2008

For Sam and Heather

Acknowledgments

Thanks to my husband Sam and daughter Heather whose support made the book possible, to my high school English teacher Mrs. Beulah Harper Nettles whose inspiration made it necessary, and to members of the Landings Writers' Group, and Rosemary Daniell who encouraged me to keep writing.

As the marsh-hen secretly builds on the watery sod,

Behold I will build me a nest on the greatness of God:

I will fly in the greatness of God as the marsh-hen flies

In the freedom that fills all the space 'twixt the marsh and the skies:

By so many roots as the marsh-grass sends in the sod

I will heartily lay me a-hold on the greatness of God...

From "The Marshes of Glynn"
Sidney Lanier

DESCENDANTS OF
ELIZABETH BRINSON LEIGH CRAWFORD

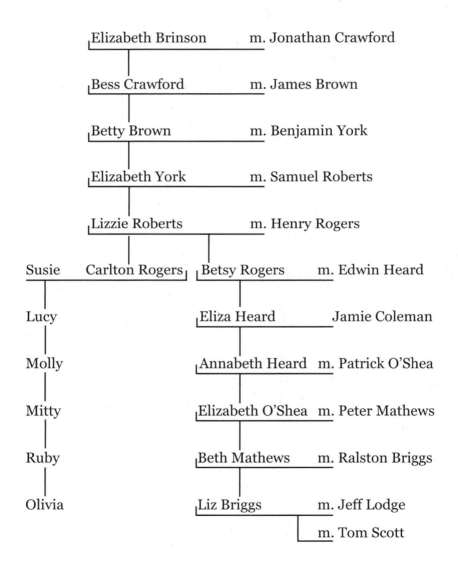

Elizabeth Brinson   m. Jonathan Crawford

Bess Crawford   m. James Brown

Betty Brown   m. Benjamin York

Elizabeth York   m. Samuel Roberts

Lizzie Roberts   m. Henry Rogers

Susie   Carlton Rogers   Betsy Rogers   m. Edwin Heard

Lucy   Eliza Heard   Jamie Coleman

Molly   Annabeth Heard   m. Patrick O'Shea

Mitty   Elizabeth O'Shea   m. Peter Mathews

Ruby   Beth Mathews   m. Ralston Briggs

Olivia   Liz Briggs   m. Jeff Lodge

                               m. Tom Scott

PART ONE

THE HOMECOMING

Skidaway

The verdant sea of marsh grass stretched to the horizon on both sides of the causeway. A shrimp boat lumbered its way through the narrows returning from the Atlantic Ocean, the nets extending like huge wings over the water. Soaring above the wake, seagulls screamed in frenzied excitement as they followed, hoping for a free meal. The mid-June sun was high overhead, its burning rays beginning to sting her bare shoulders as the last miles to her destination slipped by. Knowing she should stop and put up the top on her convertible, Liz Scott rejected the idea and continued to drive, singing along with The Platters as they crooned "Only You" on the radio.

Why have an expensive little 450 SL if you couldn't enjoy it? She'd certainly contributed her share to the firm's profitability and it was nobody's business if she blew her money on a gleaming silver little sweetheart of a car. At this stage of her life, she might as well live with abandon. What did it matter anyway? No one depended on her now except maybe Thomas, her cat.

She reached for the recorder she kept in her car to jog her memory. "Sunscreen and aloe," she said, then turned the radio louder as the continual string of beach music blared from the dash. Mocking her grandmother's words, she called to a seagull overhead, "Can't have any of those lower class freckles marring my 'to the manor born' complexion."

Fumbling for the bag of corn chips next to the recorder, Liz thought, *You really are letting yourself go, old girl! When was the last time you allowed yourself to consume a whole bag of these fat-laden things? Oh, well. You can do extra sets at the gym when you get back home.*

A mournful sound came from the pet carrier strapped in the

passenger seat. A definitely discontented face peered through the grid. Thomas' half-closed blue eyes below flattened gray ears indicated his displeasure with his prolonged confinement. In the habit of selecting the best seat in the house for his frequent naps, the huge Himalayan cat resented being in the confining and uncomfortable carrier. He also disliked the hot breeze that disturbed his fur and made an unsettling noise. His low growl was meant to remind his human of his irritation.

"I know you're unhappy, Thomas, but we're almost there. Not much longer. You're going to love it, I promise. You can go outdoors and chase the birds, sleep in the sun, do whatever you please and no one will complain."

Thomas did not respond. He was not exactly the outdoorsy type.

"Okay, I know you don't like to travel but we'll be back home by the end of the month. From what Olivia says, Grandmother is near the end. After the funeral and the legal papers, I'll put the place on the market and we'll hit the road back to Atlanta. I had to come. I'm her only heir," Liz's words were directed toward herself as much as the cat.

The feline repositioned himself as best he could in his cramped quarters in order to concentrate on taking a nap. He growled once more in annoyance and closed his eyes.

You are losing it. Explaining to a cat! Shaking her head, she turned her attention back to the road.

The air was heavy with the humidity that goes along with summer in coastal Georgia. *Boy, it must be off the charts today,* she thought as she ran her fingers through her short copper curls. Laughing sarcastically, she recalled the repetitive forecast of the local TV weathercasters—H, H, H meaning hot, hazy, and humid. *So many years and nothing ever changes on this island—not even the weather.*

The moment of levity passed quickly, however, as the acrid smell of the marsh assailed her senses and a rush of emotions whirled through her mind. She thought again about the circumstances of her reluctant return.

Though approaching her sixty-third birthday, and something

of a legend in the Atlanta legal world, Liz felt herself slipping back to her painful childhood. Memories of an orphaned child reared by a stoic grandmother hardened by the seeming injustices of her own life sent a chill through her body.

Anger once more surfaced, distorting her face as she steeled herself to deal with the task that awaited her—keeping a deathwatch over the woman who had provided for her physical needs after her parents' death but had made no attempt to give her the love a bewildered child craved. Even the way Liz was required to address her—not Nana or Gran or any of the affectionate titles children dub their doting grandparents but "Grandmother"—had established early on a formal relationship between them.

As her grandmother had preferred to spend her days with her memories and her bitterness, Liz had been cared for by Mittie, a descendant of the freed slaves who once worked the plantation before the Civil War then stayed on as hired hands rather than try to survive in an alien world. Since Mittie's death, Olivia—her granddaughter and Liz's childhood playmate—had nursed the ancient bed-ridden woman.

At least it would be pleasant to visit with Olivia and recall their girlish antics while they waited for the inevitable. According to Olivia, her grandmother was now in an advanced stage of dementia, never leaving her bed and spending her waking moments calling to the shadows as they closed in on her. At 106 years of age, how much longer could it be?

Crossing the bridge to the island, Liz saw evidence that the modern world had finally reached the secluded sanctuary of Skidaway Island. Where once stood only docks in various states of disrepair leading from the water to spacious homes half-hidden beneath ancient oaks, several high-rise condos now intruded. Liz could just hear what her grandmother would rail if she were still living in the real world, "A commercial blight on the unspoiled beauty of the island." Elizabeth Mathews never liked for anything to change. Well, things were changing now. The last generation was dying off and new heirs were somewhere sunning themselves on trendier beaches, having profited handily from the sale of a deceased relative's home place.

Liz planned to follow their lead. She would return to Atlanta as soon as the funeral was over, the will probated, and the paperwork completed. As the only heir to an estate that had been occupied by descendants of the original settlers of the island for over two hundred years, there would be no problem with changing the documents to her name and then listing the property. In the closed circle of Savannah society, word would spread like wildfire. Ambitious agents who daily pored over the local obituaries would be swarming around the door, jockeying to represent her with the eager developers who competed with voracious appetites for the dwindling supply of waterfront property in the low country. And what a trophy Marsh Oaks would be—300 acres of pristine marsh paradise ripe for exclusive condominiums, hotels, and marinas already languishing on project boards, just waiting for elderly property owners to die and the heirs to cash in.

As she turned on to the long oak-lined road leading to the old house, she tried to pinpoint just how long it had been since she had been to the island—ten years, fifteen? She had left as soon as she could with no opposition from her "loving" grandmother who was glad to write the checks that would allow her own privacy again. She attended Emory University where she received a degree in political science, then blazed through law school before landing a position in Atlanta with a prestigious firm that provided a plausible reason to be absent from the island for long periods. Soon even the annual Christmas visit was replaced with expensive gifts delivered from a catalog, a phone call, and feigned regrets. For a few more years, she maintained a "decent" relationship through obligatory cards and gifts but, as her grandmother's memories began to overpower her realities, even that requirement was waived. One less meaningless task she rationalized but sometimes she still felt a nudge of guilt— or was it remorse? Was she somehow still grieving for the love she had been denied as a child?

Don't be ridiculous! She had had enough woes in her adult life to overshadow her childhood angst. Her freedom and independence had been costly, but with her usual perseverance, she had discarded her past and carved a new identity for herself in a world her provincial grandmother could never have imagined.

Although she'd had some rough spots on the road, she'd done all right even if she did say so herself! She had loved and been loved and, even though now she was alone again, she was content with her life.

Everything had been under control, just the way she liked it, until a letter arrived from Olivia. Long a victim of Alzheimer's disease, her grandmother had recently suffered a series of strokes and the doctor felt her heart could not hold out for long, a few weeks at the most. As executor of the will, she would have legal responsibilities after her grandmother's death, but Olivia thought Liz might want to see her grandmother again before she died. Olivia had never stopped trying to engineer a reconciliation between the two people she now loved most in the world. Thus far, Liz had resisted all her efforts.

Liz remembered holding the letter in her hand as she stared out the window of her condo at the drizzling rain. Did she really want to see her grandmother after all these years? The old woman certainly wouldn't know her now, and even if she did, they had never been close. Why should she waste valuable time in that gloomy atmosphere, waiting like a vulture for her to breathe her last? She could fly down when it was over and just lose a few days from work. Besides, she had some important projects coming up.

Still she hadn't seen Olivia in years and she felt grateful to her for continuing to stay with her grandmother, an act which simplified Liz's life immensely. Finding someone to care for a demented, bed-ridden patient was no easy task, especially long distance. Liz may not have loved her grandmother, but as her only relative, she felt a moral obligation to be sure she was properly cared for.

She had plenty of vacation time accrued and someone else could handle those projects. "Alright, Olivia," she had said aloud. "I'll come for a while, but I won't stay indefinitely. If she doesn't kick off while I'm there, I'll set things up so I won't have to return when she does. That's just like the old biddy--ornery and controlling to the bitter end."

As she reached the section of the road that was still topped with crushed oyster shell, the branches of the ancient oaks sagged to within inches of the ground. She could almost hear them moaning from the weight of their centuries of life and the clinging Spanish moss that ensnared them, a moan she echoed as she struggled with a growing feeling of entrapment.

"Knock it off! Cut out the pity party! This is a *temporary* situation!" she yelled into the rear view mirror. "A week, two at the most and I'm out of here! Back to civilization and my own life!"

Feeling slightly more positive, she stopped the car a hundred yards from the house and took in the sight. Marsh Oaks Plantation, once the jewel of the island, was now merely a specter of its former grandeur. The main house, built in 1756, dwarfed a miniature structure known as the tabby house, its crumbling ruins still standing several yards behind the newer one. As the family prospered, new wings had been added, along with architectural features popular at the time. The predominant style was Georgian, with a touch of Victorian gingerbread on the back porch which overlooked the marsh.

Although badly in need of paint and some repairs, the old house was still majestic, a testimony to the glory days of the island and the once lofty financial and social status of the family. The stout white columns, once *de rigueur* for antebellum southern mansions, were flaking and showing signs of rot. Maybe while she was here she could do a few much-needed chores. Then she realized the new owners would just raze the place anyway. She felt again an unexpected twinge of—what? remorse? guilt?—then shrugged off the uncharacteristic feeling.

Without consciously doing so, Liz's gaze wandered to the second floor windows. Her grandmother had not left her bedroom for over ten years. *Still the grand lady of the manor*, Liz thought sarcastically. *Still holding court in her chamber.*

Reverie

Elizabeth Brinson Briggs—Liz to her friends—learned early in life that she was an unwelcome interloper in the peaceable kingdom known as Marsh Oaks on Skidaway Island on the Georgia coast. She never really knew the details of the accident, but she did know that her socialite parents had been killed in Italy when she was only four years old. British-born Ralston Briggs had been a visiting professor at Agnes Scott College when Beth Mathews enrolled in one of his classes.

Although studying classical literature, Beth's interests were focused more on young men than on long-dead poets. A smashing beauty with chestnut curls and sea green eyes, she somehow managed to enthrall all the young men without alienating the other girls. At the end of the semester, Dr. Briggs extended his stay and the next June married the lovely debutante in a lavish ceremony at the bride's home. They honeymooned at his ancestral home on the Cornish coast of England. One summer they left their only child with Beth's mother, the grand dame of island society, while they toured Italy, vacationing and doing research for the professor's next book—until the fatal accident.

Elizabeth Mathews was devastated. She had lost her only son in World War II and her daughter's death reopened the dreadful wound. She withdrew from social activities and received few guests. In her desperation, she distanced herself from the orphaned little girl. Liz remembered her childhood home as quiet, dark, and unwelcoming. Although she went to school every day, she spent most of her time with her grandmother's housekeeper Mittie, her granddaughter Olivia, and the few other adults who worked on the plantation. Everyone assumed that she too would grow up to marry one of the local boys and spend her life in monotonous contentment as the next mistress of Marsh Oaks. But Liz wanted more.

Touching Home

Pulling under the *porte-cochere*, Liz parked the car next to the iron statue of a jockey designed to hold the reins of a gentleman caller's horse, a holdover from much earlier days. Straightening her khaki shorts as she stood up, she removed the pet carrier from the back seat. Thomas still bore a look of disgust but was relieved at least to be out of the wind. "Just a few more minutes, I promise," Liz said, glad to be able to stretch her long legs as she walked up the oyster shell path to massive double doors wide enough to receive guests in grand style. Grabbing the ring below the brass head of a lion, she knocked soundly on the door. Deep inside the house, she heard footsteps coming to the door. *No escape now.*

Unbolting the stout door, a stately African-American woman in a neatly pressed gray uniform complete with a crisply starched white apron swung open the door. Liz had forgotten how beautiful her childhood friend was with her wide set hazel eyes and flawless skin the color of café au lait. Now, although her dark hair showed traces of gray, the short cap of curls which framed her regal face accentuated her natural beauty.

With an exclamation of joy, Olivia reached for the weary traveler and hugged her tightly. Liz relaxed against her and returned the embrace. It had been too long since she had been hugged with genuine affection.

"It's so good to see you, even under the circumstances," Olivia said when she finally released her. "I've missed you so much over the years and wondered how you were really doing. Your letters always said you were fine but I wanted to see it in your face. Let me look at you. Don't you look stylish? City life must really agree with you."

"I guess it does, but my work seems to take all my time. Climbing the career ladder is hard work. Lonely, too, sometimes. But I have my pal Thomas here to keep me company. You don't mind cats, do you?" she asked as she removed the disgruntled cat from his carrier.

"Of course not. You know I love them," she said, allowing the cat to sniff her outstretched hand, then scratching his proffered chin. "Just leave your things in the car. We'll take then up to your room later. Come on back to the kitchen with me while I fix Miss Elizabeth's custard. It needs to cool a little before I take it up to her."

With the squirming cat draped over her arm, Liz followed her down the spacious hall that led to the back of the house. Aubusson carpets in soft shades of blue and sage green covered the floors in the rooms on either side. Beneath them, the wide pine planks hewn over a century ago from trees felled on the property were carefully polished to a glossy shine. Crystal chandeliers ordered from Paris before the Civil War glistened in the sunlight coming through the transoms.

A bouquet of fresh gardenias, her grandmother's favorite flower, on a mahogany side table filled the air with their cloying scent and caused Liz to shiver. *Get a grip!* she chided herself. *Don't let this place get to you, old girl.*

"I've missed you, too, you know," Liz said as they entered the kitchen. "How do you stand it in this dreary old house on this God-forsaken island? You should at least be living in Savannah, not squirreled up in this place. And what's with the dutiful maid's garb? This country's been over that for years." Liz felt as if entering the house had hurled her into a world that ceased to exist decades ago.

"This has always been home and I'm used to it. Besides, Miss Elizabeth needs me. You know I tried living on the mainland when I was younger but I'm just more content here." Pausing, Olivia looked down at her outfit and smiled. "Grannie always wore a uniform when she was the housekeeper here. I wore one when I helped her as a girl and then, when I took her place, I just thought it would please Miss Elizabeth if I continued. I'm sure she's not aware of what I wear now but it just seems right."

Well, at least she's not still wearing a maid's cap, recalling the protests against such uniforms waged by domestic servants in Atlanta during the 60's.

"What about you? Are you planning to stay?" Olivia was asking.

"Are you kidding? Me? Stay in this place? This is the last place on earth I want to be. I've spent too many years here already. I'm just here now because I have to be. As soon as everything is resolved, I'm heading back to Atlanta. On that note, how is Grandmother?"

"She's been losing ground since last Fall but a few weeks ago she had another stroke. Doctor Wilson says she just can't hang on much longer. Her body is gradually shutting down. He thinks she has only a few more weeks. That's why I wrote you. I know things have been hard between you but you're all she has. I just thought you would want to be here at the end. She won't know you, of course. She's not even sure who I am but she knows I'm her friend. She calls me Mittie most of the time thinking I'm Grannie and she sometimes asks for your mother Beth. Sometimes she just cries. I wish I could do something but she's just in her own world now."

"Should I go up to see her now?"

"She usually sleeps all afternoon," Olivia answered shaking her head. "I check on her about three o'clock and take her some drinking custard. She only takes a few sips but she seems to enjoy it. It hurts that there's so little I can do for her now. She was always so good to me and my family. You know after my mother remarried and moved to Chicago, I stayed here with Grannie. Later I went to Savannah State, lived here, and did the heavy work around the house. Miss Elizabeth wanted me to have an opportunity to succeed in life. I bet you didn't know that your grandmother paid for me to go to college, did you?"

Liz shook her head, surprised by Olivia's very different view of the cold, disinterested woman she remembered. How strange that she inspired so much devotion from her housekeeper's family and so little from her own granddaughter.

"When I finished college and taught high school in Savannah for a few years, I started working on my masters in special education. I wanted to work with children with behavior disorders. But I missed the island and I was really needed here by then. Coming back was my choice and I've never regretted it. I've always known that this is where I belong."

Olivia's words stung Liz. *I've spent all my adult life running from this island, trying to find the place where I belong and I'm still searching. She's spent all her life within twenty miles of this house and she's never questioned her decision. How can she be so content?*

"And the classes I took weren't wasted," Olivia continued. "Later they helped me understand how to deal with the changes in Miss Elizabeth's behavior.

"When Grannie finally became too frail to work, she continued to stay here, up until the day she died. I was already living here and Miss Elizabeth didn't want her to be alone. That was before your grandmother took to her room. They would sit for hours, reminiscing about the years they had been together, both good and bad.

"Grannie meant everything to me and it made me happy to make life a little easier for her. Since she died, I've tried to do the same for Miss Elizabeth, but she's just lost touch with this world. I think she'll be happy when the Lord calls her home."

Liz stood frozen, staring at Olivia with disbelief. All these years they had exchanged letters filled with news about her grandmother's condition, the major happenings in their own lives, and unkept promises to visit. True, the letters were less frequent in recent years, but Liz had still thought she knew Olivia fairly well. After all, they were inseparable growing up. But apparently she had been oblivious to the depth of the relationship among the three women she had left behind in the house or even that her own grandmother genuinely cared for either one as she obviously had. She had been so absorbed in her own existence that she failed to read between the lines or even truly care about their lives. Could the blame for her estrangement from them be as much hers as her grandmother's? She had never even considered that she bore any responsibility but after barely a few minutes in the old house, she was starting to question her entire perception of her life. What other unsettling surprises did this old relic have in store for her?

Liz looked around the room as Olivia placed a small pottery bowl with cool water on the floor for Thomas and poured fresh homemade lemonade into a glass decorated with yellow irises and white lattice.

"This is your grandmama's special grown-up glass," she could still hear Mittie saying. "Be very careful so you don't break it." She was beginning to feel she was in some kind of historical reenactment. She had not been here for years but everything was just the same.

Although modernized some forty years ago, the room was an addition to the original house. The floors in this room too were wide pine boards. Old-fashioned bead board cupboards hung above thick wooden countertops rubbed with countless coats of linseed oil over the years. The huge copper hood still reached to the high ceiling from the now antique gas stove beneath it. Surely, those were not the same blue gingham curtains that had hung at the windows when she was a child! If not, someone had matched them precisely in an effort that nothing should ever change.

Above the cabinets and on every wall hung her grandmother's prized possession, a collection of blue and white plates. Some had been handed down through the centuries, some she had purchased new, and some were gifts. Many were very valuable, as Liz had learned when her childish exuberance had dislodged one from its appointed place, causing it to shatter into a myriad of pieces. Her grandmother had been much more distraught about the loss of her precious porcelain than the distress of her grandchild. After Elizabeth's tirade, Mittie had dried the child's tears, comforted her on her ample lap, and then sent her out to play with a healing glass of lemonade and a cookie.

"I'm sorry. What did you say?" Liz was startled out of her reverie by the sound of Olivia's voice.

"Hand me a bowl from that cabinet behind you, please."

Reaching into an upper cupboard, Liz took down a familiar pale green bowl, the same one Mittie had used when Liz was a child. *Didn't anyone else ever break anything here?*

Olivia took milk and a bowl of brown yard eggs from the old

refrigerator. Gently picking up each egg with her long fingers, she methodically struck it against the edge of the bowl. For a moment, Liz felt as if she were suspended in a time warp. Instead of a lithe latte-skinned woman with a short cap of dark curls, she was staring at a stocky somewhat darker woman wearing a red turban similar to those worn by her slave ancestors—the beloved but long-dead Mittie herself. She blinked her eyes to clear the vision. She watched as Olivia deliberately let the egg whites slide into in a small dish while she captured each golden yolk in its shell before dropping it into the green bowl.

Liz's culinary efforts were somewhat hasty and begrudging—an exercise meant to satisfy a basic human need, not one choreographed with the same passion as a ballet. With equal precision, Olivia began the ritual of beating the egg yolks to the perfect consistency. Satisfied, she spooned a small amount of the milk already warming in a double boiler into the eggs, stirred gently, then poured a steady stream of the egg mixture into the remaining milk and began a rhythmic figure eight pattern as the custard began to cook.

Olivia seemed to find pleasure in every phase of the process. And no one could fault the end result of her efforts. Mittie had been a master in the kitchen and Olivia had obviously inherited her gift.

"Remember when we were kids you wanted to have your own restaurant?" Liz asked.

"You mean the one that only served the vegetables I liked?" Olivia chuckled.

"Yeah, whatever happened to that idea?"

"I don't know. It simply never happened. It was just a childish dream."

"It's not too late. You could still do it. I mean you'll have time soon."

Olivia stopped stirring the mixture and looked past Liz, her gaze fixed on the marsh. For a few moments, she was quiet, her face devoid of expression. Then she took the pot from the burner and carefully poured the thick steaming drink into a crystal goblet etched with diamond cuts around the base.

"Do you remember this crystal?" she said holding up the

delicate glass.

Liz nodded, realizing that Olivia had deliberately steered the subject away from Elizabeth Mathews' impending death.

"Your great-great grandmother Betsy bought it in Paris on her honeymoon. She had twenty-four of everything—wine, water, cordials. She loved beautiful things and, when they first married, her rich northern husband bought everything she wished for. That was before the war when Marsh Oaks was the showplace of this island. I wish I could have seen it then. Miss Elizabeth liked her fancy possessions, too. She insisted that her meals be served on Miss Betsy's fine French porcelain. Her afternoon tea was poured from the silver teapot Mr. Benjamin's family brought from England and she used the napkins that her mother, Miss Annabeth, embroidered. She used to say using their things made her ancestors seem closer to her. I think she must have had a lonely childhood, too, since her mother died when she was born and her daddy died not too long after her, leaving your great-great aunt Eliza to take care of their baby. Grannie Molly, my great grandmother, used to tell me scary stories about the crazy spinster Eliza. The servants all thought she was 'touched in the head' as they used to say."

Liz, still reflecting on Olivia's puzzling response, stood listening with new interest. Olivia spoke about the estate and those who had inhabited it with the knowledgeable pride expected from an heir of the original settlers rather than a direct descendant of the slaves who had been forced to serve them. Liz sensed that somehow over the years, as she had lost her love for her heritage and childhood home, Olivia's love and sense of belonging had increased. It occurred to Liz that although she was the legal heir, her grandmother's companion held the greater claim to Marsh Oaks. *I'm a visitor in Olivia's domain. If I sell the place, what will happen to her?*

In her usual self-centered manner, Liz had not considered the consequences her actions might have on another person. *Rats! Why did things have to be so complicated? Maybe I could give Olivia some of the money to buy her own place.* She already knew, however, that it would not be the same. Olivia was part of Marsh Oaks. She belonged here. *Rats!*

"How about some more lemonade while I wait for that to cool a little?" Olivia said, placing the goblet on a small silver tray. "There's probably a bit of a breeze on the veranda about now. Get the pitcher from the refrigerator and I'll get the cookies. We'll have a tea party the way we used to."

Olivia picked up the plate of sugar cookies and went out the screened door to a row of rocking chairs lining the long shady porch. The sturdy columns were covered with wisteria vines, their lush purple blooms hanging like plump clusters of grapes. Birds of a dozen varieties darted between several feeders and birdbaths scattered across the back yard. Thomas crept tentatively down the steps for a better view of the feathered activity near the feeder. Unaware of the territorial nature of some birds and their instinctive dislike of furry creatures, he was dive-bombed by an aggressive mockingbird. Yowling in pain, he hastily retreated to the safety of the porch and cowered beneath Liz's chair. Licking his wound and smoothing his ruffled coat, he endeavored to salvage his dignity, deciding to watch the scene from a secure distance.

Beyond the grassy area, huge sprawling oaks gave way to the marsh along the riverbank. As a child, Liz had imagined that the Garden of Eden looked much like this. She had spent long hours here playing quietly with her dolls so she wouldn't disturb her grandmother's afternoon nap. When Olivia joined her, Mittie would warn them to whisper, bribing them with a tea party of lemonade and the same delicious sugar cookies. As Liz rocked rhythmically in the big chair next to her childhood friend, she wondered how long it had been since she had frittered away an afternoon just relaxing and drinking lemonade. She was always too busy and, besides, nobody made lemonade from real lemons anymore. Not in her fast-paced world anyway. Savoring the delectable liquid, she closed her eyes and allowed her mind to drift away, feeling the soft breeze, smelling the sweet scent of the wisteria, and listening to the birds as they wrapped her in a web of luxurious sensory pleasure. Quite a change from the usual assault on her senses—the shrill ring of the incessant phone, the blare of horns in the daily traffic gridlock, the smell of days-old garbage from the restaurant next door in the dumpster behind her office building.

After a while, Olivia rose to prepare Elizabeth's tray and Liz followed her into the kitchen, the still cringing Thomas close on her heels. "You're awful tired from your trip and this is Miss Elizabeth's worst time of day. Why don't you just relax now and go up to see her tomorrow? After all this time, one more day won't hurt. I'll start our supper before long but you have time to get unpacked if you want. I made up your old room for you. I hope that suits you."

"That's fine," Liz replied. She was ashamed to admit that she was relieved not to have to face her grandmother yet. She was tired and just being in the house had brought back painful memories. She would be able to handle the meeting better after she had eaten some of Olivia's home cooking and had a good night's sleep. After Olivia went upstairs, Liz again went out the back door onto the veranda overlooking the marsh, letting the screen door slam behind her. Funny how even sound can stir memories. When she was a child, slamming a door would trigger a lecture from her grandmother, followed by a reenactment of the proper way to close a door. Liz wondered if her grandmother could hear the noise now, and if she reacted if she heard. Part of her enjoyed a secret satisfaction at the thought as she settled into a rocker again. Thomas claimed his rightful place in her lap and finally started to purr contentedly. As she closed her weary eyes, she breathed in the distinctive and somewhat unsettling fragrance of gardenias witeia.

The sun was low in the sky, promising one of those long, slow sunsets over the marsh when she started down the path to the dock after helping Olivia clean up the supper dishes. Baked ham, sweet potatoes, butterbeans, and biscuits with peach cobbler for dessert. She needed to run around the whole island to work off that dinner but would have to make do with a trip to the dock. Still unnerved by his earlier encounter with the mockingbird, Thomas decided to follow her in case the winged attacker returned. His tender feet, however, were unused to the hard ground and he howled his displeasure.

"What a wimp," Liz teased as she picked up the complaining

feline. Satisfied, he quickly took up his usual position looking over her shoulder.

The late afternoon tide was high, the dark water lapping at the pilings of the old dock. Slipping off her sandals, she sat down, the rough boards still warm beneath her. How many times, she wondered, had she sat on the end of the dock, her bare feet dangling in the water as she cried in loneliness. Even now, that same old melancholy feeling drifted over her as she gazed across the endless marsh.

The Road Not Taken

The sound of a motor startled her as a boat came around the bend in the river. Shading her eyes, she saw it slow down and head toward the dock. *How strange. Who would be coming to this dock? No one visits here anymore.*

"Liz? Liz Briggs? Is that you? It's Jack Coleman, the nature nerd from high school. Okay if I tie up and visit awhile?"

"Jack? 'Tree hugger Jack'? I can't believe it! How did you know who I was? I haven't seen you since I went off to college. How in the world are you?" she yelled over the din of the boat motor as she jumped up, caught the line and skillfully tied a nautical knot without even thinking.

Reaching the top of the ladder, he lifted her off the ground in a bear hug just as he had done forty years ago. Beneath the faded denim shirt, she could feel his muscled shoulders. Despite the bit of gray in his sun-streaked sandy blond hair and a few wrinkles from squinting in the sun, the years had been kind to him. *Very kind indeed*, Liz acknowledged appreciatively.

"It couldn't have been anyone else on this dock with hair like that. Nobody around here ever had hair like yours and in this light it was glowing."

If he only knew what it cost in Atlanta to have Mr. Jason maintain this exact shade of copper.

"Gosh, it's good to see you," he drawled. "You look like a million bucks. Where've you been? Are you back for good? Miss Elizabeth didn't die, did she?"

"One question at a time, please! I've been in Atlanta, I'm not back for good, and she isn't dead, but she's not expected to live much longer. I came back to see her one more time." *What a strange thing to say.* She hadn't come back to see her; she came back to prepare to bury her.

As they sat down on the dock, Thomas sniffed the new arrival curiously then went back to watching the minnows breaking the surface of the water as they pursued the bugs that dared to land for a moment.

"How about you? Where have you been?"

"I've been right here for almost thirty years. I majored in forestry in college, then worked in several state parks around the South, and finally landed back here where I wanted to be all the time. I'm the manager at the state park on the island. The tree hugging paid off, I guess. You married now?"

"No, widowed. My husband died of pancreatic cancer ten years ago. We were only married a little over five years. I was too busy carving out my career before that. What about you? Is your wife waiting dinner for you?"

"No. I married Kate Brown right after I finished college. She grew up on the island. She was a year behind us but you may remember her—long blond hair and a varsity basketball player. We were married for almost ten years but we're divorced now."

"What happened, or shouldn't I ask?"

"It's no secret. Anyone on the island can give you the whole story and would be happy to, I'm sure. When we were sent back here, I was ecstatic but Kate had other ideas. She said she didn't go to college and help me build my career to end up back where she started. She called it quits, packed up our son, and went back to North Carolina near where I had worked before. I saw my son some when he was growing up but he lives in California now and that's a long trip. You have any little redheaded kids?"

"No," she said laughing. "Nor any other hair colors either, unless you count Thomas over there. I waited too late for that, I'm afraid." She tried never to think about the baby she had lost. No one even knew. It was just too painful to talk about and it was a very long time ago in a different life.

"That's too bad. You'd have been a great mom to all those little redheads. How long you going to be here or does that depend on how Miss Elizabeth does?"

"I'm not sure. I'll have to get back to work before too long. I have to support myself, you know. The doctor says her heart can't hold out much longer. We'll just take it day by day."

"That's all anyone can do," he said softly. "How do you earn your keep, anyway? You were always so smart and so determined to get away from here."

"I'm an attorney. My firm is in Atlanta but I travel a lot. The other partners have families and obligations so I do most of the out of town stuff. Works out great for everyone." Liz hoped Jack did not hear the note of disenchantment in her voice. She tried to put on a good face for others, but she was finding it increasingly difficult to lie to herself about her supposedly contented life.

If Jack doubted her glowing account of her life, he didn't let on. "Could I buy you a beer and a burger sometime?" he offered. "I'd love to hear some more about what you've been up to all these years."

"I'd like that. Why don't you give me a call tomorrow after I get my act together?"

"Sounds like a plan. Guess I'd better be shoving off. I like to get the boat in before dark. I'll call you tomorrow."

Jack swung his long legs over the side, shimmied down the ladder with the agility of a much younger man and was soon under way. The years had melted away and they had talked as if they had just seen each other the day before. He always was her best friend growing up, the one she could count on to come through for her. She wondered what her life would have been like if she had allowed their relationship to continue. He had wanted to marry her but she wanted to see the world. So much for the big wide world. And she had ultimately done him a favor. At least he was still alive, unlike the other two men she had loved.

Liz stood for a moment looking across the water in the fading light. A marsh hen swooped overhead and landed in the soft mud just above the waterline. She poked her bill into the mushy sand a few times then disappeared into the tall marsh on the other side of the river. Liz wondered if she had a nest there, hanging precariously from the reeds. Picking up Thomas, she started up the path, ready for a hot bath and the end of this very long day and the disturbing memories it had stirred.

"Jack, I really love you but I just can't marry you right now. I don't want to hurt you and I would hurt you more if I married you now. I'm just not ready." Sitting on the dock with their feet dangling in the water, she tried not to look at him as she spoke. She had gone steady with Jack Coleman all through high school and everyone expected them to get married. He had formally proposed to her last night after their graduation ceremony. The truth was she wasn't sure she wanted to marry him, not now, not ever. She wasn't sure she even loved him. He had always been her best friend, but was that enough? She dreamed of exciting new adventures in far-off places. Jack was content with a way of life as predictable as the ebb and flow of the tides.

"I know you're going to work at that camp in North Carolina this summer, but will you promise to think about it and give me your answer when you come back in August?" Jack pleaded.

She agreed with reluctance, knowing that her answer then would be the same. She was desperate to escape, not only the slow pace of island life, but also her repressive childhood, in particular her overbearing grandmother.

During the summer, her duties as a counselor kept her busy, but she felt a sense of freedom for the first time in her life. She met other young people from all over the east coast and listened to their plans for their futures in famous universities and big cities. They spent hours discussing politics and history. They recounted stories of exotic places where they intended to travel, some even hoped to stay in remote areas and teach, or work with impoverished peasants to better their lives. They had such lofty ideas and plans to make a difference in the world. Liz was spellbound. Compared to theirs, her life had been so provincial and her own future promised to be so predictable. This new awakening and the brief taste of independence had whetted her appetite for more. She needed time to be herself, to explore the vast world beyond the island.

When she returned to Skidaway, she told Jack she couldn't marry him yet. She was going to Emory University to pursue a degree in political science but she would be home for holidays. Her grandmother raised no objections, and Liz secretly felt that she was glad for her granddaughter to leave her in peace. After a frenzy of preparations, she packed her '57 Chevy Bel Air and headed across the bridge, breathing in the captivating smell of freedom as she left behind the sea of marsh and drove toward the red clay hills of north Georgia.

"Guess who I just saw?" Liz called to Olivia as the screen door closed behind her. "Tree hugger Jack."

"Jack Coleman? I thought I heard his boat," Olivia said, taking a loaf of banana bread out of the oven. Seeing Liz's surprised look, she continued, "We pay attention to things around here. We recognize the sound of a boat motor or a car engine. Know whose car just went down the road by the time of day. We're creatures of habit. That's island life. You'll get used to it if you stay long enough."

"Anyway, he invited me to go to dinner—actually for a beer and a burger. It was strange talking to him. He looked like a sixty-something year old man but he sounded just like he did the last time I saw him over forty years ago. In addition, you know what's really weird? I felt like I did then, you know, young and almost giggly."

"Why, Liz Briggs. You don't still have a crush on that good-looking lifeguard, do you?"

"Be serious. It was just seeing him after so many years. The memories just came rushing back."

"Everybody always thought you two would get married. Even I was surprised when you went to Atlanta instead. Broke his heart but he survived. Guess he still has a crush on you."

"I thought I loved him too but I didn't want to spend my life on this island. After I left, I convinced myself that it was just friendship, that it wasn't real love, the kind you build a life on. I realize now that I just wanted to run away from this island and I knew if I married Jack I would be stuck here forever."

Olivia laughed. "It's not all that bad. A person could do worse."

"I know. And sometimes I think I did. I don't mean that I regret my life. It's just...Oh, I don't know."

"You can't second guess your life. You do what you have to do at the time and learn to live with the consequences, one way or the other."

"How did you get so wise?"

"Island wisdom. I learned it from Grannie and she learned it from all the women before her," Olivia said. "Came from making the best of situations they couldn't control. One of Grannie's favorite sayings was, 'If it can't be bested, it must be borne.' She never had many choices and most of her life she spent taking care of other folks but she never let it get her down. She loved life, whatever it required of her."

Liz shivered involuntarily. The expression had been part of her upbringing too, but she had heard it as judgmental and punishing. Olivia seemed to hear it as encouragement. How different their understandings of life had been even though they grew up under the same roof.

"You were very fortunate to be so secure about her love for you. I wish my grandmother had felt the same about me," Liz said sitting down at the kitchen table. "I never told you about my years at Emory, did I? She never knew either. I was really feeling my freedom in those days, the whole hippie thing. Remember those days? I fell in love with a law student and we lived together during my senior year. We were going to get married when we graduated but Viet Nam came along, he was drafted, and he never came back. I found out I was pregnant after he left, but I lost the baby after he died. It was all over and I was alone again. I think I went to law school because it made me feel close to him. When I became a lawyer, I threw myself into my work and avoided any close relationships."

"I wondered why you stayed single so long. I had no idea you'd been through so much. Why didn't you come home or at least tell Grannie or me?" Olivia asked, reaching across the table to put her hand on Liz's arm.

"Pride, I guess. I didn't want pity. I just wanted my independence. All those years later when I met Tom, we fell in love in such a different way. We were so comfortable together. I thought we would grow old together but God had other ideas. Since he died, my job has been my life. My job and Thomas," she said stroking the cat as he slept in her lap. "I'm definitely not in the market for another man!"

Picking up the cat as she stood, Liz yawned and said, "And now, my man Thomas and I have had a long day. We're headed for the sack. Good night, Olivia. See you in the morning."

She pulled up the bed covers savoring the feel of the fine cotton sheets that Olivia still ironed by hand. Thomas circled her feet trying to determine exactly the right spot to settle. The sounds of the marsh drifted in from the open window as she relaxed into sleep, memories of Jeff and Tom filling her thoughts.

Undying Love

Beginning her college career at a time when young women were making themselves heard in a multitude of ways, Liz reveled in her newfound independence. Craving the affirmation and affection she had never received from her grandmother, she experienced a laundry list of college romances with equally needy young men. It was the era of free love and "feel good" mentality and she tasted it all! In the late 1960's she became involved with Jeff Lodge, a third-year law student from Maine who not only returned her devotion but was stable and trustworthy. They lived together in a small apartment in biking distance of the Emory campus, participated in campus protests, and looked forward to the life they would share when Jeff finished law school.

For the first time in her life, Liz felt truly wanted. She loved her new life until the day that without warning her serene world was shattered.

Curled up in the worn beanbag chair, Liz was studying for midterms when Jeff came home unexpectedly, his usual boyish grin replaced by an almost blank expression.

"Hi. I thought you were going to the library to work on your brief," she said kissing him on the cheek.

"I came home earlier to get some papers and picked up the mail when I left." He hesitated before continuing, "I got a letter from the draft board. I've been drafted. I leave for basic training as soon as I graduate and will go to Nam as soon as possible."

Liz was stunned. They knew that Jeff's low number in the draft lottery made being called up a strong possibility but she never really expected him to be sent to Viet Nam.

"You don't have to go! You can go to Canada. I'll come with you."

"You know I won't do that. I have to go. It's my duty."

"I don't care about your duty. I care about you!" she screamed hysterically as he held her close.

"Please understand. I have to go. Please don't try to stop me."

"I just can't bear to lose you. You're my whole life!"

"You won't lose me. I can take care of myself and this war can't last forever. While I'm gone, you can stay busy planning that wedding you want. I'll be back before you even miss me."

"I miss you already," she whispered as the old feelings of an abandoned child crept back into her mind.

They spent their last days together trying to do all the things they loved. When he left, she was devastated.

Liz decided to take some classes during the summer to keep her mind occupied, but she could not shake her fear that he would not return. She had loved Mittie and Olivia and she had even thought she loved Jack. She had missed them when she left for school, but nothing had prepared her for this. For one who had experienced so little affection, the passion of her first deep love was all-consuming.

At first, Liz tried to study but she couldn't concentrate. A few weeks after Jeff's departure, she began to feel tired and lost her appetite. She attributed it to missing Jeff and the stress of trying to stay focused on her classes. Several weeks later when she finally went to the clinic, she learned to her surprise that she was pregnant.

As she biked back to the apartment, she wondered how Jeff would feel about this unanticipated development in their relationship. The baby would arrive before he could return to marry her. If he still wanted to marry her now.

She wrote to him about the news. His response was immediate and supportive. Although the wedding would have to be delayed, it was still on. He vowed his undying love for her and their anticipated child.

Relieved, she told no one about the baby, deciding to delay any decisions until the term ended in a few weeks. They would have time then to make plans together.

A week before finals, Liz was struggling to review her notes when she received an almost incoherent call from Jeff's mother. Between sieges of hysterical sobs, Mrs. Lodge related the details of an ambush deep in the jungle, emergency field surgery, and death. Two days later, Liz woke in the middle of the night with excruciating cramps. Within a few hours, the baby too was lost. In the course of a few days, her life with Jeff—their love, their baby, their wonderful future together—had vanished as if it had never existed.

Once again, her peaceful world had been destroyed and she was alone with her grief. Why was God punishing her so harshly? All her life she had wanted just to love and be loved. She had taken a chance and given herself without reservation to another person and God had ripped him and their child from her.

Why am I so unworthy? What could I possibly have done to deserve such pain?

Dashed Dreams

Trying to escape from her loneliness and caught up in the era of feminism, Liz stolidly threw herself into preparing for a career that would ensure her independence. Withdrawing into a shell of indifference, she finished her degree and was admitted to the law school at Emory. She had found the law intriguing when she had helped Jeff prepare for his classes, and now saw a legal career as her key to the self-sufficient, liberated life she desired. She faced the challenge with her usual resolve and, passing the bar on her first attempt, obtained a position with a prestigious firm in Atlanta. Her exceptional work ethic caught the attention of one of the senior partners. With his mentoring and her ability to focus all her energy on her career without the distractions of family responsibilities, she rose quickly in the firm, becoming the first woman partner.

Rejecting even the constraints of a pet, she took the cases her married colleagues shied away from, ones that required her to be away for long periods of time or over holidays. She prided herself on her uncanny ability to succeed in what was still a man's world. Unencumbered by emotional baggage, she zeroed in on potential problems and worked with dogged determination without regard to weekends or holidays until the case was resolved, increasingly in her favor. Over the years, she became resigned to her "spinsterhood" and even came to see it as an advantage to her career.

Years later, as she continued her climb to the top of her field, fate dealt her another vicious blow. She had lived contentedly in her high-rise condo overlooking Piedmont Park for ten years. Decorated by one of the city's leading designers (and featured in *Southern Living*, the benchmark of southern style), her home was her haven, as welcoming after her frequent and extended trips as an old flannel robe. She was on a first-name basis with her neighbors and infrequently attended events on the calendar published by the social committee, but could in no way be considered a regular or a candidate for membership on the committee.

One December, however, having been in town for an unusually long stretch and feeling an unexplained pang of melancholy as her colleagues cleared their calendars for seasonal family gatherings, she succumbed to her friend Carole's persistence and accompanied her to the Lighting of the Yule Log Get-Together in the building. The committee had gone all out for the celebrators, many of whose circumstances were similar to Liz's. Perhaps reflecting the increased mobility of young professionals and the rising divorce rate especially in fast-paced urban communities, many of the residents found the holidays approaching without a place to go.

Entering a court room to argue even a shaky case triggered in Liz a heady sensation as she reveled in the opportunity for a new challenge; walking into a room for a social occasion triggered a somewhat different response, one more akin to panic. Surveying the dimly lit room for a safe harbor, she caught sight of an intriguing dark-haired man in an expensive hand knit sweater seated on a massive sofa and looking as uncomfortable as she felt. With deliberate slowness, she went over to stand in the warmth of the fireplace near the sofa. The firelight did great things for her copper hair and she was glad she had bothered to slip on a new burgundy satin jacket over her ivory *charmeuse* blouse. When her eyes met the gaze of the dark stranger, she didn't look away and they shared a brief moment of intimacy born of mutual discomfort. He offered a conspiratorial smile, but before she could respond, Carole swept toward her with another "fabulous" man for her to meet.

Later the other reluctant reveler approached her, bearing a mug of hot buttered rum.

"You looked as if you could use a break from the frivolity," he teased. "I sense someone dragged you here, too, and you are just waiting for the right moment to slip out."

"Am I that obvious? I thought I was faking it rather nicely."

"Maybe to those who are into this kind of thing but not to another experienced faker. I despise the forced merriment of this season. I usually just hibernate until it's over but my buddy insisted I come for just a while. Why are you here?"

"Just about the same story. I usually arrange to be on an extended business trip about this time of year but I couldn't work it out and got stuck at home. My neighbor Carole is the original party girl and insists that I would have a great time if I would just try to be more sociable. So here I am—trying. So far, it's been very trying. I'm just not much for loud music and shallow cocktail conversations."

"In that case, why don't we go down to Ernie's? You know it, don't you? The piano bar next door? At least we could hear ourselves talk. Who knows? We might even have a serious conversation." Taking her mug, he guided her to the door. Feeling like kids cutting class, they hurried out onto the street. A rare snowfall dropped a veil between them and the orange neon sign on the corner advertising Ernie's. Laughing, they darted down the block and into the neighborhood pub.

After that first evening, comfortable and unassuming Ernie's became a staple in their relationship. They often met just to talk over a drink. Tom Scott was somewhat of a novelty—a native Atlantan.

"So after law school at the University of Georgia, I came back home and started a law firm with Ted, the guy who dragged me to the party tonight. His divorce just became final and he's throwing himself into his newfound freedom. We were roommates at Georgia. His dad has loads of money so he set us up in practice and steered all his wealthy buddies our way."

"Sounds like a pretty good deal. I had to slave my way to a partnership."

"It was a pretty good deal but I paid my dues, too."

After they ordered another drink, Liz asked, "Have you ever been married, or should I say, are you married now?"

Tom shook his head. "My wife died."

"I'm sorry. I didn't mean to bring up a painful subject."

"It's okay. Jennifer died almost sixteen years ago. Or it will be sixteen years next Thursday," he said as he looked down at his drink.

"She died just before Christmas? How painful for you. No wonder you dislike the holidays."

"I'd like to tell you about it if you don't mind."

"Of course not. I just don't want to upset you."

"No, I think it might help me get through the season. People usually avoid talking about it with me and sometimes I just need to remember." He took a long sip of his Chivas and water and began his story.

"Jennifer was Ted's kid sister. I think that marrying her was an implied part of the law deal but I would have married her anyway. She was beautiful and funny. She had been given everything a lot of money can buy. She was a debutante and a cheerleader and finished at Wellesley magna cum laude. She was great at everything she did. Her dad gave us a house in Buckhead as a wedding present and she redecorated it by herself. She had exquisite—and expensive—taste. Between the growing practice and our hectic social schedule, we rarely had much time alone together. I regret that now, but we were on the way up and we thought we would have lots of time later. We all think we have unlimited time, don't we?"

Liz nodded in solemn agreement, remembering her brief time with Jeff.

"Anyway, we soon learned we were expecting our first child. I had everything I had ever wanted. We were well on our way to the good life." Tom toyed with his drink for a few minutes before continuing. "All of that ended suddenly on an icy December afternoon. Jennifer had been finishing her Christmas shopping at Phipps Plaza. It had been drizzling all day and the temperature started to bottom out. Her BMW was broadsided by a delivery truck as it slid on a patch of ice. I got the call at work and was at the hospital in a few minutes, but she died in the ambulance on the way there. She was buried two days before Christmas. Since then the holidays just remind me of the loss of Jen and our baby and I do all I can to block them out."

"I think anyone would do the same."

"You can probably guess the rest. I immersed myself in my practice. I still work long hours and spend most weekends at our mountain cabin in North Georgia with Charlie, our Labrador retriever. It's a very quiet life."

She couldn't help wondering how many beautiful and wealthy

women had endeavored to change that situation.

For the first time in years, Liz enjoyed the Christmas holidays. Not once did she go into the office or even dig into her briefcase to catch up on paperwork. Instead, she bought a live Christmas tree complete with decorations, hung a wreath on her door, and even baked cookies from one of Mittie's recipes she found buried in an old cookbook.

Although she was reluctant to become involved in a relationship, arguing with herself that her work did not allow her time for anyone else, she found herself being drawn closer to this captivating man. He shared his most intimate thoughts and concerns, allowed her to see his vulnerability, and listened compassionately as she related the pain she had felt in her life. Yet he was slow to make any physical advances toward her. Did he want only a platonic friendship? Did he not find her attractive? She wasn't exactly sure how she would respond but she realized that she certainly wanted him to try anyway.

The issue was resolved on New Year's Eve when, after a late dinner, he invited her back to his place for a drink while they waited for the stroke of midnight. She had visited him before, of course, and had been impressed with his masculine but sophisticated décor. She had wondered if one of his hopeful female friends had helped him with the decorating, only to be disappointed when she was not invited to share it. An expensive leather sofa and an oversized recliner were obviously selected for comfort. A large media cabinet housed every state of the art piece of equipment available. Tom loved music, everything from blues to opera. Rows of CD's cataloged according to genre lined the shelves. Expensive antiques were expertly placed around the room, complemented by impressive paintings and other pieces of art—the perfect retreat for a successful man.

As Tom unlocked the door, something seemed different. The lights were dimmed, the sound of romantic classics played by a piano virtuoso filled the room. A bottle of champagne stood in an ice bucket on the black granite bar top, two waiting Waterford flutes glistening in the soft light.

"You must have been pretty sure I would accept your invitation," Liz said.

Tom didn't answer but went to the kitchen, emerging with an elegant silver coffee service, two Royal Doulton coffee cups, and a small plate covered with a linen napkin. Placing the tray on a leather ottoman, he filled her cup with her favorite hazelnut coffee. "I thought you would rather have coffee now if we are going to drink champagne later. I also picked up some of your favorite chocolate walnut cookies since we didn't have dessert at the restaurant." Taking his own cup, he leaned back on the lush sofa beside her.

Savoring the taste of the rich coffee, Liz realized that he not only knew her tastes but had made a genuine effort to please her. How long had it been since she had been so pampered by someone wanting only her pleasure? She looked away to keep him from seeing the tears in her eyes. When she turned back, his dark liquid eyes were staring at her. Putting his cup down, he reached for her. He kissed her tentatively at first then with an intensity that swept away any doubts she might have had about his attraction to her. Disregarding her own reluctance, she returned his kiss and surrendered to his embrace.

They drank their toast to the New Year—a few hours late—in his king-size canopy bed. The next morning, Liz awoke when Tom drew the drapes and sunlight flooded the room.

"Wake up! The day's half gone," he said as he approached the bed with another tray, this time bearing orange juice, eggs Benedict, French toast and steaming French roast coffee for two. Settling beside her, he handed her a mug of coffee.

"You went to a lot of trouble. Do you do this all the time? Where did you learn to cook like this?"

"I've been on my own a long time remember. I like good food and there was no one else to cook it. So I took a few lessons in Paris. It's nice to have someone else to enjoy it for a change. Eat up. You insult the chef if you let it get cold."

The wedding was a very small—Liz preferred intimate—affair in early April. The ceremony took place in an old United Methodist Church down the street. Liz had not attended church as an adult, citing a lack of time as an excuse; but if she had, she would have gone to this one. She had been baptized as a child in the Methodist church on the island and had endured endless worship services seated in the hard pew, first beside her grandmother and later beside Mittie. She supposed that qualified her as a Methodist.

Only her friend Carole and Tom's buddy Ted attended the service conducted by a retired minister with music provided by his wife. Instead of a white gown, Liz chose an ivory silk suit, much more useful after the fact. Besides, she was not exactly a blushing young bride by any stretch of the imagination.

Following the ceremony, the bridal party, minus the preacher and his wife, went to Ernie's where the owner had prepared a nuptial lunch that would have made the finest five star chef proud. The staff joined in the celebration and the party lasted until time to open for the cocktail crowd. The regulars who drifted in continued to toast the newlyweds until the wee hours. The couple finally said their goodbyes in order to pack for their flight to Greece the next morning.

After sailing the Aegean for two weeks, they returned to Liz's condo and resumed their busy lives. Liz had sent Olivia a postcard informing her of the wedding and promising to write her later with details. She felt no need to write to her grandmother since she didn't even remember Liz now. Returning to her career, she turned down many new projects to spend her time off with Tom, causing her colleagues to have to tackle the undesirable holiday trips. After so many years on her own, Liz was amazed how quickly she settled into married life. They entertained frequently, attended numerous parties, and had season tickets to the symphony as well as sports events. Her life was comfortable and satisfying.

In the back of her mind, however, she kept hearing the refrain of an old song, *"Too good, this is too good to last and I'm afraid. For every joy I've ever known a price was paid."* Pushing the words from her thoughts, she focused on the positive as she had trained to do in countless motivational seminars. She and Tom were in love. They may not be young and foolish but their life together was all she could ever ask. What could go wrong?

For five years, life was wonderful. To celebrate their fifth anniversary, they planned to return to Greece and the islands they had visited on their honeymoon. The week before they were to leave, Liz came home from work to find Tom, with a drink in his hand, sitting on the sofa. His coat and tie were thrown over the recliner and his collar unbuttoned, odd behavior since his habit was to change clothes as soon as he came home. And he always waited for her to have a drink together and chat about the day. Outside the late March sky was dark but he had not turned on the lights.

Crossing the room to sit beside him, she said, "Tom, is something wrong? Why are you sitting in the dark?" She covered his hand with hers.

"Last week I saw Sam for my annual physical. He found something that concerned him and ran some additional tests. This afternoon he called with the results. It's pancreatic cancer. The prognosis is not good, two to four months, six at the most."

Fear gripped her as she said, "We have to get a second opinion. He could be mistaken."

"The tests left no doubt but he conferred with his golf buddy who's an oncologist just to be sure. The diagnosis is correct."

"We'll go to a specialist. Who's the best in the country?"

"Unfortunately his buddy is one of the best in the world. There's no surgery or miracle cure. It's the most deadly form of the disease. They'll try chemo and radiation but they just delay the inevitable. They can't cure it. I have an appointment tomorrow with the oncologist to determine the course of treatment."

Liz leaned back against him and they held each other in the dark. The words of the song replayed in her mind, *"Too good to last and I'm afraid."* For the first time in years, she was afraid.

Although the treatments were powerless against the pernicious disease, Tom endured them to gain a little more time and to please Liz. They made him weak and unable to eat. His slender frame became gaunt and a jaundiced yellow replaced his usual healthy-looking tan. He didn't want to see people—or, actually, be seen—so they stopped going out or having guests. Liz cut back on her workload to spend time with him on the good days, to drive him to his treatments and to care for him during the rough times.

Never one to give up easily, Tom was still fighting his

debilitating foe as fall approached. He spent his days listening to selections from his vast music collection, dozing on the sofa in the living room, or just gazing out the window at the changing colors of the trees in the park across the street. They sat together on the sofa for hours listening to *September Song*, Tom smiling as he whispered in her ear the words, *"These precious days I'll spend with you."*

The days were precious and far too few. As October came, he was too weak to leave his bed. The hospice people came and went, doing what they could to ease his pain, but Liz stayed with him day and night, reading to him, talking, or just sitting by his side. She had never taken care of anyone or anything, not even a pet, but taking care of him was a gift of love not an obligation. She only wished she had the power to cure him, or at least rid him of his pain. But she was impotent and she raged against the God who always caused love to be accompanied by such pain.

The first frost arrived in early November. Tom had been very restless during the night and near dawn Liz went to the kitchen to make some strong coffee, leaving Karen, the hospice nurse with him. Sipping the strong hot liquid as she stood by the window, she stared at the bare trees in the park, their leaves finally having turned brown and fallen to the ground. The overcast sky was leaden gray and so was her mood. The people on the street below were bundled up and hurrying to their destinations. Winter was announcing its dreaded approach.

The door to Tom's room opened and Karen closed it quietly behind her. She didn't have to say anything. Liz knew that Tom had finally been freed from his pain, and she was grateful, but would she ever be freed from hers? She put down her mug and went to be alone with him one more time.

After Tom's funeral, Liz took several weeks off to come to grips with this latest cruel trick of fate. When she went back to work, she found it impossible to return to the same level of commitment to her career that she had felt before. She began to refuse the projects that required long absences, even when the work would have meant another advancement. The cases that once inspired her failed to elicit the old response. She spent more time in their condominium, reading, or more accurately, reminiscing about her time with Tom. She even adopted a cat from the Humane Society, somehow feeling a kinship with the abandoned creature. She named him Thomas without consciously acknowledging her motivation.

Born to a life of ease as a purebred Himalayan with championship bloodlines, Thomas had suffered a devastating change in his lifestyle when his elderly mistress died and her daughter-in-law dumped him at the shelter. Stocky and arrogant, things had not gone well for Thomas at the shelter. He was not accustomed to such plebian accommodations. Liz arrived just in time to save him from certain disaster. He adapted with ease to his unexpected stroke of good fortune and devoted himself again to becoming a pampered feline in the best tradition. The loving care that Liz had lavished on Tom in her futile attempt to hold off his death was unwittingly transferred to the huge blue-eyed cat, an arrangement that both parties found quite agreeable.

With Thomas draped across her lap, Liz would stare at their photo albums and curse the fates that brought her this grief. She raged at the ludicrous wisdom of the old saw, "It's better to have loved and lost than never to have loved at all." Was it really better to have known such joy again, only to have it ripped as before from her grasp, daring to open her life again to another person, only to have to return once more to her "aloneness"? When she was young, her life had stretched out before her. She had managed to heal from the deep wound of the loss of Jeff and the baby to carve out a productive if not fulfilling existence. Now the wound had been reopened. Once again, her life held a gaping hole, but this time would take longer to heal and time was no longer her ally.

Gradually she regained a sense of peace and again plunged herself into her work, the only balm she had ever found for her grief. Her colleagues were delighted when once again she volunteered for the holiday trips or finished up an argument on the weekend. Secure within the cocoon of her devotion to her career, her upward climb resumed.

Then the letter from Olivia arrived and she began her trek to the sea, ironically along the same route Sherman had blazed from Atlanta to Savannah in 1864. Unlike Sherman, she was in no way a conquering hero.

PART TWO

THE CHEST

Reencounter

The next morning Liz came down to the sunny kitchen just after eight to find Olivia preparing her grandmother's tray. After the exhaustion of yesterday, she had slept so soundly that she now felt drugged and was desperate for some coffee.

"Good morning, sleepyhead," Olivia chirped as Liz shuffled into the sunny kitchen. "I didn't ask if you wanted a wakeup call so I let you sleep. If you want to see her now, I'll be taking her tray up in a few minutes. She's usually the most alert at breakfast. You have time for some coffee first, though. You look like you need it."

No avoiding it now. Might as well get it over. "Okay, but I could really use that caffeine," Liz answered pouring the dark brew into an oversized mug. She drank it slowly, willing it to work its magic.

Still in her gown and robe, she followed Olivia up the massive, curving staircase. Liz remembered fantasizing as a kid about descending those stairs in her wedding gown just like the paintings of other women in her family, including her mother and her grandmother. *Well, **that** didn't happen! Another family tradition I failed to perpetuate.*

Olivia opened the massive wooden door and crossed to the windows to draw back the cream silk draperies and allow the bright sunlight to flood the darkened room. She moved without a sound so she wouldn't startle the sleeping woman on the bed.

Although the room was quite warm, Elizabeth O'Shea Mathews lay under a quilted silk coverlet the color of the inside of a seashell, the outline of her body as tiny as a child's. The mahogany canopy bed with stalks of rice winding around its huge posters had been carved on the plantation by slaves and was still draped with mosquito netting, a holdover from the old days.

As Liz looked around the room, she thought about dealers in Atlanta who would absolutely salivate if they could see this complete suite of period furniture in its original condition. Most of the furnishings in the room had been in their fixed places for decades. Olivia had told her as a child that if you moved anything in the house, the family ghosts would put it back as it was. *They probably would*, she thought with a faint smile.

Responding to Olivia's soft voice and gentle touch, the old woman opened her eyes slowly, her confusion apparent on her face.

"It's me, Miss Elizabeth—Olivia. You have company. It's your granddaughter Liz, all the way from Atlanta just to see you. Wouldn't you like to tell her hello?" She spoke to her as she would have to a child, trying to help her remember, but her efforts were unrewarded. The woman just stared with blank eyes that peered from her gaunt ashen face.

Going closer to the bed Liz whispered, "Hello, Grandmother. It's good to see you. I've missed you."

Still no response or even a hint of recognition in her vacant eyes. Olivia shook her head, smoothed back the few tendrils of lifeless white hair and wiped Elizabeth's face and hands with a cool scented cloth. Adjusting her gown, she lifted her to an upright position against a bank of pillows covered in snow-white cotton lawn embroidered with the initials EOM. Ever the mistress of the manor, Elizabeth had always insisted that her personal linens and lingerie be monogrammed.

With an elaborate silver spoon, Olivia dipped bits of cream of wheat from a delicate china bowl and tried to coax the frail woman to eat. She opened her mouth like a baby bird when the spoon touched her lips, but then failed to close it until Olivia stroked her chin and coached her to swallow. After several minutes, the agonizingly slow process was started again. *It must take an hour to get through a meal.*

Watching as Olivia cared for her charge with such loving patience, a disturbing sensation started to rise in Liz's body. As it became an overwhelming sense of panic, she ran from the room. Escaping down the stairs, she rushed through the screen door and out on to the veranda, gasping for breath. The noise startled Thomas, who had commandeered one of the rockers for his first morning nap. She was uncertain why she panicked. It was very unlike her, but she had to get outside so she could breathe.

After she calmed down, she struggled to recall the moment. She had been studying the emaciated stranger in the bed with a feeling of disbelief coupled with intense sadness. As an adult, Liz had held on to the image of her grandmother as an unloving and autocratic woman who dominated all those around her. It was easy to be indifferent to such an ogre but the pitiful creature in the room upstairs bore no resemblance to the person she had carried in her memory all these years. She could not possibly be the proud woman who had deprived an orphaned child of love and generally ignored her. Then all at once Tom's wasted and pain-wracked body had replaced the figure on the bed and she had bolted. Tom had needed her so in those last months and she had longed to comfort him. Was she now longing to comfort her grandmother? Could she still have feelings of love for her grandmother deep inside of her? How could she continue to despise such a wretched, lost soul?

Leaning against a column, Liz remembered that as a child she, too, had been a pitiable, lost soul. When her grandmother had been harsh with her, Mittie would scoop the whimpering child up in her strong arms and shower her with affection. Liz would often sit on a stool in the kitchen as the kindhearted woman prepared the meals. Mittie had been the one who let her lick the bowl when she frosted a cake with her special fudge frosting, dried her tears when she scraped her knees, and told her stories about her family until she fell asleep at night. Liz had learned the little she knew of the history of her family not from her grandmother but from the nurturing black woman. Once when Liz had cried from loneliness and asked why her grandmother stayed in this isolated old house with only servants and her ghosts for company, Mittie comforted her with an old story.

"When the marsh hen makes her nest, she fastens it real loose to the reeds of the marsh grass," Mittie began cupping her hands to simulate the structure. "When the tide comes in, the nest rises with the level of the water and when it goes out, the nest settles back down. Fastened to the marsh grass, the nest is safe and the young birds are protected from the tide. Like that little bird nest, your grandmama is fastened to the marsh, just like all the women in this family before her. She's weathered a lot of storms in sight of that marsh out there. And just like the strength that grass gets from those roots that go down into the plough mud, her strength comes from her roots on this island, and she means to stay here until Jesus calls her home for good." Mittie paused, then rocking the miserable child, said gently, "Remember, girl. You're fastened to that marsh, too. You may not believe it now but someday you'll understand."

A middle-aged Liz sobbed aloud, "Oh, Mittie, why aren't you here to hold me now? I haven't even seen Grandmother for twenty years and she still has the power to rip my world apart. How can she have such a hold over me? I thought I had overcome my sense of being unwanted. All those years in therapy trying to put my childhood behind me overturned by one night in this house. I'm still that quivering little child you loved and protected but there's no one here to hold me now."

Unclaimed Memories

Several days later Liz awoke to a soft summer rain that had been falling for hours. Her grandmother's condition was little changed and she still did not recognize, or even seem to see, her granddaughter. Liz made only brief, infrequent visits to her room and was still struggling with her conflicting feelings about the dogmatic grandmother she remembered and the pathetic woman upstairs.

Deciding she might as well get started on her task of sorting through her grandmother's things, she took her second cup of coffee into the sitting room. The dark, dreary sky outside matched her mood. With a deep sigh, she went first to the plantation desk that had held the family's business papers for almost two centuries. She was amused to think that some people would spend a small fortune to buy other families' heirlooms and pass them off as their own. She would inherit a virtual museum of valuable antiques complete with provenance as they say and her only thought was how to dispose of it as quickly as possible. She was fighting the temptation to back a truck up to the front door and haul it all off to the dump. The precious "legacy" of her family held no fascination for her. No treasured childhood memories filled her thoughts. She couldn't wait to put it all behind her.

After rummaging for only a few minutes through centuries of records of crop yields and bills of sale, she thought, *What a family of packrats!* Abandoning the overwhelming task, she resolved to tackle the huge trunk covered with a colorful old quilt. She laughed acidly as she remembered that her grandmother had kept it locked when she was a child.

"You have no business bothering my things," Grandmother would scold, shaking an accusing finger at her. "You have your own things to amuse you so leave things that don't belong to you alone, do you hear me?"

"Well, Grandmother," she laughed icily, "I'm going to 'bother' your precious things now, all the way to the dump and you can't stop me!" Liz realized she had spoken out loud and felt a brief twinge of guilt, but it passed and she continued her task.

That's strange. The trunk seemed just to be filled with more quilts, handmade tablecloths, and other old linens. *What could a child possibly have hurt in here*? Beneath all the linens, however, she found a smaller wooden chest. At first glance it appeared quite old, probably a good reproduction of an early English piece. The pseudo-aged look was quite popular in pricey decorator shops in Buckhead, Atlanta's fashionable old neighborhood. Her own no-nonsense attitude about her physical surroundings caused her to eschew the chic obsession with faux everything and her grandmother seemed unlikely to have such a trendy fake in her sitting room where most of the furnishings were definitely in the authentic antique category.

Lifting the box out of the trunk, Liz realized that it was quite old. Switching on a milk glass lamp on a nearby piecrust table, she placed it into the pool of light and sat down on the floor beside it. About the size of a carry-on suitcase, the box appeared to be oak, the wood darkened with extreme age and worn satiny smooth from decades of polishing. Running her fingers over the top, she felt a raised area. Turning it toward the light, she could read elaborately carved letters and a date—ELB 1718. Could the chest possibly be almost 300 years old? Had it been in her family's possession all these years? Why had she never even seen it?

The tarnished brass clasp was delicately chased with a scroll design. Such a refined piece must have belonged to a wealthy person. She raised the lid, uncertain as to what she might find. Inside, beneath layers of tissue paper, were a number of seemingly unrelated objects, several small parcels and a larger one of fine cotton lawn tied with tiny silk ribbons. Should she remove them? She couldn't quite shake the feeling that she was prying into her grandmother's most personal belongings but what difference did it really make now? Soon enough everything would have to be examined and disposed of. Besides, she was oddly drawn to the mysterious collection.

She took them out, unwrapped the small packages, and laid them with care on the faded oriental carpet—old postcards from Italy, an Army Air Corps pilot's wings, a miniature watercolor of the marsh, some letters tied with a blue ribbon, and a faded dance card on a silk cord. Reaching to the bottom of the chest, she removed the larger bundle of cotton. Untying the ribbon, she folded back the cloth to reveal an exquisite baby gown, fashioned with faggoting, delicate embroidery, and exquisite lace. Although stained with age and quite worn in places, it was a beautiful piece of handwork. Staring at the dress, she recognized it from portraits of her ancestors in their christening finery. She wondered if she had worn the outfit when she was an infant. She had seen only a few pictures of herself as a child but never one with her mother or father, and her grandmother never mentioned them.

As she lifted the gown to see its full length, a small gold locket fell to the carpet. When she opened it, she gasped in surprise. Peering from the tiny oil painting was her own face! The long hair was styled with sausage curls flowing over the young woman's shoulders, but the copper color was the same as hers, or as hers had been at this girl's age. She even had the same sea green eyes. Her gown was fashioned of deep green velvet. An exquisite lace collar draped around her lovely shoulders. From the look of her, she was obviously wealthy; no working class woman would have such an elaborate gown or such porcelain skin. But who was she? Was the christening gown hers? Was she ELB, the mysterious owner of the chest? Recovering from her surprise and glancing back at the other objects, she realized how little she knew about her own heritage and now it was too late to learn. *Maybe Olivia knows something about them.* Liz went to the kitchen to find her.

Busy as usual, Olivia was engrossed in preparing chicken soup for Miss Elizabeth.

"Olivia! Do you know anything about a little old chest in Grandmother's trunk in the sitting room?"

"What chest? I don't bother Miss Elizabeth's things. You know how she is about that, or at least how she was. I've just never opened that trunk. Didn't have any need to. What did you find?"

"I'm not sure. Come look. You can let that simmer for a while longer."

Settling themselves on the floor in the sitting room, the two women examined each piece. After a few minutes, Olivia said, "I can tell you what I think I know about them, but it's not much. Don't you remember the stories Grannie used to tell us about the old days?"

"I've pretty much forgotten the details of those stories. The most important part to me was how secure I felt sitting in Mittie's lap as she talked. I didn't care what the tale was about."

"They were usually true tales about your family that her elders passed down to her. The servants always knew everything that was going on in the house."

"How appropriate that I have to learn about my family from your family," laughed Liz. "Gentry never discuss actual problems or other personal issues. What did Grandmother call it, 'airing your dirty laundry in public'? I would never have known anything about life especially female stuff if Mittie hadn't told me. What a way to live!"

Olivia laughed too as she remembered her Grannie. "She used to say the servants always knew when the mistress—or any of the women—was pregnant before she did or when any of the men slipped out to the quarters for a nocturnal visit. She swore that her family and Miss Elizabeth's were closer than most people wanted to acknowledge due to some of those visits. Guess that would explain my green eyes and light skin," she said with a sly grin.

"I always wanted a sister, but a kissin' cousin would do," Liz said. The two women laughed again, hugged each other, then turned back to the items between them on the floor.

"Now tell me what you know about these."

"Well, it's pretty clear about the postcards. Your mother sent these to your grandmother from Italy. Story goes the last one arrived the week after her memorial service. These wings must have belonged to your Uncle Jonathan. He was an Army pilot in WWII. He was young, handsome and quite the catch. Your grandmother doted on him, but he died when his plane crashed in France during the war. Then, when your mother died, too, she just gave up. She just didn't want to live anymore and here she is more than 100 years old. Life is funny, isn't it?"

"Yeah, hilarious," Liz said handing her the small picture.

"This painting is signed by Annabeth, your great grandmother. She died in childbirth and your great aunt Eliza, a strange woman if there ever was one, reared Miss Elizabeth. Remember I told you about her the other day? These letters addressed to Eliza were hers. She was in love with a Confederate soldier who died in the fighting. Folks said she eventually went crazy and shut herself up in her room till she died. I imagine it was Alzheimer's like your grandmother has. The name on this dance card is Betsy, Annabeth and Eliza's mother. She was the belle of every ball she attended but she married a rich man from the north. She's the one who bought all the crystal and silver and so on. She did love to have parties."

Picking up the christening gown and locket, Olivia continued, "And these belonged to Elizabeth Brinson, the first woman in the family to live on this island. You were named for her because your grandmother thought you looked like her portrait in this locket. She had this painted for her father when her own mother died, then she wore it when she came to the colonies after his death. She brought this beautiful christening gown over, too. The story goes that her family was well-to-do but when they lost all their money, she ended up an indentured servant in the new colony, married her master, and took care of him and the farm after he got hurt. Outlived him, too. She must have been a strong woman to survive all that." Olivia turned to Liz.

"You come from a proud family with a rich history. I'm sorry you didn't really get to know about them growing up but maybe this little bit helps. You may find out more as you sort through things. Now, I have to get back to Miss Elizabeth's soup."

After Olivia went back to her cooking, Liz sat musing about her family. A courageous indentured servant, a high-spirited southern belle, and a mad recluse—what a menagerie. She had seen her family tree recorded in the big King James Bible on the desk but they had always been just names, not living people. She was starting to regret that she had not learned about her heritage as a child. Surely, her grandmother had known their stories. Mittie had tried to tell her but she just hadn't listened.

"Soup's ready," Olivia called after a while from the kitchen. "Get it while it's hot."

Leaving the items where they were on the rug until she could replace them properly, Liz took her empty mug to the kitchen to join Olivia for lunch.

Elizabeth Leigh Brinson
1735

The marshes seemed to stretch without relief to the horizon as the sleek ship navigated the sinuous turns of the broad river. For what seemed endless hours, Elizabeth and the other weary passengers, eager to catch a glimpse of their new home after the exhausting sea voyage, jostled for space at the rail of the *Prince of Wales.*

As the ship drew closer to their destination, Elizabeth strained her eyes to take in the people standing on the shore. Although her mind knew otherwise, her senses cruelly deceived her with heady images of home—the mournful cry of the gulls as they followed the wake of the ship hoping for an easy meal; the familiar smell of the sea mingled with the stench of fish entrails rotting in the sun; the sting of the salt spray on her face. Her eyes filled with tears as she imagined herself on the quay at Clovelly watching the ships as they disappeared from the horizon.

But she wasn't on the quay and this wasn't her beloved village. After two miserable months at sea, she and the other destitute men and women were about to go ashore in the new colony at Savannah—Britain's first tentative foothold in the land touted as the New Eden.

Investors in King George's latest endeavor held high hopes that this land would prove favorable for the development of groves of mulberry trees, the preferred food of the finicky silkworm. If successful, vast fortunes could be made by supplying the fashion-conscious ladies of London's most elite salons with much-desired silk fabric. It was for this prospect that the unlanded lower classes of England faced with existence devoid of hope had abandoned their native country, envisioning a new life as landholders.

Elizabeth Leigh Brinson too had been forced to resort to desperate measures. She had once occupied a position of respect and privileged comfort, but that life was behind her now. Ahead loomed five years as an indentured servant, bound to work for strangers as free labor in a foreign land.

As the crew struggled to secure the ship beneath the high bluff, Elizabeth shielded her eyes with her hand. Even though it was December, the blinding sun shone through the chill of the winter day. Several smaller boats with sails were anchored near the wharf while even smaller ones ferried the arriving passengers to the landing.

Scanning the bluff, she wondered which of the waiting unkempt men might be her new master. Taking a deep breath and straightening her shoulders, she hugged her cloak closer as she waited with the others for her turn to disembark.

The small boat ferried them to the wharf at the bottom of the bluff. Clutching her skirts, she valiantly attempted to climb the steep steps that led up to the crude buildings at the top of the bluff without revealing her ankles to the men who stood about gawking at the new female arrivals. She feared, however, that she had failed as the raucous bystanders followed her every step with their leering eyes.

On the shore, Jonathan Crawford watched with heightened interest as the deckhands moored the ship at the wharf and the passengers struggled up the stairs. He had been assured that one of the young women would be assigned to him, but which one? Most gave the appearance of being capable of hard work, but many of them looked beaten down by the long, hazardous voyage. Then one of the women attracted his attention. She was searching the crowd as if she too were looking for someone in particular. Her elegant carriage spoke of good breeding and a genteel life spent in the drawing rooms of the wealthy, not the foul streets of London. As she walked toward the assembled crowd, a burst of wind caught the hood of her green velvet cape, revealing copper curls and flawless pale skin. *She must be the female relative of someone in Oglethorpe's company come for a visit.* He allowed his eyes to rest on her, drinking in her beauty. He had not seen such a woman in many months and had almost forgotten how exquisitely beautiful wealthy women could be. With a pang of guilt tinged with a sense of betrayal, he averted his gaze and concentrated on the assembled bondswomen.

Standing near the makeshift platform in the center of the clearing, Jonathan watched as the ragtag arrivals were assigned to their new overseers. To his shock, the lovely young creature appeared among the waiting crowd of hapless souls. He was still entranced with the mysterious woman when he heard his name called. He stepped forward as the highborn lady was directed to him. There must be some mistake. How could this woman be a bondservant? Still stunned, he took the contract handed him, gaping dumbly at the printing he could not read.

When he looked up again, he realized that the woman was staring at him, waiting for his direction. He motioned for her to follow him to the edge of the crowd. As he recovered his reason, he became anxious. Surely, she could not be the bondservant he had requested. She would not possibly be capable of surviving the rough conditions in the new colony. He desperately needed help, not another burden. How was he to treat as a servant one whose station in life was undoubtedly better than his?

Disturbed at this unfortunate turn of events, he decided to pretend he was unaware of her apparent former status and treat her as if she were a refugee from a workhouse or debtors' prison. This new world was to be a classless society. Here you earned your status and she might as well start now.

Averting his eyes from her alluring face, he introduced himself. "I'm Jonathan Crawford from Yorkshire. I'm a freeholder and I farm a plot of land on Skidaway Island. I petitioned for a woman to take care of my three children while I work my land." After a moment, he added in a low voice, "My wife's sickly."

Motioning toward the river, he said, "I've arranged our passage on the *periagua* that's taking supplies to Skidaway and Frederica. Do you have any baggage?"

He realized with embarrassment that he had been so flustered that he had not asked her name. "What are you called?" he stammered as he started walking toward the various boxes and bundles that represented all the worldly goods of the new arrivals— a pitiful collection at best.

Trying not to show her fear, Elizabeth responded, "I have only a small chest and I'm called Elizabeth—Elizabeth Brinson from Clovelly," she replied hoping she displayed more confidence than she felt.

"That's mine there," she said pointing to a small exquisitely carved wooden chest with finely wrought brass hinges resting on top of the others.

The lot had been hauled up the bluff by a crude winch with the ship's other cargo on arrival, but Elizabeth's chest would now have to be taken back down to the vessel waiting below. Recognizing the chest as one of considerable value, Jonathan became even more concerned regarding her suitability for a life of servitude in a hostile land. Uncertain whether he should hoist the chest to his broad shoulders or leave her to struggle with it, he was relieved when Elizabeth reached for one handle leaving him the other. Yoked together by the sum of her possessions, they walked to the stairs leading back down to the river.

Descending the steep stairs with a chest in a long skirt promised to be even more difficult than the exhausting climb but Elizabeth approached it with the same determination that had characterized her life to this point. Just as she was struggling to modestly grasp her skirts while holding on to the chest, a young man who had often spoken with her on the voyage stepped forward, touched his cap in respect, and, relieving them both of their load with a shy smile, carried it to the lower level. Smiling her appreciation, Elizabeth followed him down the stairs, thanking him earnestly as she reached the bottom. Acknowledging the man's assistance with a curt nod, Mr. Crawford directed her toward one of the sailed craft tied alongside the wharf. She stepped gingerly onto the rocking boat and looked about the deck for a suitable place to sit.

Although Jonathan, too, had been grateful for the man's act of kindness, he had frowned as the action reinforced his suspicion that Elizabeth Brinson's upper class breeding would render her ill-suited for a domestic's life. Jonathan had been desperate when he petitioned the Trustees to send him help, specifically an indentured servant who could prepare meals for his family, care for three children, and help out in the fields. And in their wisdom, they had sent him a delicate highborn lady who would most likely be little help and, he was beginning to believe, quite possibly a problem.

Why had he not been given one of the stocky, ruddy-faced wenches? At least, she could have handled a hoe and would definitely not have aroused feelings in him that had long been forgotten. Casting the young woman a stealthy look, he climbed into the boat and began to worry about this new burden added to his already unfortunate lot.

Elizabeth looked around her at the sailed craft Mr. Crawford had called a *periagua,* a name she supposed had been adopted from the Spaniards or perhaps the local Indians. The strange vessel appeared to be three huge logs fastened together with a small deck and a hold for cargo, apparently used to ferry colonists and goods between the new settlements. The large sails at present were strapped around two towering masts and a pair of muscular Negroes manned the oars on either side.

Before long, the captain steered the boat away from the wharf, deftly maneuvering it between the myriad of other small craft jockeying for position near the bank, and pointed the bow back toward the mouth of the muddy river. Elizabeth had been fortunate to find what she assumed were sacks of grain among the goods piled on the deck and settled herself atop the smelly burlap mound, thus providing some relief from the hard planks of the deck. Arranging her cloak with care to ward off the biting wind from the river, she steeled herself for the next leg of her journey.

The outgoing tide carried the craft swiftly along the broad channel. The sun's rays on the water sparkled like the diamond necklaces adorning the grand ladies of Bath as they sat in their boxes at the opera house, smiling and fanning. As a child, when had she wished for such finery, her father would tell her that they had food on their table, clothes on their backs, a roof over their heads, and enough coal for a warm fire. She should consider herself fortunate and give generously to those who were not so blessed as she. Elizabeth was grateful that her father was not alive now to see her present state, little more than the clothes on her back and dependent on the kindness of this solemn, brusque man for her food and shelter.

Soon the captain hoisted the sails and a gathering wind propelled the craft down the murky river toward the distant ocean. The oarsmen, released for the moment from their backbreaking task, slumped on the deck near where she sat. As she had stepped aboard, she had sensed their looks of empathy for her plight.

One of the men had removed his shirt as he rowed. His muscular shoulders testified to the manual labor that was an integral part of his daily life. His ebony skin, glistening with sweat, was marred by stripes of lighter tones, the obvious marks of severe beatings. His downcast glances bespoke his subservient station. The other man, older and less physically strong, lay exhausted beside the first.

Since slavery was forbidden in the new colony, they must be either slaves or former slaves from another colony, perhaps Charleston. As her father had often railed against the evils of slavery, she was aware of the repugnant institution but she had never actually seen a slave. Now, confronted with the degrading reality of the abhorrent practice, she felt a sense of revulsion. Whatever their current status, their browbeaten demeanor and scarred backs indicated they had known reprehensible lives of servitude. Would she, too, become such a creature, cowed and beaten down by the life she would now be forced to lead?

Pushing such thoughts from her mind by sheer determination, she heard again her father's words, "What cannot be bested must be borne." She had borne the untimely loss of both of her parents, the sudden destruction of her comfortable world, and a demoralizing existence in the sordid slums of London. She would bear, with the grace of a merciful God, whatever peril lay in store for her in this new land.

Bowing her head, she earnestly prayed again as she had all her life—but with renewed vigor in recent months—for the assurance of God's comforting presence at her side. Then, exhausted from her journey and the uncertainty of what lay ahead, Elizabeth closed her eyes as the gentle rocking of the boat lulled her weary body to sleep.

Nodding to the other worshippers already seated, Elizabeth Leigh Brinson preceded her father down the long aisle to their customary pew in the old stone church in Clovelly. As she sat down, she smoothed the folds of her new deep green velvet cloak, a Christmas gift from her widowed father. She loosened the lavish velvet bow at her neck and allowed the hood to settle on her shoulders revealing her hair. Though not a prideful person, she had to admit that she was pleased with the way the rich color accentuated her best attribute—her long curls the color of newly polished copper. Feeling a flush of guilt for entertaining such vain thoughts, she quickly looked down at her prayer book with rapt attention.

After the prayers and the hymns, Elizabeth listened with concern to the visiting clergyman from London as he issued a "charitable appeal" to the congregation to aid the "distressed persons" of England. Their financial contributions for the development of a colony in the New World, he expounded, would provide land to Britain's "honest poor families." The result of such action would benefit all: the poor would be able to provide for themselves; the wealthy would have a sense of having satisfactorily fulfilled their Christian duty; and, by no means least in import, the country would be relieved of their support. According to James Edward Oglethorpe, the colony's founder, "England would grow rich by sending the poor abroad."

In his appeal, the vicar drew a beguiling image of a virtual Garden of Eden where settlers would live an idyllic life. In later years, Elizabeth would recall—with a feeling akin to bitterness—his enticing words.

As she and her father walked home after the service, snowflakes began to dance in the air again, adding a clean new layer to the snow already covering the ground. She pulled her hood close against the gathering wind.

"You seem very quiet, my dear," her father said as they neared their home on the high street. "Are you unwell?"

"No, Father. I was just thinking about the vicar's words. Is the plight of the poor really so desperate? I've seen you giving money to men who come to see you, the ones who are out of work. And I often went with Mother before she died to take food and even money to widows or families with sick children. I know you've always taught me that God has blessed us and we must share that blessing with others less fortunate, but I didn't know so many were so wretched. Is it true, Father?"

His daughter's questions disturbed him deeply. A devout man of profound faith, Robert Brinson had long been concerned about the plight of the poor. In the cozy kitchen of the family's comfortable home, he had helped his wife and daughter pack baskets of food and together they delivered them to poor families in their village. After her mother's death, he had encouraged Elizabeth to become even more involved in acts of charity toward the less fortunate in her village. He realized now that her experience of the world was quite limited. In her little sphere of drawing rooms and charitable deeds, the ills of society could be solved by baskets of food and small loans. She had no conception of fortunes that were made and lost in a day and lives turned upside down by an imprudent investment.

"I fear the number of impoverished souls is rising, my child," he said as he slipped her hand through his arm and they continued home in silence.

Following the clergyman's appeal, a special offering had been taken for the proposed humanitarian project. Overcome with compassion, Robert Brinson, a wealthy and respected tradesman, had made a generous contribution, never suspecting the profound impact the projected philanthropic venture would have on his own descendants.

Although Elizabeth had been quite moved by the stirring presentation of an idealistic vision of a new life for England's struggling masses, she soon forgot about it as she went about her daily round of lessons, charity work, and overseeing her father's household while he conducted his business as a successful wool trader. In the evenings, she sat by the fire doing her needlework while her father read aloud from one of the many volumes in his library. Her life was secure and pleasant, her routine varying only with the seasons.

After the activity of the Christmas holidays, life in the village continued its phlegmatic pace. As winter gave way to the warmer days of spring, Elizabeth's father seemed to change. Usually a jovial man who always took time each evening to have tea with his daughter and share with her the news of his day, now he often returned home long after teatime. Even when he came home as usual, he seemed rushed and anxious to withdraw to his study alone until he retired at a very late hour.

One evening in the late summer, he came home in time for tea. As she sat opposite him in the parlor, Elizabeth could see how pale and drawn his face had become. The lines on his forehead had deepened and his hands shook almost imperceptibly as he took the delicate cup and saucer from her.

"Father, you've been so busy that we have not talked for weeks. You're working much too hard. I'm worried about you and Mother would be, too."

As he looked at his daughter, the late afternoon sun making a halo of her glorious hair, his saw his lovely wife and his heart ached remembering how much they had loved each other.

"I've just had pressing business in recent weeks, my dear. Nothing for you to be concerned about," he said trying to dissuade her concern.

Going to the window to collect his thoughts, he said, "I noticed you talking to young Dudley after worship last week. Has he asked to call on you?"

"Yes, he has indicated that he wished to call, but I told him that I am quite busy with my studies and my household duties," she said hoping to end the discussion.

Though not of the aristocracy, for generations her family had been prosperous and well respected. Several young men in the village called on her often but, in the two years since her mother's untimely death from pneumonia, her primary concern had been the proper supervision of her father's household. A serious courtship would just have to wait.

"You know how appreciative I am of your devotion but you deserve to have suitors. It's high time for you to be thinking about marrying and managing your own household. And young Dudley's family is quite prosperous. He would make a very suitable husband. You should encourage his attentions."

Elizabeth was puzzled by her father's words. They had always joked that she would be content to remain a spinster and spend her life caring for him. Now, strangely, he seemed very interested in finding a husband for her.

As autumn approached, Elizabeth noticed that a large oil painting was missing from the library. After dinner one evening, she brought up the disappearance of the piece.

"Father, one of the paintings in the library is gone, the one of the cows in the pasture. Did you move it to another room or take it to your office?"

At first, her father frowned and then forcing a smile said, "I gave it to a friend who has always admired it. Seems it reminds him of his family's farm in Hereford. You don't mind, do you?" Robert Brinson failed to mention that the "friend" was actually the butcher who had agreed to take the painting as payment for an account much in arrears.

"Of course not, Father. It is your painting to do with as you please. I was just concerned."

Sometime later she missed a bronze statue of Hermes that had stood on a pedestal in her father's study since she was a child. Weeks later as she checked the silver closet in preparation for their annual Christmas gathering, several large serving pieces including a very valuable samovar reputed to have belonged to a Russian nobleman could not be located.

Fearing they had been stolen, she sought out the cook.

"Mrs. Moore, I've just come from the storage closet. I can't find the samovar. Have you already taken it out to polish?"

"Oh, no, miss. I don't go in there without you, but your father went in there several months ago and come out with a big sack. Looked heavy, too, it did. I thought you knew."

"He must have taken it to be repaired and forgotten to mention it. I'll just make other arrangements and let you know. Thank you, Mrs. Moore," she responded somewhat shaken. Why would her father take the items and where were they? His strange behavior of late was beginning to trouble her.

She did not see her father that night as he returned long after she had retired. The next morning she met him in the hall as he was leaving with a large portmanteau.

"Father, why are you leaving so early? What have you in the bag?"

"Just some old books, my dear," he replied uncomfortably. "I'm taking them to the church for the vicar." Giving her a quick kiss on the cheek, he hurried out the door with his burden.

Elizabeth watched him descend the front steps and cross the street. He had seemed so ill at ease that she had not questioned him, although she didn't quite accept his story. Going into the library, she inspected the volumes on the shelves in the dark oak paneled room. Robert Brinson was an educated man who prided himself on his extensive collection of books, including many first editions. He was meticulous about his valuable books and had arranged them with great care on the shelves. With a gasp, she saw that her father's first edition of the work of John Milton was not in its accustomed place. It was one of his most valuable volumes and he would never allow anyone to take it out of this room. With apprehension, she looked for *Pilgrim's Progress* and *The Iliad*, both among his favorites. They too were missing. Her father would never part with those. Something was very wrong. She closed the door and, for the rest of the day, tried to keep herself busy with household duties until her father came home.

That afternoon he came in as Elizabeth was waiting in the parlor for Mrs. Moore to bring in the tea tray. Greeting her warmly as usual, he took the daily mail from the mantel and began sorting through it.

"Will there be anything else, Miss?" the cook said as she set the tray in front of Elizabeth.

"No, Mrs. Moore. It looks delicious as always. Thank you very much."

Effie Moore closed the door behind her and stood for a moment in the hall. She had been with the Brinson family for over twenty years, coming to the house as a young woman fresh from the country, and had seen them through births, sicknesses and deaths. She cared deeply for them and had for sometime sensed trouble. Tonight the mood was especially grim and she feared something was very much amiss.

When they were alone again, Elizabeth poured the tea from the heavily chased teapot into the delicate bone china cups her mother had loved. "Lemon or milk, Father?"

"Milk, I think, my dear," he responded coming to sit across from her.

"Father," Elizabeth began with apprehension, "I have begun making preparations for our Christmas party to be sure that the linens are freshly laundered, the silver polished, and so on. Today when I went to the silver closet, the samovar was missing. I asked Mrs. Moore if she knew where it might be but she had no recollection. Do you know where it is?"

Hesitating as if collecting his thoughts before answering, he replied, "My dear, you know we use the silver so rarely. It just sits in the closet most of the time and it has such monetary value. I decided it could be used to feed many destitute families so I sold it. I didn't think of discussing it with you. I really didn't know you were so fond of it. I apologize for not considering your wishes."

"Is that what you did with the bronze statue and your first editions as well? I didn't think you would ever part with your books."

He rose and walked to the window, staring out into the gathering dark. After a long pause, he turned to face her, his eyes full of despair. "I might as well tell you the truth. I forget you are a grown woman and much too clever for subterfuge." He came to sit beside her on the sofa taking her hand in his. "The truth is I sold them to pay off some of my accounts. I had hoped I wouldn't have to tell you."

Elizabeth stared at him in disbelief. Why would a man with his wealth have to do such a drastic thing?

"Several years ago I purchased a large amount of shares in the Charitable Corporation. A fund was created to provide small loans to poor people trying to establish themselves in a trade. The corporation's intentions were honorable, many people were helped to climb out of poverty, and the value of the stock experienced steady rise so I continued to invest in it. Over the last year, the profit from the wool trade has been falling and I borrowed against the stock to cover the shortfall. Unfortunately, in recent months, control of the fund fell into dishonest hands and an official absconded with the money. The stock crashed and I'm afraid I lost a great deal of money. With the stock worthless, I am not only without cash, I am deeply in debt."

Taking her hand in his he continued, "I sold some of our most valuable pieces to try to make some restitution. Now that my situation is known in my business circles, however, my creditors are pressing me to settle my accounts forthwith. I am afraid, my dear, the situation is rather bleak." He lowered his head and, for the first time in Elizabeth's memory, her father, who prided himself on his erect posture, allowed his shoulders to slump.

Elizabeth put her arm around his shoulders. "Don't be so glum, Father. We will manage. You will think of something. You always do," she said. "And are you not fond of saying, 'What cannot be bested must be borne?' Whatever the future brings, we will bear it together. We have each other and we have our faith. We are blessed," she said willing her tears not to flow.

Not since Elizabeth was a child had the Brinson family failed to host their annual Christmas party. True, Robert Brinson was in poor health—the excuse generally given for not hosting the much-anticipated fete—but his illness was in reality a convenience, not the actual reason. A more truthful explanation would have proved much too embarrassing. Although the rumor of his plight was already common gossip in the village, few wanted to believe that the man who had always been so generous with others now faced financial ruin. Even though the local merchants were slow to dun the one who had often been a benefactor to them, London creditors were much less sympathetic. Elizabeth watched helplessly as her father's health continued to decline.

Returning from the market on an particularly bitter March day, Elizabeth shook the icy rain from her blue wool cloak and hung it in the hall before taking her basket to the kitchen. As she passed the door to her father's study, she felt a cold shiver, an instinctive feeling that something was wrong. Putting the basket down, she tapped on the polished oak door. Hearing no answer, she turned the big brass knob and eased the door open.

"Father, are you resting?" she called as she entered the dark study. Across the room, she saw her father sitting in the great wing chair by a dying fire. "Why are you sitting in the dark? And the fire has almost gone out! Are you ill?" As she moved closer, she gasped.

Her father was staring at her with sightless eyes, his face ashen and his arms limp at his sides. Running to him she cried, "Father! Father!" She touched his hand and quickly drew back. His flesh was cool and he was not breathing. Hurrying to the door, she screamed to Mrs. Moore, "Send for Doctor King! Father is very ill! Quickly!"

When the physician arrived, he verified Elizabeth's worst fears. Robert Brinson had suffered a fatal stroke.

Two days later the village gathered at the cemetery next to the ancient stone church as the master of Heather House was laid to rest. The frozen ground, already covered with a crust of snow, crunched beneath the mourners' feet. Above, the leaden gray skies threatened more precipitation. As Elizabeth dropped the handful of dirt into the grave as tradition required, the biting wind chilled her to the bone and icy tears stung as they flowed down her face. The vicar pronounced the benediction as . . .Whapp!

The loud slap of the oars against the hull startled Elizabeth out of her reverie. Touching her face, she realized that she had been dreaming but the tears on her cheeks once again were real. She hurriedly drew her scarf around her as she fought to compose herself. After all these months, the pain of her loss was still almost unendurable.

Diverting her mind from such troubling thoughts, she forced herself to study the man who would control her life for the next five years as he dozed on the deck near the bow. His angular face was quite handsome but his weathered skin testified to long hours in first the biting wind of the moors and then the burning sun of the New World. Beneath his worn hat, his dark hair curled untidily over his frayed collar.

She considered herself fortunate that Jonathan Crawford's need was primarily for a nursemaid not a field hand, although he probably needed that as well. Having learned from her kindhearted father to be attuned to the concerns of others, she sensed the man was as uncertain of their contractual relationship as she. He obviously had little prospect in England or he would not have undertaken such a daunting challenge as carving out a new settlement in this wilderness. His hesitancy, too, indicated that he was not used to directing servants. Still there was something about his manner that spoke of pride in himself. At any rate, he certainly didn't seem abusive or drunkardly. Somewhat reassured, she relaxed against the rough sacks and watched the unfamiliar scenery as it slipped by. From her vantage point just above the surface of the water, she could see only the endless line of brown reeds interrupted at intervals by palms and scrubby oaks that indicated small islands as they passed.

Jonathan Crawford closed his eyes against the glare of the sun on the water. Or had he closed them to avoid the sight of the dejected slaves as they slumped over their oars, temporarily released from their never-ending labor? His calm exterior appearance belied the inner turmoil he was feeling.

He had reached the depths of self-hatred when he petitioned the Trustees to grant him a bondservant to care for his wife and children. He had vowed to Charity—and to himself—that he would never hold another person in bondage. When he made that vow, he was thinking of the despicable system instituted by white businessmen of the kidnapping and enforced slavery of African Negroes to work in the sugar cane fields in the Caribbean islands. He still could never own a slave, but he was desperate for someone to care for his ailing wife and sickly children. The men and women coming to the colony were seeking a new beginning just as he had but they were hoping to find it by working as bondservants for the settlers. They came by choice—perhaps in desperation as he had— but they were only indentured for a limited time. They would not be in bondage forever. Still, his conscience had plagued him as he watched the hapless souls disembarking from the ship. Now just the sight of these wretched men had rekindled his feelings of guilt over petitioning for a bondservant.

To make matters worse, having come to grips with his deplorable decision, he had been assigned person who could not be less suitable for his needs. She was too high-classed, too frail, and far too beautiful. She had attracted too much attention from the men at the wharf and she had even caught his eye in a most unsettling way. He had imagined that having a strange woman living in their small house would be difficult at best but this woman he feared would be impossible. He had expected a sturdy, country woman such as his wife; he had been given a red haired beauty who was even now disturbing his thoughts. He had left Skidaway hopeful that he would return with much-needed help; now he worried whether his already desperate situation had worsened.

Pulling his hat over his face, he reclined against a crate and struggled to clear his mind of his guilt. *God, forgive me, but I have no other choice. I swear I will treat her as kin.*

Jonathan Crawford's muscular appearance testified to his lineage. He was of strong yeoman stock, the last of a long line of Yorkshire sheep farmers and one of the multitude of victims of England's unstable economy. Like hundreds of other small farmers, his ancestors had worked their modest bit of land since before the Norman invasion. His family had never managed to rise above a meager existence, but the increasingly desperate times threatened his ability to eke out even that. Finally, his only recourse seemed to be to move his wife and children to London and seek employment wherever it was to be found.

Pulling his coat closer against a frigid blast of wind from the moors, Jonathan walked wearily through the yard, his mood as gray as the ancient fieldstone of the house that had sheltered Crawfords for more generations than he could count. Glancing at the sky, he frowned, for the dark clouds promised more snow before morning. The sheep had little enough grass to eat now and new snow would make their foraging even more difficult. Each day seemed to bring another trial.

In the dark kitchen, Charity Crawford ladled the soup into the few remaining brown crockery bowls. To call the liquid "soup" required imagination since it consisted of one potato chopped fine and simmered with the last bit of mutton. The two girls ran to greet their father and, even though his back ached from the long strenuous day in the damp cold, he lifted the toddler Lucy high in the air and hugged his older daughter close to him. Abigail, mature far beyond her eight years, took his coat from him and hung it on a peg by the door before helping Lucy into her chair.

After the meager meal, Charity put the children to bed once again with half-empty stomachs then returned to the kitchen where her husband sat dejectedly before the dying fire.

"Jonathan, we have only a few more potatoes and I used the last of the mutton tonight. What are we going to do to feed the girls? I can go without but they are too young to understand why they are always hungry."

"I know, Charity. I talked with Robert Durham today. He's giving up and going to London. He says he's heard there's work to be had there and help for those who are hungry." He sat silently for a few moments then continued softly, "I think we should go, too."

"Oh, no, Jonathan! Your family has held this land for centuries. We can't leave! What about your brothers and their families?"

"They'll keep struggling for a bit I suppose, try to prove they can hang on without me. Thomas would have had the land one day at any rate since I have no son to follow me."

His words stung Charity when he talked about a son. She had borne him three boys and another girl but they all lay in unmarked graves in the churchyard now and, after Lucy's difficult birth, the doctor warned Jonathan that her weakened body could bear no more children. One day Thomas or one of his sons would be head of the family. She knew Jonathan longed for a son but he never shamed her for her failure to provide a healthy male child. He didn't have to. She bore enough guilt within herself and she had felt his unspoken grief each time they buried one of his sons.

"But it doesn't really matter now," Jonathan continued. "He'll lose it anyway when the tax man comes 'round."

So, driven by hopelessness, Jonathan, frail Charity, and their two girls packed what belongings they could carry and moved to London. Once there, he discovered, however, that waves of other now landless countrymen had already flooded the city, scrapping for whatever work was available. Jonathan found himself in a veritable sea of displaced families sinking deeper each day into a quagmire of poverty, disease, and desperation. Countless honest men and women, once staunch examples of moral piety, had resorted to petty thievery, prostitution, or worse. Those fortunate enough to find employment in workhouses labored from dawn to past dark, seven days a week for barely enough to buy food for a day much less a week.

Unwilling to resort to crime and unable to find other work, Jonathan was desolate when, on a rainy afternoon in October, his fortune changed. While wandering the streets in his futile search for work, he chanced upon a man seeking indigent families to establish a settlement across the Atlantic Ocean. The fortunate encounter opened the possibility of a new world to him, the New Eden in the British crown colony of Georgia.

As the girls slept on a filthy blanket in the corner of the dark room they shared with several other families, Jonathan told Charity about the rumor he had heard from the well-dressed man passing out pamphlets on a street corner.

"The gentleman claimed to represent a land company looking for families to establish a British settlement in the New World. The New World, Charity, think of it! It's to be named Georgia in honor of George II, the one that's king now. It's between the Carolinas and the Spaniards in Florida." But the names had no meaning for Charity who knew nothing of the world's geography.

Seeing Charity's misgiving, Jonathan continued excitedly, trying to paint a picture of a fertile region with an agreeable climate in the mind of a woman who had lived her life in a place where the grass had been shorn almost bare by generations of starving sheep and winter winds painfully chapped her face and hands. "The trustees for the colony say the land is just waiting to be turned into lush groves of mulberry trees heavy with silk-producing worms."

Realizing that she could not possibly visualize such a paradise and already envisioning himself returned to his role as landowner, he said, "We would not only have our own land again, but we would have the prospect of becoming wealthy planters, just like those on the great plantations in the Caribbean islands." *At least that's what the man said*, he thought to himself. "We might even get some slaves to help with the hard labor."

Immediately Jonathan saw the look of horror on Charity's face and wished he could take back his words. For years, they had lived as close as human beings can to slavery yet still be free. They owed every farthing they managed to earn and went to bed hungry more often than not. His master was not an individual but a system that kept men enslaved to land that no longer produced and taxes that rose every year to fill the pockets of the indolent wealthy in London.

"I didn't mean that, Charity. You know I could never hold another person in bondage for my profit. I just got caught up in hoping that I could provide a better life for you and the little ones. Please say you forgive me," he begged.

Charity, a frail woman perhaps because of the difficult life she had been forced to endure in her 26 years, somewhat prone to hesitation and fear, counseled against his decision. "Jonathan, how can you say such a thing and how can you be so reckless? We know nothing about this New World. I've heard horrible tales about monsters and wild savages that eat people. Please say you are not serious about going there."

"Those are just sailors' myths told to frighten foolish folks. The Trustees say it's a wonderful place, just waiting for hardworking settlers. Charity," he argued, gripping her shoulders so tightly that she flinched, "we have nothing left. Even the uncertain possibility of a better life in the New World outweighs the certainty of our continued miserable existence here in England."

Eventually he prevailed and signed on, already seeing himself in his mind's eye not only returned to his role as landowner but a wealthy one at that. Charity, terrified but submissive to her husband's wishes, prayed that he had made the right decision. She could not rid herself of her fear as their departure approached.

With high hopes for their bright future, the bedraggled family set sail aboard the *James*, Jonathan and the girls full of enthusiasm and Charity filled with apprehension. For over two months the voyage took its toll on the would-be colonists, many of whom had never even seen the ocean until they viewed it from high on the ship's deck.

Charity, never a robust woman even with an adequate diet, suffered from violent spells of seasickness that left her body dehydrated and her spirit flagging. As she agonized below the deck in the large wooden cradle assigned to their whole family, Jonathan refused to be discouraged. He tended to her needs as well as managing the two children who also experienced bouts of illness though not as debilitating as their mother. Having spent most of their young years on meager rations, their underdeveloped bodies required little to survive.

"Charity, you must try to take some of this soup. You haven't eaten a bite in two days," he urged her.

Retching at even the smell of the broth, she begged him to give it to the girls. "I just can't, Jonathan. Maybe tomorrow," she said smiling weakly.

Jonathan knew that tomorrow, too, she would refuse. He watched her grow weaker but was powerless to help her. He became more fearful that she might not survive the arduous voyage. "One of the crew told me he saw a land bird today," he lied hoping to cheer her. "We should see land any day now." He knew that they were perhaps weeks from their destination but surely God would forgive his lies if they helped her.

Jonathan's spirits soared when, several days later, a sailor did see birds and, from high above in the crow's nest, the lookout spied land. Standing eagerly at the rail, he wondered which of the many small islands might be his future home as the ship haltingly made her way down the snaking river to the settlement. Finally, he spotted the bluff where the settlement called Savannah had been established. *At long last, a new life begins,* he thought as the crew secured the ship and made ready to unload the weary passengers.

After resting for a few days in Savannah, the five families and six single men assigned to Skidaway Island were ferried to their new home on a *periagua* along with their paltry supplies. Put ashore on a small beach that gave on to a forest of pines and oaks towering over dense, mangled undergrowth, they were jolted by the task before them. The site had been chosen by Oglethorpe whose first concern was defense of the settlement at Savannah, not farming. From this point, the settlers could monitor any traffic on the river which provided access to the town.

Given a map of their designated plots, the men were instructed to build a guardhouse immediately to house them while they cleared their fields then were left to their own devices as the boats returned to Savannah. The excitement that had given them hope on the long voyage, quickly deteriorated into despair. It was as if they had gone into battle as little David when he fought Goliath, but even a miraculous slingshot could not defeat the seemingly impenetrable foe before them.

Eventually they cleared enough land to build the guardhouse and finally focus on preparing their fields in time for planting season. The land too was nothing as Jonathan had envisioned. Clearing it had been backbreaking, but he was working his own land again. During the short winter days, he often worked many hours in the dark, cutting down the tall pines and sturdy oaks to build a house and get the fields ready in time for spring planting.

Once a small field was cleared, Jonathan was again dismayed. The Trustees had touted the fertility of the soil, so "impregnated with fertile Mixture that it requires no Manure." He found however that even the most potent manure would not render this sandy soil productive.

He was unprepared as well for summers in the southern part of the New World. The long days in the heat of the blistering sun sapped his strength, the biting insects tormented him, and the deadly snakes slithered menacingly in the thick underbrush. He was used to hard labor but not under these hellish conditions. But he was the owner of these fields or, as he imagined himself, the lord of this manor or at least the one he dreamed it would become. His body gradually adapted to the conditions, his muscles became stronger, and he flourished with renewed health and optimism.

Charity, however, found the difficult circumstances much harder to bear. Her fragile health, after years of poor nutrition and labor much too hard for her wasted body, followed by her devastating illness during the voyage, continued to decline. To her dismay, in the early spring she had recognized the familiar signs that she would bear another child before the end of the year.

One evening when darkness forced Jonathan from the fields and the girls were playing a game with the other children by the fire in the guardhouse, she told him quietly about the coming child. She watched his face as his first reaction was one of dread.

Jonathan's heart sank. Conceiving had never been difficult for her, but carrying and bearing each child had taken a dreadful toll on her frail body. She was still sickly and could barely manage now. The possibility that she might not be able to survive another pregnancy filled him with fear. He blamed himself for the sinful failings of his flesh. How could he have been so stupid! He should have not touched her until she was stronger.

"Are you sure? How far along are you?"

"Far enough to be sure. I waited to tell you until I had no doubts."

When he realized that she was watching him, he took her in his arms and, with feigned delight, said, "That's wonderful news, luv. When will it be?"

Charity, having seen his initial despair, burst into tears. "After the harvest," she sobbed.

"Don't cry, luv. It will be all right. We'll have our first harvest and our first child born in the New World. Maybe it will be a boy this time." *Please, God, let it be a boy this time*, he prayed.

Once again, Charity was reminded of her failure to give him a son as she sank down onto the bench.

Jonathan had already turned away as he called, "Abigail! Lucy! Come here. We have a surprise for you." Taking both girls on his lap, he said, "Guess what? We are going to have a new baby. Won't that be wonderful? A little baby for you to play with and love. You can help your mother care for him."

Little Lucy jumped down and ran to hug her mother. "Oh, Mother. May I hold him? I'm big enough."

As Charity held her, Jonathan watched Abigail with concern. The older girl had not reacted to the news with excitement. She still sat on his lap with a worried frown knitting her brow. Lucy was too young when the other babies came, the ones who died, but Abigail was not. Surely, she remembered how her mother was so sick before the births and how she suffered for months afterward. Each time she had feared that her mother would die, too. This time he sensed that she was even more frightened. He prayed that her fears—and his, too—were unfounded.

Through the stifling heat of the long coastal summer, Charity dragged her bloated body through her necessary chores. The girls were excited about a new baby, maybe a brother this time, but their parents awaited the birth with grave concern. Jonathan worked even harder to complete the house so Charity could give birth in their own home rather than in the communal guardhouse where all the settlers lived together. By the first frost, the Crawford family was under their own roof, but Charity's physical condition continued to worsen.

As the days grew shorter, Jonathan came home late one chilly afternoon, unable to work in the growing darkness. As he opened the door, he saw Sarah Whyte standing over the bed where Charity lay, pale and still. Alarmed, he bounded across the room to her side.

Sarah touched his arm to keep him from disturbing his sleeping wife.

"You have a son, Jonathan," she said, trying to be cheerful as she wiped the blood from her hands and arms on her dingy apron. The wife of another settler, Sarah served as midwife for the women of the colony. She had seen enough births to know that the chances of survival for both the new arrival and his ailing mother were slight. She had done all she could for them. They were in God's hands now. "He's wee but he's alive," she said softly. The hoped-for boy had arrived two months too soon—a tiny, weak creature unfit for his harsh world.

Charity lay motionless, the frail babe tucked into her arm for warmth. Her pale hair was wet from perspiration and clung to her ashen face. Her shallow breathing was the only sign that she was even still alive.

"What about Charity? Is she all right?"

"She's sleeping now," Sarah whispered. "She's very weak, but with good care she may live. I'll stay for a while and try to get her to take some broth. She's had such a hard time, poor dear. I'll give her a little laudanum before I leave so she'll rest for a few hours."

Jonathan stood staring at his wife and son, uncertain what to do.

Putting her hand on Jonathan's shoulder, Sarah urged him toward the door.

"You go now and tell the girls about their new brother. I sent them over to the guardhouse awhile back for something to eat. Tell my eldest to get your supper, too."

While Jonathan Crawford dozed, the captain steered into a smaller, less traveled river that seemed to follow the contour of the mainland, high ground on one side giving way to marsh on the other. On a low bluff, Elizabeth could see the few ramshackled structures of one of Mr. Oglethorpe's outposts such as the one where she would live on Skidaway Island. The settlement that had been described to her was not dissimilar to sketches her father had shown her of primitive villages in Africa brought back by British explorers. She shuddered as she recalled the pity she had felt for those poor benighted people as she listened to his stories of their desperate existence. Was such a place now to be her destiny too?

Past the settlement, the course of the river appeared to lead away from the high land into a vast plain of marsh. Sometime later, the sail furled once more, the Negro men took up the oars again as the boat left the river and veered into a lesser channel. Again, she could see only great expanses of marsh broken sporadically by low islands, some with narrow sandy beaches and wind-blown trees. The tide was beginning to rise again and the water was slowly consuming the muddy banks. On one bit of shore, decaying trees lay bleaching in the unrelenting sun. Suddenly what appeared to be a log stirred and slid noiselessly into the murky water, disappearing below the surface.

"Just a 'gater, miss. River's full of 'em," the captain chuckled when he saw Elizabeth recoil. "They're powerful mean if you get too close but they're skittish, too. He won't bother you none in the boat. He's more interested in grabbin' a big fish or one of them birds."

Dirty and foul-smelling, he was a tall, sinewy man who handled the sails or the rudder with equal facility. He also made Elizabeth very uncomfortable when he looked at her. Inexperienced as she was in the ways of men and women, his sneering stares made her ill at ease and she sensed he was not to be trusted. She curtly turned her back to him, inwardly thankful that Mr. Crawford did not instill the same fear in her.

When her heartbeat slowed again, Elizabeth settled back against the bag of grain. Ahead of the boat, schools of silver fish broke the surface, the resulting ripples reflecting the setting sun in ever widening circles. Gangly pelicans bobbed atop the swells or, with their wings tucked close to their sides, plummeted swiftly beneath the water, only to rise again with their catch wriggling in the pouch of loose flesh hanging below their bills. Other waterfowl, swooping and diving after the fleeing fish, squawked their displeasure at being disturbed in their pursuit. Regal herons on stilt-like legs stood as motionless as statues in the shallow water watching for small unsuspecting minnows to swim by. Lurking somewhere beneath the shimmering water, that monstrous primitive creature waited to attack his unwary prey.

The eternal struggle for existence, reenacted here everyday just as it had been in England, every creature—man and beast—striving to survive whether in the fetid streets of London or in the pristine beauty of this exotic wilderness. The "New Eden" the promoters of the colony had described was a land of fertile soil, delicious fruits, abundant wildlife, and "never subject to excessive Heat or Cold." Shivering from the rapidly chilling air, Elizabeth prayed that their words were true, but a specter of doubt was already creeping into her subconscious mind.

Finally, the captain guided the vessel into an even smaller cut in the forest of reeds, expertly steering in the direction of a huge stand of trees. With skillful maneuvers, he headed toward a narrow beach fringed by dense marsh. Mammoth oak trees covered in a strange web-like growth reached out over the water and loomed over a path that led away from the river. The remains of other trees lay along the shore like fallen soldiers on a battlefield.

With a jolt, the boat came to a stop on the beach, making a curious grinding sound as the bottom came to rest on the sand. Below on the beach, Elizabeth saw hundreds of tiny creatures scurrying in every direction. Although less than the size of a farthing, each had one enormous claw which it waved in a semblance of a threatening motion. They may have intimidated each other but their weapons were useless against this massive intruder. Perilously vulnerable on the sand, they scuttled frantically into small holes to escape the destructive invader. Elizabeth shuddered at the excruciating sound as their fragile bodies were crushed beneath the prow of the boat. Unexpectedly, she felt an affinity with the pathetic fleeing warriors, for beneath her deceptive façade of confidence, she too was distressingly vulnerable in this alien world—this New Eden.

Holding on to her long skirts, Elizabeth accepted Mr. Crawford's hand as she stepped over the side of the boat. Her shoes sank into the soft sand as she strained to keep her balance. She was relieved as Mr. Crawford and the boatman carried her chest and some other bundles leaving her to manage just her portmanteau. Straightening her cloak and securing her scarf against the chilling breeze, she followed the men to a path leading through the ancient trees that was almost obscured by the same strange growth hanging from the low branches.

The little party passed a guardhouse where several haggard-looking men were gathered after a day spent working in their fields. They eyed Elizabeth at first with curiosity and then with obvious appreciation as she followed Jonathan. Just beyond were several huts, clustered together for some semblance of protection from attack by Indians or Spaniards. Again, she felt that nagging twinge of fear. Up to this moment, she had chosen to ignore the possibility of danger, but now it could no longer be denied. The island had for centuries been occupied by aboriginal tribes. She had tried not to listen but frightening tales of the colonists' encounters with them had enlivened the long hours on board ship. Unfortunately, she had heard enough to be frightened now. Besides the savages, it was well known that the Spaniards had already colonized the land to the south and were unlikely to welcome British neighbors. The small band of poorly armed settlers would be no match for heavily armored Spanish troops. Seeing these pitiable structures, she understood the reality of the threat and was, for the first time, afraid.

As they neared one of the huts, Jonathan announced, "This is my house. You'll stay here with my family. It's small but it's dry. It's better than living in the guardhouse with all the other settlers."

The house was indeed very small and constructed in the familiar wattle and daub style used in the English countryside. The roof, however, was covered with dried palm branches quite different from the thatch used at home. Although dark smoke was rising from a chimney at the far end, the scene was in no way welcoming. Beyond the cleared area, the branches of massive oak trees spread out from their trunks like the tentacles of some fabled sea creature, the ever-present gauzy growth eerie in the fading light. As if their weight were too much to bear, some of them almost touched the ground.

The melancholy scene was proving too much for Elizabeth's resolve. All day long, she had managed to keep her emotions in check, but weary from the stress of the day, Elizabeth felt a tightening in her throat and chest. Struggling to retain her composure and sensing that her posture was betraying her emotional distress, she straightened her shoulders, lifted her chin, and started toward the door. From deep within, she heard once more her father's words of reassurance, 'What cannot be bested must be borne.'

Mr. Crawford called out as they approached the house. At the sound of their father's voice, two children opened the planked door and looked out. Their sallow appearance startled Elizabeth. They looked like the waifs who roamed the streets in the sooty slums of London—malnourished and empty-eyed. When they saw her, they drew back into the doorway, wary of this stranger.

"Don't mind them. They don't see many new people here. The oldest one is Abigail and the little one is Lucy. The baby George is inside with his mother. Mistress Crawford spends most of her time in bed now. She tried to keep going but she just never got over the voyage. She was sick the whole trip and ate almost nothing," he said shaking his head dejectedly. "Just couldn't keep it down, not even water. That's why I petitioned the Trustees for help," he said as if justifying his loathsome action. "I can't work the land and take care of them and I've got to get more land cleared before spring. Come inside. The house is small but we'll manage," he said without conviction.

Even in her worst times in London when she had felt so desperate, Elizabeth's accommodations were not as mean as this. Rather than a lodging, it was little more than a hovel. She wondered just how wretched his situation in England had been to make him willing to live like this.

Slowly Elizabeth's eyes adjusted from the glaring sunlight to the dim light inside the room provided by a dying fire in the small fireplace. The room contained a rough plank table littered with dirty wooden bowls surrounded by three stools hewn from large tree trunks. A rasping cough drew Elizabeth's attention to a another wide plank piled with clean straw in a darkened corner. On it wrapped in dirty linen lay a woman no larger than a child, straining to breathe. A small bundle of equally dirty rags rested next to her—apparently the other child. As the woman attempted to lift her head, a new spasm of coughing seized her and she collapsed from the effort.

"This is my wife Charity and our youngest, George," Jonathan said motioning toward the makeshift bed. "The baby came too soon. He was so weak he couldn't even cry. Charity has had a rough time, too. She just hasn't been able to get her strength back. Maybe now that you're here she can rest without worrying about me and the girls. She just needs a little time." His words were positive but his eyes betrayed his true fear that Charity would never recover.

Elizabeth looked at the forlorn man, the stricken woman on the mat, and the sickly children. She had fled her own seemingly bleak circumstances in the hope of finding a better life only to land in a situation far more desperate than any she had known.

Hanging her cloak on a peg, she took in her new surroundings with a false air of confidence after sending the children outside to collect branches to coax the embers into flame. Surveying the scarcity of cooking vessels and eating utensils, she thought sadly of the shelves of pots and pans, china, and pottery that had stocked the kitchen in her home in Clovelly. Swinging the iron pot over the embers, she started to peel the meager root vegetables in the bowl on the solitary table. How she wished her education had included more culinary training and less of the classics.

Through the winter, Elizabeth nursed Charity and her weakening baby but their needs were greater than watery soup and tender care could cure. As Charity became unable to nurse the infant, the child became more lethargic and his brief life ended as quietly as it began. Just days later, no longer feeling that her life was necessary to sustain another's, Charity too released her fragile hold on the world that had dealt with her so cruelly.

Jonathan comforted his motherless children, mourned the loss of his wife and baby, buried them in a grave beneath a huge oak tree near the marsh, and went back to his fields. Grief was a luxury he could not afford. The land had to be cleared by planting time. The survival of his family depended on his ability to wrest a meager harvest from this begrudging ground. Already his dreams of being a prosperous landowner were fading only to be replaced by recurring nightmares of failed crops and starving livestock.

After Charity's death, for the sake of propriety, Elizabeth moved to the guardhouse with the others who had not completed their houses. During the day, she cared for the girls, kept Jonathan's house, then shared the meal with them. Through the coming months, Elizabeth watched as Jonathan stolidly worked his unyielding plot and held on to the hope of producing crops. She grew to love the forlorn girls who, though still hollow-eyed and frail, smiled occasionally and seemed to be growing stronger. Gradually her respect for their father deepened as they worked together to prevail over this inhospitable place.

After clearing away the supper things, Elizabeth bid the family good night and, instead of going to the guardhouse, she walked out to the edge of the marsh in the still sultry heat of a summer evening. Leaning against the trunk of the great oak, she gazed over the marsh to the vast water beyond. The setting sun cast a golden glow on the horizon. With her mind's eye, she saw across the ocean to the shore of her beloved Devon. Though she tried not to yield to it, a wave of homesickness overwhelmed her and the long pent-up tears flowed down her cheeks. Would she ever go home again? Had she made the right choice? What would become of her in this desolate place?

She was so lonely. After working all day in the tropical heat and humidity, the settlers had little energy left for socializing. On rare occasions when they gathered for worship or a shared meal, she found she had little in common with the other women who were content to spend their lives as they had spent them in England, working in the fields with their husbands. She longed for time to read a book or engage in spirited conversation, but she knew in her heart that such pleasures would never be hers again.

After a few minutes of self-pity and tears, she straightened her shoulders and rebuked herself for such thoughts. She reminded herself that this too she must bear. She had no other choice and she must make the best of her circumstances.

As she dabbed her apron at her tears, she heard a sound on the path. Alarmed, she strained her eyes in the direction of the sound. Lost in her reverie, she hadn't realized the sun had gone down. Settlers were warned not to wander about after dark for fear of attack by wild animals or even Indians. She had never seen an Indian but they were rumored to be watching the settlement. Just then, she heard Jonathan's voice as he came toward her.

As he approached, he said apologetically, "I didn't mean to frighten you but I was worried about you alone out here after dark. I know you like to walk alone but it's dangerous at night." He watched her every evening when she left his house. He told himself he was assuring her safety, denying his true motive.

"I'm sorry I caused you worry. I didn't mean to tarry so long. I suppose I was just lost in my thoughts and didn't realize the sun had set." Wondering how he knew she was still there, she continued. "The marsh is so beautiful and the smell of the sea reminds me of

Clovelly. I'm just missing my home," she said, then added, "Life is so different here."

Jonathan came nearer as he too stared out at the marsh. "Yes, everything is very different here. All the old rules don't seem to matter here. At home we had time to do things properly but here survival is all that seems to matter." Jonathan took a few steps toward her, then hesitated.

In the moonlight, her copper hair glowed as if on fire. Her loveliness took his breath. The first time he saw her on the wharf in Savannah he was struck with her beauty. Since that day, he had struggled not to look on her as a desirable woman but he could not control the thoughts that haunted him in the night. She had nursed Charity with tenderness and patience. She had cared for him and the children, even teaching the girls their letters and helping out in the fields when she finished her other chores. He had never really thought of her as a servant and, after Charity died, more than once he had felt a twinge of desire when he looked at her. Now emboldened by the moonlight, he could not hold back his thoughts.

"Elizabeth, even though you came to us as a bondswoman, I've never thought of you as a servant. In three years, you will have finished your obligation to me and you'll be free to go wherever you choose. I know I don't have much to offer you but I can give you a home. The girls love you and you clearly care for them. I know Charity has only been gone a few months and I don't mean to be disrespectful of her memory, but we never really loved each other as a man and wife should."

Jonathan's voice became choked as he spoke about his dead wife. "Before we were married, she had her heart set on a boy in the village, but our fathers arranged for us to marry when I was seventeen and she was only fifteen. Her father was a sheep farmer like my father. He had the grange next to ours. They hoped that joining the family holdings would help both our chances to hold on to the land, but we lost it anyway. Charity and I just did what our fathers wanted. She was broken-hearted, but she was an obedient daughter and her father was a stern man. I never had time to think about whether I loved her. I didn't really know what love was then."

He came to stand beside her as he continued. "You have made me know what it means to love a woman deeply. I can't stop thinking about you. I push hard in the fields just to spend more time around you. You make me smile and feel hopeful that I can make a good living here for you and the girls. What I'm trying to say is I love you, Elizabeth."

Elizabeth stood motionless, overwhelmed by his confession of his feelings for her. For months, she had felt a strange sensation when she spoke with him or brushed against him as she served the meals. She had planned her chores in a manner that allowed her to be near where he was working, but she, too, had little experience in affairs of the heart. The young men who called on her in her father's home had produced no such effect on her. Could she be in love with him, too?

Embarrassed by his own words, Jonathan moved away from her, nervously grabbing at a low hanging branch with his strong hands before continuing to speak. His words were rushed as if he feared he would lose his nerve if he took too long to express his feelings. "If times were different, I'd court you properly. That is, I would take a long time for you to get to know me and maybe come to care for me. But life is hard here on the island and my girls and I need you. It doesn't seem right for you to keep caring for us, you a pretty young woman and me without a wife and," his voice dropping as he continued, "I don't know how long I can bear this longing for you. The pain is becoming insufferable. I don't want you to go back to the guardhouse each night. I want you in my house, lying next to me."

As she felt the color rise in her face, Elizabeth was grateful for the darkness. No one had ever spoken to her with such boldness. She could see only the outline of his muscular body in the moonlight, but she imagined the look of distress on his gentle face. She wanted to say something to him but she didn't trust her own voice.

All at once, Jonathan seemed to lose his nerve. Scraping the hard ground with his boot, he looked again at the well-bred young woman with the flaming hair. "What I'm trying to say is, Elizabeth, will you live with me as my wife?"

Yes, Elizabeth thought dolefully, *things are very different in this new Eden.* Her early years had been devoted to being groomed to be the wife of a middle-class businessman—not part perhaps of the society class but respectable enough, with a house in town and servants. Instead, she now stood as an indentured servant herself on a dirt path thousands of miles from her beloved home as a struggling farmer asked her to be the mistress of a one room house and mother to his two frail children. No need for Latin phrases, Shakespearean sonnets, or drawing room manners in this wilderness. Even so, Jonathan was a good hard-working man who treated her with respect. He was still young and quite handsome in a rough-hewn way. She had on more than one occasion allowed herself to watch him with admiration as he washed the dirt of the field from his powerfully built body. He would never share her love for poetry but...

Her hesitation caused Jonathan to fear she wished to reject his proposal but was afraid of offending him. Her soft reply was barely audible.

"I would be honored to be your wife, Mr. Crawford."

"Jonathan," he whispered as he reached for her hand.

Elizabeth had never been kissed by a man before. She had not hesitated to rebuff any such advances from the young men who courted her in Clovelly. But she responded to Jonathan's embrace without reservation. His kiss at first was tentative, but the emotion he had held in check for so many months overtook him and his kisses became hungry with desire. Charity had been a dutiful wife to him, but their relationship had not been a passionate one and he had never forced himself on her. But he was no awkward young boy; he was a healthy man who had fathered several children. He felt such passion for Elizabeth, however, that he feared he would frighten her and, when he felt her body tense, he released her and stepped back.

"Forgive me, Elizabeth. I love you. I don't want to hurt you. Forgive me."

Astonished at the depth of her own emotion, she answered, "There is nothing to forgive." She put her arms around his neck and pulled his face close to hers. "I have been in torment. I have had strong feelings for you since I first came but I knew it was wrong to care for you in that way. I put such thoughts aside and tried to find my place here. Then after Charity died, you sent me to the guardhouse and I thought you didn't want me near. But all that time I loved you too, Jonathan, and I do so want to marry you."

As they walked to the guardhouse hand in hand, Elizabeth thought, *Yes, life is so different here. Different and wonderful.*

When the Anglican priest from Savannah next visited the island to examine the religious state of the settlers, he performed the simple service. Miss Elizabeth Leigh Brinson, indentured servant, formerly of Heather House, Clovelly, was joined in holy matrimony to Jonathan Crawford, farmer, formerly of Ramsdown Farms, Yorkshire, beneath the great oak overlooking the marsh on the island of Skidaway in the Province of Georgia.

Elizabeth wore not the fashionable gown of her dreams but a plain muslin dress more suitable for her new life. Her lustrous hair was tied back with a bit of blue silk ribbon, a gift from her groom. The marriage was solemnized in the presence of the other colonists who took a brief respite from their labor to drink a toast to the couple's health, a serious concern among the few surviving original settlers. Several members of the settlement had already succumbed to the fever that plagued the struggling new colony.

Soon Jonathan too kissed his bride chastely on the cheek and walked back to his fields with the others as Elizabeth and the girls returned home to begin the evening meal.

In the months after their marriage, Jonathan's spirits seemed to lift. The promise of a new and productive growing season filled him with hope as he spent long hours in his fields. He laughed easily, played with the children, and spoke with increasing hope about the future of the farm. That summer the Crawford family worked together caring for the struggling crops. Corn, potatoes, and melons basked in the long sunny days and were cooled by showers late in the afternoon.

As they sat together in the evening, Elizabeth and Jonathan allowed themselves to dream about a prosperous future with burgeoning crops and fattened livestock. Maybe such dreams really were possible. The reality however, was that though they worked as hard as their bodies could bear, the results by the end of the growing season were still disappointing.

As the blistering days became shorter and the morning air held a slight chill, Elizabeth sensed changes in her body. Although naïve about such things, she instinctively knew that she had conceived a child. She sought advice from her neighbor Mary Smith who had borne six children although only four had survived. Mary, herself pregnant again, confirmed her suspicions.

As they filled the storehouse for the long winter, she felt the child move within her. The spring would see the arrival of a new baby, perhaps this time the son Jonathan longed for. Elizabeth prayed devotedly that this child, unlike so many island newborns, would be strong and able to endure their strenuous life.

After the barrenness of the winter as tiny shoots struggled to emerge from the fields, Elizabeth Anne Crawford was born. Though not the longed-for son, Bess as she was called was robust and happy.

In spite of the stifling heat of the coastal summer, Bess flourished, a sharp contrast to the older girls who suffered from the suffocating heat. Elizabeth made every effort to improve their diet, hoping proper nourishment would strengthen their gaunt bodies and bring color to their faces. With Elizabeth's loving care, the girls grew a little stronger, but she feared they would never fully recover from the difficult times they had endured.

On a late summer afternoon, while the older girls played with Bess, Elizabeth was tending the small patch of ground near the door which produced a welcome variety of vegetables for the table. Her basket was almost full of green peas and yellow squash when she heard the frightened voice of Jenny Smith, the ten-year-old daughter of their nearest neighbors, screaming her name.

"Mistress Crawford! Mistress Crawford! Come quick. Mum's fallen down and she dropped the baby. Help!"

Leaving her basket by the door and instructing the older girls to mind Bess, Elizabeth ran after the terrified girl to the Smith's house. Reaching the door, she saw her friend Mary lying face down on the floor, the infant boy wailing nearby.

"Jenny, pick up the baby and try to calm him. Is he bleeding?"

"I can't see no blood, ma'am, but his face sure is red," she replied rocking the baby in her arms.

"That's because he's crying so hard. Put him in the cradle and go fetch some water from the well. Where's your father?"

"He's in the field plowing."

"Well, get the water first, then go tell him to come home. Go!"

"Yes, ma'am," she said settling the still whimpering baby and starting out the door.

"The bucket, Jenny. Take the bucket!"

"Yes, ma'am."

As the child scampered from the house, Elizabeth focused her attention on Mary. Turning the stricken woman over, she was shocked to see her flushed face. Her friend, an Irish lass with delicate ivory skin, looked as if someone had thrown scalding water in her face, blistering her horribly. Touching her arm, Elizabeth realized she had a raging fever, the colonist's greatest fear.

"Mary, it's Elizabeth. Jenny has gone for Alfred and she's bringing some cool water from the well. The baby's back in his cradle. He's quiet now. He was just frightened." Elizabeth hoped her words were convincing. She feared the baby had stopped crying because he was unconscious. "You're going to be fine. You just need some rest. You've been working too hard in this heat. You just lie here and rest until Alfred gets here to get you in bed. I'll bathe you with some cool water and you'll feel better in no time." Mary gave no sign that she heard the words of comfort but lay lifeless as Elizabeth tried to fan her with her apron.

When she picked up the baby, she saw no obvious wounds but he was just too quiet. The poorly constructed windowless house was stifling in the late afternoon heat. Elizabeth too began to feel dizzy but willed herself to ignore it. She had to care for her friend until help arrived. She was relieved when she heard the sound of Alfred's voice outside. As soon as possible, she hurried outside and stood in the shade of a tree as she wiped the perspiration from her face with her apron.

After bathing Mary and feeding the children, Elizabeth returned to her own home. She would pray that Mary would recover but she feared that she would not. The crude cemetery was a silent witness to the deadly effect of disease among the settlers and few survived such a high fever.

Two days later Mary and her baby were laid to rest together. The tiny boy had sustained a severe blow when he tumbled from his mother's arms, but it was difficult to know whether he died from the blow or the fever, as he never regained consciousness. Mary, after two days of delirium and hallucinations, closed her eyes in peace. Her grief-stricken husband and bewildered children stood motionless beside the yawning grave as one of the islanders said a few lines of scripture. Another life beaten down by the hardships of this promised Eden, another life extinguished too soon, another unmarked grave, another distraught family. Elizabeth wondered if it would ever be easier. Would their dream of a promising new life ever be fulfilled?

After supper several weeks later, Jonathan and Elizabeth sat talking together before bed. Jonathan told her that he had heard about a way of building that the local Indians had used for centuries. Although Elizabeth never complained, Jonathan felt that the house he hastily built when he first arrived on the island was not suitable for his gently bred wife.

"The Indians crush oyster shells then mix them with sand and potash to form a plaster-like material they call tabby that will withstand the rain and wind. The structures stay cooler in summer and warmer in winter. Will Coleman and I plan to make up a batch to see if it really works. If it does, I can build you and the girls a proper house so the weather won't be so hard on you. I'll have to work on it after I finish in the fields so it will take awhile to build. If I can start soon, we may be in it before the worst of winter sets in."

"You work so hard, Jonathan. You don't need to take on an extra task to please me. Our home is fine. The girls love the loft and this room is quite large enough for the baby and us."

"You grew up as a lady. You were accustomed to fine things and elegant houses. I was just a sheep farmer and now I'm trying to eke out a living from this hard ground. I can't give you a beautiful parlor and fancy furniture, but I can give you a better home than this, one that will keep you warm and dry and even cool in this heat. Maybe Mary Smith and her boy wouldn't have died if she could have gotten some relief from this blasted heat. I love you, Elizabeth. I don't want you and the girls to get sick and die. I know you don't expect much, but I'm a proud man and I need to provide the best I can," Jonathan insisted.

So, every afternoon, Elizabeth and the girls filled burlap sacks with oyster shells from an ancient Indian midden on the edge of the marsh. When Jonathan finished his work in the fields, he burned the shells to produce lime, then mixed the crushed shell with sand and water and poured the mixture into frames to form bricks. Slowly the new house took shape, including a small bedchamber separate from the keeping room. By late fall the home was complete. As Jonathan had said, the walls provided excellent insulation from the cold and the following summer the little house was equally effective against the pervasive heat.

The object of the other islanders' admiration, Jonathan was well pleased with his craftsmanship and enjoyed the attention. As was his manner, he gladly helped the others to improve their houses and the morale of the dispirited band of settlers rose above their increasingly difficult circumstances for a time. By consensus, Jonathan became the accepted leader of the isolated community.

With the addition of the new baby, Elizabeth and Jonathan worked even harder on their plot of intractable land. Elizabeth was content with her life. But on the rare occasion when she had a moment alone, she longed for a stimulating conversation or an idle afternoon spent in a gallery and wondered if such an indulgence would ever be a part of her life again.

The monotony of Elizabeth's regimen was occasionally broken by visitors from a passing boat. Located on the water route from Savannah to Fort Frederica, travelers frequently stopped at the island to wait for the tide to change or foul weather to pass before continuing their journey.

In April, an Anglican priest came ashore to wait out a spring thunderstorm. The brothers John and Charles Wesley arrived in

Savannah in February that year, full of missionary zeal and intent on preaching to the savages. Oglethorpe, however, had thwarted their attempts, occupying their time with clerical tasks since literate men were rare in the colony. Charles was finally dispatched to Fort Frederica near the border with the Spaniards to act as his secretary while also serving the spiritual needs of the settlers.

On this day, John was in route to the fort to visit his brother and perhaps make contact with the Indians in the area. His departure from Savannah had been delayed first by the tide and now by the approaching storm.

That morning Elizabeth was preparing the mid-day meal. Though the supply of provisions was still limited, Jonathan's skill with a musket supplemented their fare with small game and on occasion one of the wild boars on the island. She applied herself to the task of cooking with the same devotion with which she tackled any challenge. Her skill was rapidly improving and she enjoyed cooking for her family.

"Mum, Jenny Smith says there's a preacher at the landing." Abigail cried as she burst into the house, her sister Lucy trailing behind her. "And he's coming this way."

"Coming this way? What on earth for? Who is he?" Elizabeth turned from stirring the pot of stew she was tending.

"Jenny says he's coming here to eat because you're the best cook in the village."

Just then, a man appeared in the doorway. Slight of statue, his finely chiseled features and graceful stance gave him an almost feminine air. Shoulder-length auburn hair and a clear, healthy complexion identified him as a scholar or, as Abigail had said, a clergyman, not a laborer who spent his days in the scorching Georgia sun. His dark suit was quite serviceable in cut and fabric, suitable for a man of the cloth.

"Good day, Mistress Crawford," the man said politely removing his tall black hat. "My name is John Wesley. Pray forgive the intrusion but I was informed at the landing that I might prevail upon you to provide a meal while the captain of my conveyance waits for the threatening storm to pass over."

Elizabeth acknowledged his presence with a nod, momentarily disconcerted by his unannounced arrival. Recovering her composure, she motioned for him to enter.

"Please come in, sir. Sit here by the fire," she said drawing the chair close to the hearth. "We are unaccustomed to guests but you are welcome at our table. My husband Jonathan will soon be in from his fields."

"I am on my way to Fort Frederica to visit my brother Charles and to assist him in caring for his flock at the settlement there. My departure from Savannah was delayed and I am forced to break my journey since the captain will not press on in the face of a storm. I have been asked in the meantime to say evening prayers while I am here on the island."

"I have only local ale to offer you to drink, sir, but I am told it is somewhat acceptable."

"I am sure it is quite fine and would be most welcome."

Taking the minister's hat, Elizabeth hung it on a peg as she led him to a chair by the hearth. She poured ale from the crockery pitcher into an elegant pewter goblet, its smooth surface pitted with age. Handing it to her guest, she noticed the puzzled look on his face as he took it from her.

"I brought it from my father's house in Devon. I treasure it greatly," she said wistfully as she turned back to the pot on the fire.

"Pardon my rude inquiry, mistress, but how does a woman of such obvious breeding and education come to be in this primitive colony? Your careful speech belies the appropriateness of your present surroundings and the possession of such a costly goblet presupposes a former privileged lifestyle."

Replacing the lid on the iron pot, she sat down in the chair opposite the preacher who was watching her with great interest. She was drawn to his inquiring eyes and elegant manner. Such men did not often stop on the island.

"No one is exempt from falling on difficult times, sir. Whatever privilege I may have once enjoyed is but a poignant memory now and my future is here with my yeoman husband and my children."

"Forgive me, but I would hear more of your history if you are wont to speak of it. Conversation with another of your obvious intelligence is rare in this environment and I implore you to prolong my pleasure. Pray speak, mistress."

The longing for intellectual conversation that Elizabeth had so painstakingly suppressed since her arrival in the New World overtook her restraint and she found herself reliving the difficult years before she left her homeland.

"You are correct, sir. Such a life was never envisioned by my late father or myself. My widowed father was a successful wool tradesman in Clovelly, not landed or of noble class but wealthy enough and well respected. He valued education highly; I was tutored at home and given religious instruction by our parish priest. My father was a very compassionate man who anguished over the plight of the poor. He invested heavily in the Charitable Corporation and I am sure you are aware of the fate of that venture. The unfortunate collapse of the wool market in the same year rendered him unable to recover his losses. The stress was too much for him and he suffered a fatal stroke. His creditors seized all of his assets and I found myself not only penniless but homeless as well. My only recourse was to try to find employment in London," Elizabeth paused as she recalled that wretched period of her life.

"Once there I discovered that I was ill suited for any position. I was about to enter a workhouse when I learned of Mr. Oglethorpe's venture and took the only avenue open to me, indentured servitude. I was contracted to Mr. Crawford to care for his ailing wife and their children. After her death, we were wed. Thus came I here," she said, her voice trailing off as she finished.

"You are an admirable woman. You express in your recounting no anger against God or even remorse as most persons would at being brought so low to your present estate."

"I do not take your meaning, sir. God did not bring about my misfortunes. The greed of unscrupulous men, the failing economy in England, and the overgenerous and naïve nature of my dear father brought me to this state. I cannot fault God for all of that. My dear father believed that what cannot be bested must be borne. I am powerless to change my circumstances but I can determine how I respond to them. I am quite content with my husband and my family here in this New World." Elizabeth rose and returned to the pot on the fire, her attention focused on the task of preparing the evening meal for her family and guest.

For a few moments, the young minister sat quietly, considering the depth of faith the young woman displayed. Frequently suffering from periods of doubt regarding his own salvation, he was truly amazed at her unrelenting trust in God and her calm resignation to her unfortunate circumstances.

Wishing to continue the conversation, he said, "I am led to understand that the village has no spiritual leader."

"Your understanding is correct, sir," she replied continuing to stir as the steam rose from the pot.

"And your children have no religious instruction?"

"I read the Bible to them each evening and try to instruct them as I was instructed as a child. I have taught them their prayers and the Ten Commandments, but I fear I have little more to offer them."

"God be praised that they have such a devout mother in this seemingly God-forsaken place. You have done well. Perhaps I may be able to give you guidance for their instruction when I am traveling between Savannah and Fort Frederica. I will gladly bring you some of my books which you may find helpful."

Guiding her tutelage of the children would both further God's kingdom and allow him to spend time in her company. A most satisfactory arrangement indeed. Always appreciative of feminine beauty and accustomed to the intelligent company of his mother and sisters, he was grateful to the disobliging storm that had forced his party to overnight on Skidaway. He was eager to engage this intriguing woman in further discourse. He feared, however, that, truth be known, she might rightly be the tutor and he the student.

When Jonathan came in from the fields, he too welcomed their guest. After the meal as the priest was leaving, he said, "Mr. Wesley, my wife has recently given birth to a daughter and she has not been baptized as yet. We would be honored if you would baptize the infant while you are here."

"Mr. Crawford, I am always available to receive a new soul into the family of God. Kindly bring the child to the guardhouse.

I will begin the service as soon as I have greeted the other parishioners."

John Wesley baptized the new Crawford baby, lavishly clad in the elegant christening gown that so many in Elizabeth's family had worn and she had lovingly stored in her chest. Fashioned from the finest cotton lawn, the dress was trimmed with delicate roses of silk ribbon and imported Venetian lace. The tiny tucks which formed the bodice and sleeves had required hours of tedious handwork. The matching cap was tied with silk ribbon held in place by the same tiny roses. She had forfeited precious space in her chest to keep it, but it represented for her an unbreakable link with her past and a token of hope for her daughter's future. Perhaps Bess's child would one day wear the gown in a proper setting.

For the present, it connected her with her lost past, the memory of which was fading daily. When she tried to recall details of her home or her village, the images were blurry and unclear. She feared that in time she would forget everything about her former life. She had adapted to her new circumstances, she loved Jonathan and the girls, and she had even learned to manage without some of the things she once thought essential, but she would always miss England. Her roots, her history, her heritage were there. She had been formed by the stories of her ancestors and the values of her staid British culture. In this new land, she had no history, no roots. She had been required to put her old life behind her and begin anew. With determination, she vowed that she would begin a new heritage for her child. Bess may not have been born in her ancestral homeland but she could build a good life here. Elizabeth had loved the sea and the beauty of the marsh in Clovelly; she would learn to love them here. She would make certain that Bess would grow up proud of her birthright.

True to his word and never one to miss an opportunity, the Reverend Wesley stopped frequently at the island to preach to the raucous settlers. Such occasions, without exception, included an opportunity to instruct his most adept pupil and share an excellent meal at her table.

"Good morrow, Mr. Crawford, Mistress Crawford. I trust you

and your family are well?" Mr. Wesley said greeting the family as they approached the guardhouse for worship.

"We are well with the exception of Abigail who is prone to croup this time of year," Elizabeth said putting her arm around the child. "And you, sir?"

"Quite well and I am looking forward to another splendid meal with your family today."

Elizabeth blushed. The preacher was so effusive in his praise of her cooking that some of the other women had begun to take offense. "Come, girls," she said, ushering them into the building before he could say more.

Later, after the meal, Jonathan suggested that they walk to the dock and try to catch some fish. The girls ran ahead with their father as Elizabeth and the priest lagged behind and settled on a low hanging tree trunk to watch. She wondered why Mr. Wesley had been unusually reticent at table. More often than not, he regaled them with amusing tales of happenings in Savannah and any news from England. Today he had been polite but not as garrulous as was his custom.

After a few minutes, he began to speak in a soft, almost droning tone. "I fear I have been quite rude today. I apologize for my poor temperament, but I am quite vexed by my circumstances."

"Why are you troubled, sir?"

"I came to Georgia not with the purpose of attending to the spiritual needs of the colonists but to bring the word of God to the heathens who inhabit these shores," Wesley began. "Thus far, I have been ill-effective in saving the souls of the settlers and Mr. Oglethorpe has put impediments in my path such that I have been unable to even encounter Indians with the exception of the small number who come to Savannah to trade. Those few, having already been corrupted by the sinful activities of the townsfolk, show no disposition to even hearing the message I bring. I am thus becoming quite discouraged."

"Surely Mr. Oglethorpe does not with intention thwart your efforts. Have you made your concerns known to him?"

"Most certainly I have but each time I am dismissed summarily. He argues that I cannot leave Savannah without a minister."

"Of a certainty, the settlers could manage for a short while. You must make your petition again. On the morrow," Elizabeth said becoming agitated.

"I fear that will not be possible. Mr. Oglethorpe leaves on the morning tide for England to report to the Trustees. He will not see me again and I am not wont to disregard his wishes. I have begun to question the wisdom of continuing in a mission for which I no longer have a passion. I now feel my mission in Georgia was ill-fated from the start."

Before Elizabeth could respond, Lucy caught a large fish and the girls came running to her to show off the prize. "Will you cook him for us, please?"

"We will feast on him tonight," she said laughing as Jonathan joined them. "Mr. Wesley, will you join us?"

"I am sorry to miss such a repast but I fear the captain will be ready to depart on the tide. Thank you for the exceptional meal. God bless you all," he said as he walked off to find the captain.

"You and Mr. Wesley were deeply engaged in conversation. Is he unwell?"

"No, but I feel he is gravely troubled about his work here. He longs to preach to the Indians but Mr. Oglethorpe will not allow it."

"Mr. Oglethorpe is a very intelligent leader. I'm sure he must have his reasons," Jonathan said taking the fish from the girls and heading down the path.

Elizabeth followed, still concerned about the priest's apparent disillusionment regarding his mission. He seemed to be questioning not only Mr. Oglethorpe but himself—and even worse God.

Late one summer afternoon Elizabeth was preparing the evening meal. Humming as she waited for the water in the big iron pot to boil, she was surprised to hear visitors approaching the house. She watched as the men neared the open door, removing their hats and nodding respectfully to her.

"Evening, mistress." The man was William Coleman whose fields adjoined theirs on the south. Twisting his hat nervously, he continued. "I am pained to have to be the one to bring the news but there's been an accident..."

"Jonathan!" she screamed. "Is he all right? He's not dead, is he? What happened?"

"He's not dead but he's hurt pretty bad. He was huntin' for hogs down near the marsh on the other end of the island. He must have been trackin' a pack and they run down there 'cause he don't usually hunt that far off. He shot a big boar but he just wounded him. The beast charged him and run him through with his tusks. Hit him just above the knee. Tore up his leg real bad. Some of the young boys were down there catchin' crabs or we might not have found him for a while. The boys are bringin' him now but we come ahead to tell you."

As he spoke, she saw the other men carrying Jonathan home on a makeshift stretcher fashioned from tree limbs. His eyes were closed and his right leg was drenched in blood and twisted at an unnatural angle, obviously broken. Mercifully, he was unconscious.

"Bring him in here," she called as she rushed into the house ahead of them. "Can any of you set his leg?"

One of the men stepped near the bed. "I'm not a doctor, mistress, but I've put bones back in place before. I'll see if I can help him if you want. He's unconscious so he won't feel too much pain."

The boar's tusk had broken Jonathan's leg just above the knee and ripped the flesh to reveal the white bone through the torn muscle. In the next few days, he slipped in and out of consciousness. Even when he slept, he moaned when he tried to move. During his waking moments, his face was distorted with pain. Elizabeth kept watch by the bed, offering sips of water through his parched lips and wiping his face with a cool cloth when the excruciating pain caused his body to sweat. She feared infection, but the gaping wound remained clean.

Gradually the pain subsided as his broken bones healed, but, although their neighbor had done his best, his leg remained useless. Jonathan was unable to stand without support and pain shot through the leg when he tried to put his weight on it. Another neighbor made him a pair of crutches and helped him learn to use them. Elizabeth prayed that his condition was temporary, but as weeks stretched into months, it became apparent that Jonathan would never again walk alone—and if he couldn't walk, he couldn't work. How would she handle the farm with just the girls for help? Again, she was faced with what appeared an insurmountable situation. But she had managed in the past and she would manage this. But how?

As the sun was starting its descent in the western sky, she instructed Lucy and Abigail to tend to the baby and, throwing her shawl over her shoulders, walked down to the old oak that stretched out over the water. Leaning against a low hanging limb, she felt tears stinging her eyes. "Lord, how are we going to survive in this difficult place if Jonathan can not work our land? I am not strong enough to plow the fields and, even if I could, the girls still need my care. How am I going to manage? You've always been with me no matter how taxing my trials, but this time I cannot see my way. Show me what I am to do."

Shivering from the early evening chill, she started back toward the house. From the marsh, she heard the sound of a marsh hen calling, searching for its mate. As she neared the door, she repeated her father's words, "What cannot be bested must be borne." Wiping her tears, she entered the house to serve her family the evening meal she had left simmering over the coals.

With increasing regularity when the Wesley brothers stopped on the island to conduct services, they took a meal at the Crawford home and were quite generous upon returning to Savannah in praising Elizabeth's exceptional ability to make the paltriest fare tasty. When passengers and crew of other boats broke their journeys ashore to wait for the tide to change or for inclement weather to improve, they too sought a meal at the table of Mistress Crawford. Several times, she had provided a warm fire, a simple meal, and even a place to sleep for stranded female travelers during a storm.

When John Wesley next visited the island, he was shocked to hear of Jonathan's injury and hastened to the home to express his concern. Jonathan was sitting in a chair by the fire with his leg propped on a small stool.

"Mr. Crawford, I have just learned of your grave injury. How are you faring?"

Jonathan winced in pain as he adjusted his leg but tried not to let the visitor see his discomfort. "I have survived the worst and with Elizabeth's fine care I have escaped infection. I hope to be back on my feet before long. Planting season will be here soon."

Behind his back, Elizabeth exchanged a look of concern with the priest. She was beginning to fear that Jonathan would never be able to walk again, much less work in the fields but she kept her own counsel and said nothing to her husband.

"Will you join us at table, Mr. Wesley? Please tell us the news of Savannah. We seldom hear anything here."

"Thank you, Mistress Crawford. I always welcome the opportunity to enjoy another of your excellent repasts."

Later Elizabeth went outside on the pretext of watching the girls while they played near the marsh. Saying his farewells to Jonathan, the priest walked toward the river with her.

"Jonathan seems to think that he will recover completely and be able to work as he did before. I am not as optimistic. I am concerned that he may not even walk without his stick again," she said. "I fear for our future on the island. I cannot physically manage by myself and the girls still need my attention. I pray every day, sir, but God has yet to tell me what I am to do. I have no skills; I came here from England for that reason. And even if I had, there is no work for a woman on the island. The women here just keep house for the men, cook and care for the children. I have found satisfaction in my life here, but all has changed now."

"You say you have no skills but you set an admirable table. My brother and I have dined well with you. As commerce between Savannah and the settlement at Frederica increases, more boats will be putting in here en route. Could you not prepare meals for them to supplement your income until you can make other arrangements? You have a gift for gardening as well, for I have observed evidence of a fine garden by the side of your house. Since travel from settlement to settlement is quite rough, most travelers are men who would be quite willing to pay generously for a superb meal served by such an exceptional hostess." He paused a moment to gauge her response. "And since your husband is at present an invalid, there would be no impropriety in welcoming gentlemen into your home."

Elizabeth reflected on his proposal. "Perhaps Jonathan would not object, since it would be a temporary arrangement." She glanced at Wesley who gave no indication that he also knew that the proposal would be more than temporary.

"I pray you, discuss the plan with him. He is a reasonable man and he will most likely see the merit in it. Until I come again, God bless you," he said and turned back toward the dock.

Elizabeth stood gazing at the water. She could not work the fields by herself but she could run a public house and care for Jonathan and the girls at the same time. The girls could even help her serve the meals. Kneeling by the huge oak tree, she prayed, "Dear God, I believe that you sent Mr. Wesley to reveal your plan to me. Please let Jonathan favor it. I don't know how we will survive otherwise."

Thus, Elizabeth became the proprietress of the island's public house. Customers were few, but she was able to collect enough cash to buy meager provisions to supplement the vegetables from her small garden. Her gift of hospitality was such that even the somewhat Spartan meals were downed with gusto and travelers often arranged a deliberate stop at Skidaway just to enjoy a meal and the lively conversation at Elizabeth's table. As Mr. Wesley had predicted, most of her guests were men, often wealthy, sophisticated men who found their charming hostess well worth any delay in their journey. Women of Elizabeth's caliber were still rare in the colony and many of the men had been away from the pleasures of polite society—and beautiful ladies—for many months. Elizabeth often smiled when she remembered her girlhood lessons on being the perfect hostess, keeping the conversation lively, avoiding unpleasant or controversial subjects, and subtly flattering a gentleman's ego. Maybe her genteel education was paying off after all. She was certain, however, that her tutors had never intended it be used in such a fashion.

Secretly relishing the intellectual stimulation she had so

longed for, Elizabeth seemed unaffected by the effusive attention she received from her appreciative customers and flourished in her new role. Military scouting parties often brought rumors of Spanish soldiers encroaching from the south or sightings of marauding Indian bands nearby. New arrivals from England conveyed news of political happenings and gossip about the nobility. The Wesley brothers were inclined to expound on the virtues of the Christian life at length, requiring Elizabeth to skillfully redirect the topic of discussion lest her other diners become irritated. And, Elizabeth flourished.

The effect of the new enterprise on his wife was not as pleasing, however, to Jonathan. Still unable to walk without crutches, plagued by constant pain, and brooding over his loathsome state, Jonathan became withdrawn and moody. He often sat as silent as a shadow in the corner while his wife served her guests. Elizabeth watched his suffering but was unable to cajole him into participating in the spirited conversation that often filled the room.

He had never been her intellectual or educational equal but when he was the provider that didn't seem as important. They shared the joys of watching their children grow, celebrated each little success with the crops, and encouraged each other when the going was hard. Most of all, even though the workday was long, at night they held each other and talked about their dreams for the future. Now many nights Elizabeth was so tired she fell asleep as soon as she came to bed. He often spent hours listening to her soft, regular breathing and drinking in her beauty, her long copper curls framing her face, released for the night from their usual chaste cap. The limited physical activity of his days now caused sleep to elude him, leaving him with long lonely nights and lingering thoughts of failure.

Before the accident, life was tough but he was doing his best. He had placed great store in being able to provide for his family even in this hostile environment. During the frightening time in London, he had managed to find enough work to keep his family from starvation. In the early days on the island, he had cleared the land, built the house and planted the fields single-handedly. Now he could do nothing without assistance from someone. Now he was trapped in a useless body while his wife earned their keep. Why hadn't he just died when the boar gored him? Elizabeth could have easily married again and not been forced to work so hard. As it was, she was saddled with another burden.

In the coming months, Elizabeth grieved that her increasing responsibility was taking a toll on their relationship but she had to give her attention to their only source of livelihood. Still her heart ached when she looked at her despondent husband.

Elizabeth's English parlor education was also beneficial in another way. After their mother's death, Elizabeth had begun teaching the girls the alphabet, in part to instruct them in basic reading skills but also to help them deal with their loss. As the other island families learned that she was teaching Jonathan's girls to read, they began to want the rudiments of schooling for their children as well. Hard cash was rare and far too precious to waste on schooling when more than likely the island children would spend their lives trying to scratch out a living from the begrudging land, the same as their parents. On occasion though, a farmer might produce enough sweet potatoes, corn, or other crops to feed his family with a small amount extra. A good marksman sometimes bagged a deer or wild boar large enough to share. A man with several strapping sons could perhaps allow one of them to do some manual labor for a neighbor down on his luck. Thus, Mistress Crawford and her invalid husband were the grateful recipients of vegetables, meat, and help with heavy chores in return for instruction in reading.

Through the winter, Elizabeth continued to operate the public house. After Christmas, Jonathan developed a fever and a rattling cough in his chest. Fearing the dreaded illness that had sent so many of the settlers to an early grave, Elizabeth nursed him through several crises with nourishing soups, hot toddies, and foul-smelling plasters.

"My dear, please take some of this broth. It will help to break your fever and strengthen you. Mistress Jones gave me some herbs to put in it that will soothe your cough and let you sleep. Please, my love, try to drink it."

Jonathan made an effort to sip the broth, more to please his beloved wife than to satisfy his own needs, but even his effort to sit up to drink produced another spasm of coughing. When the cough abated, he collapsed against the pillow in exhaustion. His look was one of apology as he closed his eyes once more.

"Mistress Jones also gave me herbs for a plaster to loosen the congestion in your chest. Let me apply it then you can sleep," Elizabeth said as she smeared the malodorous concoction on his chest, feeling his ribs so prominently beneath his feverish skin. Trying to conceal her worry, she said, "Now then, my love, when you wake in the morning, I'm sure you will feel stronger." She kissed him on his forehead and blew out the candle by the bed before he could see the tears in her eyes. "Good night, my love. Sleep well."

In desperation, Elizabeth prayed for an early spring. Without doubt, fresh air and warm sunshine would cure Jonathan's cough and perhaps even lift his spirits. As if in answer to her prayers, spring arrived ahead of schedule. The woods were filled with bursts of dogwood and wild azaleas. Tiny bulbs pushed their way up around the door as the sun warmed the earth after the dreary winter. As always, the new season filled her with a sense of hope. She begged Jonathan to go out into the sun and he struggled outside to please her, spending long hours just sitting in the warmth of the sun. But Elizabeth's devoted nursing and the warmth and hope of the new season were not enough to restore his health. The rattling cough worsened and his once muscular body continued to dissipate. The dark circles under his listless eyes and the sallowness of his skin increased. By summer, he no longer even went outside, but sat almost motionless by the cooking fire wrapped in a blanket to ward off frequent chills.

In late autumn, Wesley came for several days to preach to the growing congregation. As had become his custom, the preacher joined the Crawford family in their home for the midday meal. Wesley walked ahead with Elizabeth while the others followed, Jonathan struggling proudly on his crutches and the girls playing tag as they made their way to the house.

"I fear, Mistress Elizabeth, that I may not visit Skidaway again," he blurted out as they walked.

"Mr. Wesley, pray why not?" Elizabeth asked in surprise.

"The magistrate, Mr. Causton, is conspiring to bring charges against me. He has filed a list of grievances against me in court, cataloging numerous incidences of misconduct. I know, however, that he bears me ill will regarding my performance of my duties as minister. His anger in actuality stems from my refusal, in response to my own conscience, to serve his niece due to the state of her soul when she presented herself to receive communion."

Elizabeth did not respond, pretending instead to concentrate on the leaves of red and russet that had fallen on the path. Skidaway was removed from the settlement of Savannah, but news of the town still found its way to the island. She had heard that Mr. Causton and her friend had been involved in a dispute for some weeks now. The gossipers insisted that the clergyman had spent the past year engaging in Bible study and French lessons with the comely Miss Sophy Hopkey, niece and ward of Magistrate Thomas Causton. When after some months, Mr. Wesley had failed to offer a proposal of marriage, the impetuous young woman wed a more willing man. In the following weeks, the priest repelled her from communion, alluding to inappropriate behavior on her part but the local hags swore that his actions were those of a spurned suitor.

"What will you do?" she asked.

"I am persuaded that God is calling me to return to England. The reason for which I left is no longer possible so there remains no purpose for my habitation here. I shall post my intentions in the square and begin preparations to depart as soon as I can book passage," he said his voice quivering with emotion as he spoke. "My futile efforts here are at an end. I came to convert the heathens, but I fear it is I who is in need of conversion."

"Sir, you must not speak so. Surely, you do not feel that you have failed God?"

"My soul is deeply grieved and my body is weary from the conditions in this New World. I long to return to my home where I may restore my body and my soul. I desire now only the sight of my beloved England."

The two continued to walk in silence toward the tabby cottage. Elizabeth frowned as she thought about how she would miss the priest. He had provided brief glimpses of the life she too had left behind, but unlike him, she did not have the option of returning to England. He was choosing to turn his back on Georgia with no apparent regrets. Would she do the same if she had the choice? Just then, she heard Bess squeal as Abigail swooped her up in her arms. *No, my life is here with Jonathan and our girls in our little house by the marsh.* She would miss her friend and, on occasion, she missed her past life in England, but she knew in her heart that her future was in the New Eden.

A few weeks later, word came that John Wesley had left Savannah in the middle of the night, fleeing from the wrath of the magistrate. After spending several days lost in the maze of small streams between Savannah and South Carolina, he had arrived safely in Charlestown and set sail for England.

The winter after Wesley left Savannah was bitter and to Elizabeth it seemed unending. Jonathan's health continued to decline as cold weather set in. The week after Christmas, his racking cough returned and he slipped into a deepening coma. On the fourth day of the new year, his labored breathing stilled and he was finally at peace. She sat by his bed, allowing herself to recall the brief time they had together until the setting sun cast long shadows across the room. Their future had been so full of promise, but it was not to be.

Aware of voices from the other room, Elizabeth kissed the gaunt cheek of her beloved husband for the last time, then pulled the blanket over his pallid face. She returned to the keeping room where she found her friend Sarah Whyte talking with her children as they finished the meal she had prepared for them.

"I thought you could use some help tonight. Sit down while I get your plate."

Although she had no appetite, she sat down with the girls as they ate. After sending the girls up to bed, Sarah opened the door and her husband Ethan entered carrying a worn blanket. Two other men followed him, nodding to her as they crossed to the bedchamber. In a few moments, they returned bearing between them Jonathan's body wrapped in the blanket. They would take his body to the guardhouse for the night then serve as both gravediggers and pallbearers in the morning.

Later the two women shared steaming mugs of chamomile tea as they sat by the fire.

"Drink all of that tea, Elizabeth. It will help you sleep. I'm sure you need it."

"Yes, I suppose I do. You are a dear friend to leave your family to come help me, but we'll be fine."

"I don't know how you'll manage now. Goodness knows you've had a heavy burden to bear and now you're alone. You took such good care of Jonathan and kept food on the table. I just don't understand why God keeps making you suffer so."

"Sarah! God isn't making me suffer. Suffering is just a part of living. Everyone has some sadness in their lives."

"Well that may be, but you've had more of a run of bad luck than most. You lost your mother, then your father, then you were turned out in the streets with no way of supporting yourself. I grew up in the streets of London. Lived there 'til Ethan brought me here, but I learned real early how to survive. You didn't. You're a lady. Seems awful unfair to me."

"You're right, Sarah. I did have days when I wasn't certain I would survive, but I never blamed God. I learned to trust Him more and I became stronger. And I've had a wonderful life with Jonathan and the girls. Please don't worry. God will guide me now. I know He will."

"I hope you're right," Sarah said as she hugged her friend and, pulling her shawl around her shoulders, went out into the wintry night thankful that Ethan was waiting for her at home.

Sitting alone before the dying fire, the reality of Jonathan's death gripped her. She longed for the comforting presence of the absent John Wesley. She missed his friendship and grieved that he had left the colony tormented by the belief that his mission to convert the heathen natives was a failure. She hoped that he had found peace in returning to England.

In the early morning, a heavy frost covered the ground as the men dug a new grave under the huge oak tree near the edge of the marsh. Jonathan Crawford was laid to rest next to his first wife Charity as Elizabeth, Abigail, Lucy, and little Bess along with the few remaining settlers mourned his untimely death.

For another year, Elizabeth struggled to stay on the island she had come to love. She continued to operate the public house but sensed that some of the other settlers questioned the propriety of a widow engaging in such an endeavor. They respected her too much to criticize openly but she felt their disapproval and, in secret, she questioned the wisdom of her actions as well.

For the second time in her life, Elizabeth felt compelled to leave her home but her journey this time would not take her far. Many of the original colonists had already abandoned their efforts to settle Skidaway and moved to the mainland. Defeated by the harsh conditions of the island, some had even returned to England. Ethan Whyte and his family were living in Savannah, where he had received a lot and they were beginning to make a new start. She wrote to them asking to share their home until she could find work. When, without hesitation, they opened their home to her and the girls, she started her preparations to depart.

In the lingering warmth of Indian summer, she stood by Jonathan's grave as the girls waited impatiently for her near the boat that would take them away from the island. They were excited about going to the home of their former neighbors and seeing their friends. The older girls had only vague memories of their lives before coming to Skidaway and Bess had never left the island. They were too young to realize that their stay with the Whytes would be brief and that they were without a home or a means of support. To them it was an adventure.

Elizabeth looked out at the marsh and thought of her life on the island with Jonathan. She had left England only a few years before but she had lived a lifetime in those years. She had learned to love—and be loved by—a wonderful man, had borne one child and become a mother to two others, and had discovered her own strength that had carried her through difficult times and even the loss of her dear husband. Confronted once more with adverse circumstances, Elizabeth was changing course again and, with the three girls, leaving behind her island home. Her future was once again uncertain, but she would face it with boldness as she had in the past. This time, however, she added Jonathan's strength to her own.

In the sound of the rustling leaves, she heard again her father's words, "What cannot be bested must be borne." She straightened her shoulders and lifted her chin. Picking up Bess, she called to the older girls to hold hands. As she walked toward the waiting boat, she passed for the last time beneath the ancient oak near the edge of the marsh, just as she had when she first arrived as an indentured servant.

The tide was turning as the craft slid away from the beach. Plough mud and exposed oyster beds lined the banks of the estuary as the small party floated by. Rising from the mud, the long stalks of the marsh grass obscured their view. Wading birds crept along the edge of the water as glittering schools of tiny fish swam near the boat. Startled by the intruders, a marsh hen flew from between the reeds, emitting a shrill cry as she rose. Somewhere in the dense grass was the nest she was so reluctant to leave. With a sad smile, Elizabeth felt a kinship with the frightened bird. She too was fearful at being forced to leave her home on the marsh, but like the sturdy nest of marsh hen, her heart would be forever fastened to the marsh.

Unopened Journal

Returning to the sitting room after indulging herself with a second bowl of Olivia's delicious chicken soup, Liz decided to rewrap the items in fresh tissue paper before replacing them. As she removed the remaining faded tissue from the chest, she discovered several old books underneath. The volumes were of embossed leather with gold-edged pages of fine parchment. Opening the cover of the top book, she read *The Journal of Elizabeth O'Shea Mathews, Volume One.* She was tempted to abandon her project and begin reading the journals, but somehow she didn't feel right exposing her grandmother's private thoughts while she lay dying upstairs.

Probably just some silly girlish musings or dull accounts of her boring life anyway. I doubt she ever had anything exciting to write about, she thought as she put them back in the box with the other items and closed the lid.

PART THREE

THE ANVIL

The Buckle

The phone rang as Liz was sorting through yet another pile of papers in her grandmother's old desk in the parlor. She heard Olivia answer it and went back to her chore. A few moments later, Olivia called her to the phone.

"Good afternoon," Jack said. "Olivia said you were shuffling papers again."

"Yes, I'm rifling through this never-ending cache. I think she kept everything she ever received, important or not."

"Well you'd better be glad she did. You wouldn't know most of what you know if she hadn't."

"I suppose you're right. I just wish she had been a little more discriminating."

Jack laughed. "Are you about ready for a break?"

"Maybe. What did you have in mind?"

"Do you remember Jim Johnson? He was in our class. He runs a dredging company now and he's doing the work at the new marina down the river from your place. They're developing that stretch into condos with a big dock on deep water so his company is dredging along the bank."

"I've been curious about that development. I really would like to know more about it. I'm going to need to do something about this place someday, you know," Liz said, feeling a little disloyal even thinking about it while her grandmother was still alive.

"Anyway, his crew had a problem with one of the big hoses yesterday and had to stop work when it became clogged. When they went down to check it, they found a hunk of iron wrapped in some old chain. Jim knows I'm interested in old wrecks so he called me to come check it out. He said they had brought up some other objects, too, so I'm going to see what he has. I just thought you might like to ride over with me."

"I guess a break would do me good. And I am interested in the project."

"Great! I'll pick you up at the dock in about fifteen minutes. Don't forget your sunscreen. It's really bearing down out there."

Olivia was rolling out the crust for an apple pie when Liz walked into the kitchen.

"I'm going to ride over to the new development with Jack," Liz said. "He's going to look at some artifacts they've dredged up and I'm interested in finding out more about what they're going to build. I hope it will increase the value of this place when I decide what I'm going to do with it after ... well, you know."

Liz thought she saw a slight frown on Olivia's face when she mentioned the future. They had not really talked about what would become of Marsh Oaks when her grandmother died but surely Olivia knew she wouldn't stay on the island. She hadn't given any thought to what Olivia might do. *I wonder what she will do,* Liz thought. *She's just like me, the end of the line. No children, no siblings. Two pieces of driftwood, bobbing with the tide.*

Pushing that disturbing thought aside, Liz continued, "Okay if I ask him to have supper with us tonight? Do you have enough?"

Smiling again, Olivia said, "I always have enough for one more. Jack seems to turn up pretty regularly around here these days." *I hope he'll keep coming and make you want to stay for good,* Olivia mused as Liz headed out the screen door and toward the dock, waving.

Olivia finished the pie then fixed the tray to take upstairs. She knew when Liz came that her plan had been to stay until her grandmother died then sell the property and head back north. The longer she stayed on the island, however, the less she talked about getting back to Atlanta. She was changing in other ways too. Ways that were subtle but sure. In Atlanta, city people ate dinner; on the island, folks ate supper and Liz had asked about supper. *Yes, she's changing.*

As she picked up the tray and started upstairs, she whispered aloud, "Miss Elizabeth, you just hang on a little longer and I think we can bring her around. I know you would want her to stay here where she belongs, so you just hang on, honey." Then she prayed silently, *Dear Lord, please let her hang on long enough for Marsh Oaks to work its magic on Liz. I know my happiness is here and I truly believe hers is too.*

"Hang on, Miss Elizabeth. I'm comin' now," she sang out as she climbed the long staircase. "Hang on, Missy."

In the blazing July heat, Jack maneuvered the boat to the ladder while Liz climbed down. Smearing on the heavy layer of sunscreen her fair skin required, Liz squeezed the last of the lotion from the tube and laughed. "I don't think I've used a whole bottle of sunscreen a year in all my adult life and now I can't keep enough of it."

"Sounds like you spent too much time indoors. You need to be out enjoying God's creation more. It's good for the soul."

"The soul, maybe, but it's doing a number on my face. I'm going to look like a withered old crone!"

"Never happen. Your face is much too beautiful," Jack called over the roar of the engine.

Liz felt herself blush under the floppy straw hat she was wearing. No one had called her beautiful in years. She almost giggled. *Don't be ridiculous. He's just making conversation.* Still she had to admit she liked the compliment and the sensation it produced.

Smiling to herself, she watched the waterfowl as they soared overhead scouring the water for schools of fish until the boat reached the work area. Jack tied up to the huge barge that held the dredging equipment and they climbed up the rope ladder hanging over the side.

"Glad you could come over, Jack," a large man with a deep tan in khaki shorts, soiled camouflage tee shirt, and a red baseball cap with a bulldog on it called as they came aboard.

"Thanks for giving me a call, Jim. You remember Liz Briggs from school, don't you?"

"The redhead you used to go with?"

"The same," Jack teased, putting his arm around her shoulder. "The red hair's under the hat."

"I thought you moved away after school, Atlanta or somewhere. You living here now?"

"No, I'm just here for a visit. I really don't know how long I'll be here." She hoped he would change the subject. Somehow, she just didn't want to talk about her situation today, especially with someone she barely remembered.

"You better watch out. Lots of folks come to visit and just never leave. Saltwater gets in their blood."

Jack seemed to sense her discomfort and came to her rescue.

"You said you had found some interesting stuff. Is it on the barge?"

"It's over here," Jim said going over to a plastic bucket sitting next to some rusted chain. "We've dug up the usual pieces of broken china, some nails, a bunch of bottles but this length of chain is what caused the problem yesterday. Look at those links. They've got to be hand forged. They were wrapped around this old anvil like it was meant to weigh something down. The boys said it must have been a body," he laughed. "You know like the Mafia or something. Ever seen one like it?"

"Well, these links are definitely hand forged and I would guess Civil War period," Jack said as he turned the heavy links in his hands. "They must have been made by slaves on one of the plantations around here, but it does seem odd that someone would deliberately sink an anvil. They were just too valuable to waste," Jack said. "Maybe someone did want to dispose of a body."

Liz felt a shiver as she ran her finger over the piece of chain Jack held out to her. How strange to touch an object from another era and think about who might have forged it and how it came to be on the bottom of the river all these years. She wondered, too, if her family had owned the slave who crafted it or if Olivia might be his descendant.

She was still lost in her thoughts when she realized Jim was speaking to her.

"We found this, too. It was covered with rust but I took it home last night and cleaned it up."

He held out a large brass belt buckle. "On the back it has the guy's initials and a date—HCR, 1844. Wonder who he was?"

Again, Liz shivered as she remembered a name in the family tree inscribed in the family Bible—Henry Carlton Rogers, her grandmother's great-great uncle.

Carlton and Susie
1845

Elegant carriages bearing the socially elite—
and filthy rich—families from the other plantations on the island
rumbled up the long drive lined with ancient oaks, their moss-
covered branches interwoven above the crushed oyster shells like
a leafy canopy. Slaves holding lanterns greeted the guests and
ran alongside the coaches to light the way. Music spilled from
the French doors opening on to the veranda as the guests drove
under the porte-cochère and entered the massive front door. Few
declined a coveted invitation to spend an exhilarating evening at
Marsh Oaks, the gracious home of Henry and Lizzie Rogers. The
ladies delighted in an opportunity to display their newest gowns
from Paris and New York and the gentlemen appreciated the fact
that Rogers never skimped on the food and libations he served his
guests. This evening was no exception.

Henry, the master of the plantation, owed his enviable status
to his fortuitous marriage to Lizzie Roberts, the last surviving heir
of Elizabeth and George Roberts. Through a long series of unusual
circumstances, the plantation had passed down through the female
line since 1739. Following the death of the original settler Jonathan
Crawford, his widow Elizabeth and her daughters Abigail, Lucy,
and Bess left the island. The widow later found employment at
Bethesda, the orphanage founded by George Whitefield on land
just across the Skidaway Narrows from the Crawford farm. In
1742, a yellow fever epidemic took the life of Lucy and two years
later Abigail died in childbirth. Although women were not allowed
to inherit property, the land somehow remained in the hands of
Crawford's youngest daughter Bess and her husband. Several
years later, they returned to the island, renewed the attempt to

cultivate the land, and named their home Marsh Oaks. Succeeding generations managed to make the farm profitable until by the early 1800's the estate had become the showplace of the island.

Henry Rogers enjoyed opening the beautiful old house to his many friends. On this night, the occasion was ostensibly a ball marking the end of the harvest season, but such an occasion also served to remind the other families on the island of Henry's very prosperous plantation and the fact that his lovely daughter was, in effect, up for bids. Dressed in a gown of crimson taffeta trimmed with a profusion of beads that sparkled with each coquettish movement, sixteen-year-old Betsy was enjoying the limelight, flirting with every eligible young man in the impressive ballroom.

"I do say that Betsy Rogers is a fine specimen of blossoming southern womanhood. I'd like to get her behind the barn one moonless night." Slurring his words as he spoke, Will Coleman was already feeling the effects of numerous cups of the potent Chatham Artillery Punch Henry Rogers served with pride on such festive evenings.

Grabbing the collar of Will's jacket, Carlton Rogers, son and heir to Henry's considerable fortune, drew the shocked man's face close to his and hissed, "How dare you make such a scurrilous remark about my sister's virtue? I ought to take you out back and tan your hide!"

"Take it easy, Carlton! You know he's just drunk," cried Sam Jones, Carlton's best friend. "He didn't mean any disrespect to Betsy. Let him go."

Carlton relaxed his hold but continued to glare at the other young man. Will straightened his jacket and said with his head down, "I'm sorry. I just wasn't thinkin' about her being your sister. I didn't mean nothin' by it."

"Taste of your own medicine, eh, ol' boy? Dare say you've made the same remark about most of the young ladies on this island. Stings when it's your sister, doesn't it?" Sam said recalling an evening when his own sister had been the target of Carlton's lustful words. Only Sam could rebuke his friend without drawing a blow. They were as close as brothers and each minced no words about the other's shortcomings. "Let's go have some more punch then go out on the veranda for a smoke."

His handsome face still distorted with anger, Carlton growled. "Just keep that dirt farmer away from me."

Will's face flushed red with fury at his supposed friend's remark, turned on his heels, and stormed out of the house.

"Good riddance," Carlton snarled. "He's not good enough for her, even in his wildest dreams!"

Sam put his arm around his friend's shoulder and guided him across the room to the punchbowl.

The harvest moon slipped behind a cloud as Carlton Rogers eased the back door of the big house closed and moved as silent as a ghost across the veranda. The lack of moonlight presented no problem as he made his way down the familiar path to the row of slave cabins that separated the main house from the fields. At this time of night all the houses were dark and quiet. Not that he needed any light, even though he was feeling the discomforting effects of his overindulgence in the infamous punch earlier in the evening.

He was still stinging from Will's remark about his sister. True, his beautiful but vain little sister was approaching marriageable age and his father was beginning to cull the crop of eager young suitors hoping to wed and bed the delicious young heiress, but he would brook no lewd references to her, particularly from the son of a dirt farmer, friend or no friend.

Will Coleman's father James farmed the land that adjoined the Rogers plantation. His family had been among the early settlers of the island but, unlike the owners of Marsh Oaks, their descendants had never been able to rise above the level of simple farmers and had never entered the elite ranks of Skidaway society. Carlton and Will were hunting—and drinking—buddies. Will was allowed to join in on some of the social events at the Roger's home, but everyone knew that he was not a true member of Carlton's circle.

The plantation would one day belong to Carlton, but his father's wealth was such that Betsy and her future husband would also inherit a fortune. Henry Rogers would allow only a very financially secure gentleman from a family with an impeccable heritage to marry his princess. No low class dirt farmer or penniless fortune hunter would profit from the wealth of Marsh Oaks. An obedient girl who would do as her father asked, not to mention one oblivious to the politics surrounding her eventual marriage, his sister's only concern was that her fiancé be handsome and charming—and an excellent dancer.

As he stumbled down the path, he was now eager to exercise his right as the future master of the plantation. Reaching the second house in the row of cabins, he stumbled up the ramshackled steps and shoved open the flimsy door of the room where Susie and her two younger sisters were sleeping in a rusty iron bed.

"Where is she? Where's she hidin'?" Carlton bellowed, his drunken state causing his words to slur almost unintelligibly.

Startled by the unexpected intrusion, Susie sat up in bed, covering her distended belly with the tattered quilt. Having been a house servant for several years, she knew very well who the intruder was. She also feared why he was there.

"Who you callin' for, Master Carlton?"

"You know who I want. That young gal. What's her name? Sally, that's it. It's time for her to be broken in," he laughed crudely.

"She's asleep. Please, Master Carlton," Susie pleaded. "She's only twelve. Please let her be."

"You should have thought of her and rid yourself of that bastard you got in there when you could. I can't stand you like that so I'll have to take her. Can't be helped. Get her up and send her outside. Now!" he barked as he staggered out the door. "And send a blanket with her. It's a beautiful night."

Too distraught to move, Susie sat immobile for a moment. She couldn't bear to give him her precious younger sister but she dared not disobey the young master. He had complete control of her life and her sisters' lives as well. Filled with rage but powerless to ignore his summons, she reached for Sally who was already awake and cowering under the cover. Susie held the trembling girl in her arms and tried to console her but what comfort could she possibly offer her?

This was not the first time he had stormed into Susie's cabin in the middle of the night. Several years before Susie had caught the eye of Carlton's father who had "broken her in" then passed her on to his son. It didn't pay for a nubile serving girl to attract attention to herself. Nocturnal visits to the slave quarters by the men of the household were an accepted practice on many plantations. Such visits were never discussed in polite company, but were considered a "rite of passage" for a young gentleman and generally continued even after he took a bride.

"Baby, I wish I could stop him but I can't," Susie whispered to the terrified child. "You just keep your eyes closed and pray to Jesus to take care of you. Don't fight him. It just makes him meaner. It'll be over soon."

Slowly Sally stood, her gangly arms hanging limply by her side, a mere child with no hint of a woman's body. Why did he want to hurt her? She was so young! With a look that begged Susie to save her, the innocent virgin went out into the dark night.

Susie sat on her bed, clutched her still sleeping youngest sister to her, and keened bitterly. How long before he tired of Sally and came for this little one, too? It just wasn't right!

Since Carlton had started coming to the quarters for her, she had prayed that, even though she hated him, she could continue to satisfy his lust and he would leave her little sisters alone. She had relied on Mama Juba's magic potions to keep her from conceiving for a long time, but her luck had finally run out. She would have his baby before spring came. The last time he took her, he cursed her for her swollen body and snarled that he had no interest in carnal relations with a bloated cow. Susie had been relieved to know that she would have a few months of freedom from his lustful attention. He might even find another slave to satisfy him. She never dreamed that he would force himself on her little sister.

"Mama," she wailed, "I promised you I'd take care of the girls after you were gone and I'm tryin' to protect 'em, but what can I do?"

She was still holding the sleeping child when she heard the sound of his boots on the crushed shell as Carlton, having finished his disgusting deed, started unsteadily back to the big house. The door creaked open. A sliver of icy moonlight cast an eerie glow in the room as Sally stumbled through the door and collapsed on the floor whimpering, her shift torn and splotched with blood. How could the Lord let him do this to her sister? Why did she have to stand back and allow him to rape her and not do anything?

Gently Susie bathed the blood from the child's bruised body, put a clean shift on her, and rocked her until she fell asleep. Then she covered the sleeping girls and, wrapping a worn gray shawl around her shoulders, walked out on the steps. In the chill of the early autumn night, she pushed her hands against her aching lower back as the child inside her pressed painfully against her ribs. She wished desperately that the baby were Jacob's. They had both grown up at Marsh Oaks and were planning to jump the broom, in the African tradition, when she discovered she was pregnant with the young master's child. She could not expect Jacob to take her as his wife now but he insisted that he still loved her and wanted to be her husband.

Her face still damp with tears, she looked up at the waning moon.

"I don't know how I'll stop him but I swear on my baby's life, he will never touch my little sister again!"

As the Christmas holidays approached, the Rogers began a round of festive occasions that took them to most of the other plantations on the island. They attended parties as well in Savannah, necessitating a stay of several days with friends. Even the slaves were excited as Master Henry, in a gesture of generosity, gave them three days to celebrate and rest before the new year began. The plantation hummed with preparations. Decorations were hung throughout the manor. A steady stream of smoke rose from the cookhouse as meats were roasted and an infinite variety of sweets was produced for the anticipated guests.

On Christmas Eve, the family was preparing for the traditional worship service and dinner party at the Wilson plantation across the island. As they gathered in the sitting room before their departure, Carlton, still suffering from the effects of the previous evening's excess, staggered into the room.

"Father, I'm afraid I am unable to accompany you this evenin'.

I am quite unwell. Must have gotten hold of somethin' that didn't agree with me," he said anticipating his father's displeasure.

His mother tensed, expecting another unpleasant scene between her husband and her strong-willed son. Henry was determined that his heir should conduct himself in a suitable manner, but Carlton seemed bent on defying him at every turn. He and his friends spent their days hunting or fishing and their nights drinking and playing cards until all hours. Her son was often away from home for days, eventually turning up unshaven and smelling like a wild creature. She prayed constantly that he would change but she feared he would not.

"Yes, I imagine you did, but I suspect it was more like something you drank," his father said turning his back on his wayward son. "I am most perturbed that you intend to stay at home but, considering your most unsavory appearance, that seems to be the only alternative. I shall extend your apologies and try to put a good face on it. But I remind you, I am most displeased."

"Oh, Carlton, I had a special gift made for you to wear this evening," Betsy said in a peeved voice. "Since he won't be with us, Father, may I give it to him anyway?"

Henry might often be irritated with his son, but his daughter was the light of his life. He rarely refused her anything. "If it will make you happy, my dear. I'm sure you are disappointed that your brother will not be joining us," he said, glaring angrily at Carlton.

Handing her brother a small package wrapped in gaily-colored fabric, she said happily, "Merry Christmas, Carlton. Open it now. I had it made for you in Savannah. I hope you like it."

From the wrapping, he removed a shiny brass belt buckle bearing his initials—HCR—on the back side. "It's fine-lookin', Bets. How sweet of you," he said removing the old buckle on his belt and attaching the new one. "I shall wear it always," he said in an exaggerated gesture of appreciation. Kissing his sister's forehead, a bleary-eyed Carlton wandered back to his bed. By late afternoon, the rest of the family had departed and would not return until the early hours of the morning.

Rousing from his alcohol-induced sleep late in the evening, Carlton pulled on his boots, put on his coat, and headed for the slave quarters, delaying just long enough to grab a bottle of brandy from his father's study. The night was unusually cold for coastal Georgia and Carlton warmed himself liberally with the brandy. In the moonlight, the new buckle glistened. By the time he reached Susie's cabin, he almost fell up the steps and hurled himself at the door, cursing in a loud voice.

Susie and her sisters had been sitting by the fire when she recognized his voice. "Quick! Hide on the other side of the bed," she whispered to her sisters then opened the door.

"Where is she?" Carlton bellowed.

"My sister's not here."

"You're lyin'. Where is she?"

"Look for yourself," Susie taunted as she moved toward the fireplace.

"She's hidin' under the bed, isn't she?" he growled as he leaned down to peer under the iron frame. "Come out of there, now!"

Reaching behind her, Susie grabbed the pointed iron rod she used to stoke the coals and, holding it tightly with both hands, she raised it above her head. As Carlton straightened and turned toward her, she rammed the rod with a downward motion into his midsection with all her might. As he staggered back, blood spread across his fine linen shirt and ran down over his new buckle.

"You crazy bitch! You tryin' to kill me?" he yelled, grabbing at his chest.

Susie quickly withdrew the weapon and struck a blunt blow on his forehead. With his sense of balance impaired by pain and his inebriated state, he pitched backward and collapsed against the brick hearth, striking his head again as he fell. Susie stood over him for a few moments with the rod still poised to hit him. When she was sure that he was dead, she wiped the blood from the tool and carefully placed it back on the hearth.

Calling to the terrified children, she said, "It's alright now, girls. You can come out. He won't bother us anymore."

Susie was trembling and her back ached but she dared not stop. She had sent Sally to fetch Jacob and begun to clean up the blood on the floor immediately. When Jacob reached the cabin, he took her in his arms, then stood staring at Carlton's body for a few minutes.

"Wrap his coat around him and button it. You got an extra blanket?" he asked calmly.

Susie nodded her head and waited.

"Put the girls to bed an' I'll be back in a minute," he said as he closed the door behind him.

The girls were too frightened by what they had seen to argue with their sister. Susie covered them warmly, kissed them both, and told them not to get up for any reason.

She found the ragged blanket and was relieved to hear Jacob's footsteps outside. He knocked softly then came into the darkened room with his brother Enoch. Both men carried ropes.

"You get in bed, too, and stay warm," he said as he took the blanket from her. "It's powerful cold out there, too cold for you in your condition." He hated Master Carlton for robbing him of fathering Susie's firstborn, but he loved her and bore her no ill will. The child would grow up as a slave to work in the fields with him, in spite of the white blood that flowed in his veins.

Without a word, the two men wrapped the body in the blanket, tying it securely with some of the rope. Then they slipped out the door, their shrouded burden slung over their brawny shoulders, the white man's indolent body no match for the muscular frames hardened by years of back-breaking labor in his fields.

At the end of the dock, Jacob climbed into a small rowboat tied to a piling.

"Hand him down, Enoch. Careful, he's heavy," Jacob said as he laid the lifeless body in the bottom of the boat. "Now hand me them chains. Don't forget the anvil."

The two men wrapped the heavy chains around the body. Enoch worked as Juno's helper in the blacksmith shop. He would probably be blamed if the smithy discovered the hand-forged chain was missing but they couldn't worry about that now. They would think of something then. Right now, they needed to get this body out of sight before the master and his family returned home.

Without a sound Enoch rowed the boat out into the river,

around the bend, and away from the cabins so the other slaves would know nothing of the events of this night. Master Henry was a kind man not given to beating his slaves, but Jacob didn't want to take any chances.

When they reached their destination, Enoch slowed the boat. The moon was behind the clouds but Jacob kept a nervous watch just in case anyone should be on shore.

"Fasten that anvil real secure. If we're lucky, the crabs and fishes will take care of him soon, but we don't want him floating up to the dock one day," he said. They watched in silence as the young master's body slipped beneath the turbid water.

When the family returned in the early morning hours, Carlton was nowhere to be found. His mother was concerned, but his father, too familiar with his son's errant ways, reassured her.

"Don't fret yourself, Lizzie. I'm sure Carlton and the other young bucks on the island have just gone off for a few days. You know how they are. I can't say I approve but they don't mean any harm. Jacob says his horse and saddle are gone so I guess they just went on an adventure for a few days," Henry reassured his wife. He didn't mention that a bottle of his best brandy was also unaccounted for. Nor did he tell her of Jacob's uneasy manner when he questioned the man about the missing stallion.

Following the holidays, the smithy discovered that an old anvil was missing as well, but as he had others, he thought nothing of it. After a week, when Carlton had not returned and none of his friends was missing, Rogers informed the sheriff and a search was conducted, but neither the horse nor the heir to the estate was ever located.

An uneasy feeling continued to haunt Henry about his son's disappearance. He blamed himself for Carlton's behavior—his laziness and drunken crudeness, his constant fights and lewd language, his sometimes sadistic treatment of the slaves. He had tried to reassure himself that the boy would mellow as he grew older, but no amount of discipline seemed to change him. Somehow Henry had always feared for his son's future and now his old fears had surfaced again.

But he had no evidence of any foul play. The boy had just vanished. Henry questioned all of his slaves but learned nothing. True, Jacob had seemed anxious when he questioned him, but being interrogated by the master would unnerve any slave and his most trusted man had never been violent. Besides, why would Jacob have anything to do with the young master's disappearance? Henry had to conclude that his son had ridden off drunk and fallen prey to robbers or met with an accident. He resigned himself to the fact that he would probably never know Carlton's fate but he felt sure he would never see him again.

In the early spring Susie gave birth to a beautiful daughter she named Lucy. A few weeks later, she and Jacob jumped the broom and Jacob came to live with Susie and the girls in their cabin.

Betsy Rogers
Boston, 1847

A Negro woman in a starched uniform answered the door of the elegant brick mansion in Beacon Hill. Beyond her in the hall stood a woman Betsy felt sure must be her Aunt Virgie, even though she couldn't remember seeing her before. Short and plump with blond sausage curls a bit too youthful for her advanced age, the woman wore a deep brown bombazine dress trimmed in soutache that surely came straight from Paris.

Betsy had often heard her mother brag to the other planters' wives about her widowed sister-in-law's elaborate wardrobe of French creations and her elegant lifestyle as part of Boston's elite inner circle. She had reminded her husband that in order to visit Boston at the height of the social season, she and Betsy would require new wardrobes—soft wool ensembles for chilly daytime calls on Aunt Virgie's lady friends, fine silk dresses for the numerous dinner parties, and elegant gowns for the fancy balls. It would not do for them not to be properly attired when the Boston doyenne presented her kinswomen to her snobby friends.

With a squeal of delight, the woman rushed toward them—as much as a woman of her age and amplitude could rush—her arms flung wide in welcome.

"Henry! Lizzie! I'm so happy to see you!" she shrieked as she pecked each of them on the cheek.

"And this must be little Betsy!" she cooed as she clutched Betsy to her abundant, lavender-scented breast. "My, how you've grown. I haven't seen you since you were a baby. You were such a beautiful baby and you're just as pretty as you were then! I'll bet you have too many suitors to count."

Betsy saw her mother wince at her aunt's words. Apparently,

her father had not shared with his sister the reason Betsy had been allowed to accompany her parents on the trip. Never mind the reason, she still felt so grown-up.

"Henry, Patience will show the ladies their rooms while we go into the parlor and you tell me all about your lovely plantation. Just tell Patience if you need anything," she called as Betsy and her mother followed the young Negress up the stairs.

As the two women went to rest before the evening's festivities, Virgie led her brother into the parlor.

"Henry, Betsy is a beauty! The young men must be clamoring at your door to court her."

"I'm afraid, Virgie, that's not quite the case. In fact, I brought her on this trip hoping that spending the high social season here in Boston would lift her spirits, and, to be frank, perhaps produce some new candidates for her hand."

Virgie looked surprised as she poured him a glass of sherry from an exquisite crystal decanter, settled into her chair by the fire, and motioned him to the chair opposite hers.

Continuing, he said, "Remember, Sister, we've been in quite a turmoil since Carlton's disappearance. Even though we've never found his body, realistically I've had to assume that my son is dead. We've been in mourning and Betsy, of course, couldn't accept social invitations or receive gentlemen callers. I don't mean to be indelicate but you know how impatient young bucks can be. As a result, her more suitable beaux have by now taken brides and, unfortunately, I'm not favorably inclined toward any of her remaining suitors. Her mother is becoming more anxious every day now that Betsy's passed her eighteenth birthday for fear that she'll be a spinster. I know you never remarried after Lowell died, but that was your choice. Betsy thinks of nothing but having a husband and children. And I need a son-in-law to take over the plantation someday."

As he sat down and bowed his head in despair, he felt again the overwhelming sadness that had been a part of his daily life since his son's disappearance.

His sister came to him and, stroking his back to soothe him, said, "Don't you worry, Brother. Your big sister is going to take care of things just as she did when we were children. Don't you worry."

For the first time since the nightmare began, cleansing tears flowed down his face as he acknowledged the depth of the grief he had not been able to reveal even to his wife and daughter.

It was all just too exciting! The days were spent either driving in Aunt Virgie's magnificent carriage, attended by two men in fancy livery, to call on an endless round of matrons and their unwed daughters or receiving the same women in her elegant parlor where they munched on an infinite variety of tiny sandwiches and cakes. At night, they went to elaborate dinner parties or Aunt Virgie entertained at home.

Tonight they were going to a ball, the highlight of the season. Excitement raced through Betsy's body. The porte-cochère was ablaze with lanterns as music poured from the doors and windows. She had attended balls in Savannah but never one as grand as this.

The gown she was wearing was her favorite—a periwinkle blue to match her eyes. All her beaux at home said no one had eyes as blue as hers. Yards and yards of tulle floated around her with every move. Above her shoulders, chestnut coils danced when she walked, her naturally curly hair responding easily to the sausage curls so fashionable this season.

As she glanced down, she was pleased by the low cut neckline which revealed the silken paleness of her bosom—a difficult condition to accomplish when she loved to spend time outdoors in the sun. Her nearly perfect beauty was marred by only one flaw—a sprinkling of freckles across her nose that had resisted the strict regimen of broad-brimmed hats, long milk baths, and expensive powders her mother forced her to follow. Signs of exposure to the sun were considered a stigma of lower class women who were forced to labor outdoors. No well-bred young lady bore such marks.

"Mind your gown, Betsy," her mother warned as her daughter stepped down from the carriage. "And keep your dress pulled up on your shoulders. You're not used to such a plunging neckline. You don't want to be exposed."

As she entered the ballroom, Betsy felt the eyes of the other partygoers follow her—some with admiration and some with envy.

She had never had many girlfriends because they were all jealous of her. She really didn't care though, because all that mattered was attracting a suitable husband and settling down to become an accomplished hostess. Although Betsy knew she was not clever, she did know that her future social success depended on her beauty—and her father's profitable plantation.

Standing near the door, Edwin James Heard surveyed with gathering disappointment the usual offering of available anxious young women waiting around the edge of the dance floor. His gaze stopped abruptly on a vision of loveliness in a cloud of periwinkle blue. She appeared to be with Mrs. Virgie Adams. He remembered hearing that the wealthy society maven's brother and his family were visiting, a planter from some God-forsaken island in the South. He had been invited to a dinner party to welcome them weeks ago, but he rarely responded to such invitations. Wasting an evening with some backwoods farmer and his homely daughter was by no means his idea of worthwhile *divertissement*. But this was no unmarriageable spinster. Time to exchange pleasantries with Miss Virgie and her stunning niece.

Striding toward the party, Edwin kissed the woman's pudgy hand and purred in his most amiable tone, "Why, Mrs. Adams, you do look lovely this evening. You must save me a dance."

"Edwin Heard, you don't fool me one little bit! You just came over to meet my beautiful niece," she laughed, swatting him playfully with her fan. "Dears, may I present Mr. Edwin Heard, bachelor *extraordinaire*! Mr. and Mrs. Henry Rogers of Marsh Oaks Plantation and their daughter Betsy."

With an elegant motion, Edwin gave a deferential nod to the gentleman, then kissed the hands of the ladies, staring boldly into Betsy's eyes as he did so.

"All the young ladies are infatuated with him but no one has been able to trap him," Virgie continued. "We're fortunate to have him here tonight. He spends most of his time traveling on the continent."

With a smile, Edwin said, "I hope you are having a pleasant visit, sir. Boston can be quite entertaining during the season. I'm certain Mrs. Adams is keeping you amused. I believe I am fortunate enough to be invited to a dinner party in your honor at the Cabots next week. I shall look forward to seeing you and your lovely family again, sir. Until then, may I have the honor of a waltz with your charming daughter?"

With a chuckle, Rogers replied, "I think you'd better ask her, but, from the look on her face, I believe she would be delighted."

As Edwin led Betsy onto the dance floor, Virgie whispered behind her fan to her brother about young Heard.

"Edwin comes from one of Boston's finest—and oldest—families. His ancestors came here in the 1600's and became very successful in business. His older brother Nathan runs a shoe factory that supplies the army. Until their father died a few months ago, Edwin lived in the family mansion on the hill, but he's been abroad since then visiting old friends from Harvard. I'm not sure what his plans are now, but every woman with an unmarried daughter has her eyes on him."

Henry Rogers watched with guarded pleasure as this young Bostonian guided his daughter around the dance floor with marked confidence and grace. He had clearly dedicated much of his time to perfecting the ballroom manners designed to charm the anxious mothers and win over the wary fathers of the most eligible maidens the city's upper class had to offer. By the time the dance ended, it was obvious that Betsy was taken with him and Henry wanted nothing more than he wanted his daughter's happiness. Still, he felt a bit uneasy about this enigmatic young man.

The following Tuesday, having assured Evelyn Cabot that his failure to respond to her kind invitation had been an inexcusable oversight, Edwin managed to sit next to Henry Rogers in the gentlemen's parlor as they enjoyed after-dinner brandy and excellent cigars. In the relaxed atmosphere, the older man responded to Edwin's polite inquiries about the Rogers plantation.

Accepting the light the diligent Edwin offered, Henry launched his dissertation on the virtues of his beloved plantation.

"Marsh Oaks is the loveliest spot on earth to me. I don't mean to sound boastful but I raise some of the finest cotton in the South. You may not be familiar with our island, but Georgia was once called the New Eden. Climate's mild, growing season's long, and my slaves are good workers. We have a real close society among the other planters. I can't imagine a more agreeable situation." He hesitated a moment and then continued. "My only bad time has been the loss of my son. You couldn't know, but my son Carlton disappeared two years ago. Just vanished one night while the rest of us were visiting on another plantation. I have to assume he's dead, but I'll always wonder what happened to him."

Henry took a linen handkerchief from his pocket and wiped his eyes. The passing years had not lessened his pain. He missed his only son as much today as he had the night he disappeared.

A sympathetic Edwin feigned surprise and concern. In fact, he was well aware of the old man's loss. Since meeting the planter, he had been engaged in obtaining as much information as possible about his holdings. In doing so, he had uncovered the story of Carlton's mysterious disappearance, a circumstance that made his younger sister the only heir to a very prosperous plantation on the obscure southern island. Recognizing a most fortuitous opportunity, he had set about to win the heart of the lovely heiress and the approval of her adoring father.

Edwin settled into a large leather wing chair and leaned forward, positioning himself close to his companion. In a low voice, he said, "I can only imagine your grief, sir. I believe you know I lost my father some time back. I miss him terribly, much as you must miss your son." Edwin's remorse, in fact, was not at all the same. True, his father had died recently, but the effect on the young man's life had been more practical than emotional. Until his father's sudden heart attack, his life had been one of privilege and idleness—a situation that suited him quite well.

"I still live in our family home with my brother and his wife, but it's just not the same. That's why I've spent so much time in Europe." That and the fact that his elder brother had inherited the family mansion as well as principal ownership of the factory. Although he was well provided for financially and would be able to continue his indolent lifestyle, Edwin had unexpectedly found himself a guest in his ancestral home. His sister-in-law Elfira—the possessor of a viper's tongue to match her venomous personality—had been quite clear about her desire for him to seek other accommodations. For his part, the very thought of looking upon her pinched features and listening to her whining voice at table each day had been sufficient motivation to devise a suitable solution regarding his future lodging place.

"I am deeply grieved by your loss and I sincerely hope that your time in Boston will help to assuage some of the pain you have endured. If I can provide any diversion during your stay, please feel free to call on me. I pray I do not offend, but I am a member of several clubs and can offer a relaxing evening of cards if you are so inclined, say tomorrow night."

Henry was indeed missing the camaraderie with his friends back home and tiring of the constant company of the ladies. "You may have something there. I've missed my regular card games on the island. An evening out might be just what I need. I'd be pleased to accept your invitation."

"Splendid. I'll call for you at nine," Edwin said cheerily. "May I get you another brandy?"

With luck, befriending the sad old man would rend him favorably disposed to Edwin's hasty betrothal to his charming if rather vacuous daughter. Now, to woo the willing young woman.

Edwin pursued the naïve belle by daily visits, carriage rides, and dinner parties in her family's honor at the homes of his most socially acceptable friends. Many of the most suitable young ladies and their mothers watched with gathering despair.

Betsy, bedazzled by her suitor's constant attentions, soon confided to her mother, "I'm in love with Edwin. He's the most wonderful man I've ever met. He's so much more sophisticated than the boys I know back home. Don't you agree, Mother?"

Her mother hesitated before responding. He certainly was attentive and he seemed to be from a good family. Having spent many anxious moments regarding her daughter's marital prospects, she was most eager for her daughter to find a suitable husband, but she was still concerned. "I hope you are not wearing your heart on your sleeve. He may just be enjoying your company because you are visiting. You have no idea whether his intentions are either honorable or lasting. Just be cautious, dearest."

"Mother, please don't spoil it. I believe he truly loves me. I just know he does."

"I hope you are right, darling. Time will tell."

After a delay of several weeks, the Rogers family was preparing for their departure on a rainy afternoon. Henry and his sister sat discussing their time together in the parlor while the women supervised the packing of their trunks.

"I do hope Lizzie and Betsy enjoyed their visit," Virgie said. "I had hoped to introduce Betsy to several eligible young men but she seemed so taken with Edwin Heard that the others were discouraged and Edwin certainly did his best to entertain them both. I pray she won't be too unhappy to part from him. He has his pick of all the young ladies in Boston but he seems to prefer the bachelor's life, for the present at least."

"Yes, she does seem smitten but then she's a flighty and quite emotional little thing. She'll probably mope for a few days but she'll get over it."

As they were talking, Patience tapped lightly on the door as she opened it. "Mr. Edwin Heard is here to see you and Mr. Rogers, Miss Virgie."

"Well, show him straight in, Patience, and bring us some tea. And some whiskey, too." Glancing quickly at her brother, she said, "How unusual for him to call unannounced. I was expecting him later for dinner but not this early. I wonder what is so urgent."

Edwin entered the room with his usual air of confidence. "Good afternoon, Mrs. Adams, Mr. Rogers. I trust you are both well. And Mrs. Rogers and Miss Betsy," Edwin said kissing Virgie's hand as he bowed to Henry. "Forgive me for intruding but I have a matter of importance to discuss with you, sir, if you will permit me to impose on your time."

"I'm sure Henry will be glad to speak with you. I'll go hurry Patience with your tray and let you men have some privacy." Virgie smiled knowingly at her brother who still seemed somewhat puzzled by this unexpected visit.

Henry returned to his chair while Edwin stood by the hearth and began his petition. "I know, sir, that we met only a few weeks ago and you are justified in thinking my action somewhat rash, but I assure you that I have given considerable thought to what I am about to say. I am 32 years old and have seen quite a bit of the world and made the acquaintance of a considerable number of suitable young women. Even so, I have never known a woman with whom I would like to spend the rest of my life. At least, not until now."

Edwin paused to look at the older man who seemed unable to comprehend what he was saying. At that moment, Patience entered the room with the tray, sat it on the tea table, and left.

Crossing the room, Edwin continued, "As I was about to say, I would consider it an honor if you would grant me your permission to ask your daughter to marry me. If she accepts, I would be willing to relocate to Georgia since I know how much her home and family mean to her." *And, how vast I now know your holdings to be*, he thought. "If you would care to check with my solicitor and my banker, I will be happy to provide their names. I think you will find that I am quite well-fixed financially and am assured of a steady income from my family holdings both here and abroad."

Henry seemed taken aback by Edwin's request. A few minutes ago, he was preparing himself to console his lovesick daughter and now he was being asked to give her hand in marriage. Young Heard would make a most suitable son-in-law and, even more importantly, a most acceptable future master of Marsh Oaks. How quickly situations can change!

"I admit I am a bit surprised by your request as I was unaware of your intentions toward my daughter. I agree that we have not been long acquainted but my sister speaks highly of you and vouches for your reputation and good family connections. I have in fact become somewhat fond of you. You remind me of my dear lost son. I am also pleased that you would be amenable to coming to Georgia. I'm sure you realize that, in years to come, my plantation will need the hand of a new strong master. Therefore, I raise no objection to your speaking to Betsy regarding your affection for her, but the decision, of course, will be hers."

As the two men shook hands, Henry quipped, "I hope you will win her heart as easily as you have won my permission."

Edwin smiled at his future father-in-law. *That will be no*

chore. The little ninny would have run away with me the first evening had I asked her. She should prove an obliging and docile wife. Besides, she's quite a beauty. A landless, second son could do worse.

To the seeming gratification of all parties concerned, before the Rogers party left Boston, the couple was betrothed. Mrs. Rogers was a bit perturbed at the brevity of the courtship, but she had no complaints about the suitability of the gentleman—good looks, wealth, and the highest social standing. By their departure, she was already planning how she would let her friends know that young Heard was such a catch as a son-in-law.

Plans were made, too, for the prospective groom's extended visit to the plantation prior to the wedding—time for him to meet the other families of the Rogers' acquaintance. Time, too, for him to survey his future domain. Yes, Edwin was well pleased with the season's turn of events.

Rounding a bend in the river, the small boat glided closer to the shore. On the bluff above the marsh, an ancient oak tree leaned precariously over the water. Shading his eyes against the bright sunlight, he could make out the figure of a young woman in a rope swing suspended from one of the low-hanging branches. Her flowing white dress floated around her as she sailed through the sultry air. Spying the boat, she jumped from the swing, waving with excitement as she ran toward the dock. Taking a deep breath, Edwin James Heard gave a respectful wave to his betrothed, Miss Betsy Rogers, heiress.

Once he stepped on to the dock, he would begin a journey to the fulfillment of his lifetime dream to be a landed gentleman, a dream that his standing as the second son had denied him until his propitious encounter with Henry Rogers and his eligible daughter.

At last, his ungodly journey was almost over. Days of being jostled in coaches and fighting seasickness on a storm-tossed schooner had further piqued his inability to endure unpleasantness in any form. Since the majority of his waking hours were spent at a gaming table or in a ballroom, hours of intense sunlight and raw winds had produced a somewhat painful ruddiness on his usual pale face. His dark wavy hair fell in limp curls above the collar of his once impeccable linen suit, now quite rumpled with an indistinct stain on one pant leg.

Slapping at the side of his face, he cursed. "Damn these blasted creatures! Are they always like this? They're sucking all of my blood and raising whelps all over my face."

"Them's no-see-ums, sir," Jacob answered with exaggerated respect as he rowed the boat toward the dock. Although a slave, he had the master's trust and was often sent alone to Isle of Hope to fetch a special shipment of supplies or ferry visitors to the island. "You'll get used to 'em." Secretly laughing at the stranger's discomfort, he doubted that his irritable passenger ever would. Miss Betsy's intended was a person who did not take well to discomfort.

A keen judge of character, Jacob held that you could tell a great deal about a person from the way he reacted to some of the "peculiarities" of island life, especially the "no-see-ums"—the relentless sand gnats that attack their victim's eyes, nose, and any other unprotected body part. They were a fact of life in the Low Country and a newcomer might as well take them in stride. Thus far, Mr. Heard was not handling them well. Jacob would have a good laugh with Susie and the children at the supper table tonight when he recounted the tale of the future groom's undignified arrival.

When the master and his family came home from the trip to the north, everyone had been surprised by Miss Betsy's engagement. The family's wealthy friends and their slaves alike speculated about her fiancé. The socially elite islanders conjectured about the suitability of his family tree and his ability to fit into their very closed local society, but the slaves on the Rogers' plantation had a more practical concern. As Miss Betsy's husband, he would one day be master of Marsh Oaks and their fates would be in his hands. That thought, in light of the young gentleman's behavior so far, made Jacob very uneasy.

Guiding the boat to the dock, Jacob tossed the rope around the piling and secured the craft.

"Watch your step, Mr. Heard, sir," Jacob called as his future master climbed from the rocking boat and, in a brusque manner, adjusted his somewhat disheveled traveling ensemble. "Watch your step."

Once on the landing, Edwin surveyed the area with a practiced eye. As a young boy he had learned to assess his surroundings—both animate and inanimate—with a thought to courting people or controlling things which held the potential to advance his position and discarding who or what would not. His acute awareness of his unfortunate birth rank spurred him to focus all his efforts on securing his desired status in society. His brother may have the family home in Boston, but he would control a vast plantation in Georgia.

This will do nicely, he decided, *very nicely indeed.*

The bank sloped gradually from the marsh to the low bluff. Huge oaks dotted the shore, their heavy branches draping down toward the water, the tendrils of the Spanish moss brushing the tops of the marsh grass. A profusion of flowering shrubs lined the oyster shell path leading away from the dock, their lush shades of magenta and fuchsia giving way to pure white near the house.

Standing sentry above the marsh, a magnificent mansion—far grander than he had envisioned—came into view. With typical Brahman superiority, Edwin had assumed even the wealthy in coastal Georgia resided in little more than cabins with dirt floors. The edifice before him was no cabin. Almost blindingly white in the mid-day sun, the façade stretched more than a hundred feet across. Massive Corinthian columns lined the shady veranda where several pairs of French doors allowed a cross breeze to cool the interior of the house.

His reservations about life in the South were rapidly dissipating. The young woman in the swing, her chestnut curls flashing in the sunlight, was bounding eagerly toward him. Yes, his approaching wedded state was becoming more agreeable by the moment. Removing his hat in a sweeping motion, he smiled contentedly as his soon-to-be bride approached.

Gathering up her flowing skirts, Betsy raced down the dock. Her mother would scold her if she saw such an impetuous, unlady-like manner. Her mother was a stickler about lady-like behavior and admonished her frequently regarding her spirited actions. But she couldn't contain her excitement. Her fiancé was here at last! For two months, she had regaled the other island girls with exhaustive accounts of her triumphant introduction to Boston society followed by a whirlwind courtship and a much-admired betrothal. At last, they would see for themselves her handsome, desirable future husband.

Edwin adapted quite well to the life on a plantation. His days were filled with riding alongside his father-in-law overseeing the work of the slaves in the cotton fields, and his nights were often spent playing cards with the other planters. Betsy was a devoted wife and, just three months after their wedding, she greeted him one afternoon full of excitement.

"I'm going to have a baby! Isn't that grand? Aren't you excited?"

"Of course, my love. That's wonderful. When will it be?"

"Mama says it should be in the spring. That's the perfect time! I won't have to suffer through the heat of the summer. I just couldn't bear it, I don't think."

As her mother had reckoned, Betsy should have given birth in late April, but in the predawn hours of an early March morning, a chilling scream pierced the silence. Betsy contorted in pain as blood soaked her mattress.

"It's alright, dear. Susie and I are here. The pain won't last long and you won't even remember it," her mother reassured her.

The women tried to comfort her and ease her pain, but she labored all day before giving birth to twins.

Edwin was ecstatic and not a little pompous when he announced to his friends that he was the father of twins, a boy and a girl. His joy, however, was short-lived. Although Eliza, rosy-cheeked and healthy, grew stronger with each day, little Edwin was tiny and pale.

"How is he this morning, Susie?" Edwin asked. The wet nurse lowered her eyes and did not answer. She was afraid to tell her master that the boy was weakening and could not nurse. Pushing her aside, he rushed to the crib and was horrified at the sight of the frail infant gasping for breath. Lifting the baby, he rushed to his wife's bedroom and thrust him into her arms. "Do something! You're his mother!"

Sobbing inconsolably, Betsy held him to her bosom, but she could do nothing to save him. The boy failed to thrive and died two days later as his parents and grandparents watched helplessly.

Edwin had been devastated but, having regained his composure, he attempted to comfort his wife.

"Darling, we are young and there will be more sons. As soon as the doctor permits, we will try again."

"I'm so sorry I disappointed you. I know how badly you wanted a son, but we will try again. And, Edwin, we are so lucky to still have our beautiful, healthy daughter."

Edwin turned away before Betsy saw the scowl on his face. No daughter would ever take the place of a son and heir. Betsy must give him a healthy son.

Soon Betsy was pregnant again but the baby girl was stillborn. Her next pregnancy ended prematurely and the infant boy lived only a few hours. Then, after a difficult confinement, Edwin was overjoyed when at last a very healthy Henry Rogers Heard was born.

On little Henry's first birthday, Jacob brought a dappled pony up to the veranda.

"Edwin, you'll spoil him. He's too young for a pony," Betsy laughed as the child squealed with delight when his father placed him on the animal's back.

"Every boy needs a pony. He must learn to sit his horse so he can oversee his plantation. He'll be fine." He held his son securely as Jacob led the pony around the yard.

Four-year-old Eliza watched the scene unobtrusively from behind her mother's rocking chair. As the procession circled the lawn and returned, she asked, "May I have a pony, Father?"

Casting a disinterested glance at her, Edwin replied, "Girls don't have ponies. They stay inside with their mothers and do their needlework so they can grow up and make a suitable match." Turning his attention back to his son, he said, "Come, son. Let's go see if Susie has a sweet for you in the kitchen." Holding the boy in the air, he walked toward the kitchen.

"May I go, too, Father?" Eliza called.

Edwin continued on his path without responding. Betsy took her tearful daughter on her lap and rocked her, smoothing the child's copper curls as she hummed softly. Although the child was only four, she seemed to feel her father's indifference toward her. Since Henry's birth, Betsy, too, had felt the loss of her husband's affection. His obsession with his son left little room for others in his life.

The master lay in his darkened upstairs bedroom, bathed in sweat and besieged with a raging fever. The house slaves moved quietly as they went about their duties. Conversations even in the outbuildings were whispered and the children were warned not to make noise.

Anyone who had been alive in Savannah in 1820 knew the reason—the dreaded yellow fever. Thirty years ago, the last epidemic had wiped out ten percent of the city's population and the current outbreak threatened to equal the devastation of the last. In recent weeks, unrelenting rain had again halted work in the fields and caused standing water around the plantation. Mosquitoes swarmed in the yard and infiltrated the rooms of the big house, each carrying the deadly virus. They clung to the screen doors and buzzed angrily as they became entangled in the netting that swathed each bed in the house.

In the kitchen behind the big house, Jacob placed another bucket of cool spring water on the rough wooden table, then filled the china pitcher with a dipper. "Master doin' any better?" he asked as his wife took more clean cloths from the cupboard.

"Not that I can tell," Susie replied shaking her head in despair. "He just lays up there in that bedroom, drenched in sweat and ravin' with fever. Miss Betsy just sits by her daddy's bedside day and night, bathin' his face with cool water and tryin' to coax him to sip a bit of broth or at least drink some water. But he just seems to get weaker every day. She keeps clingin' to the hope that the fever will break and he'll get better, but, Jacob," she said wiping her eyes,

"I think he's gonna die."

"You be sure you take care, girl. I don't want you gettin' sick," he said softly as he took her in his arms and comforted her.

"You know I'll be fine, but I'm worried that Miss Betsy might get the fever, too. She looks so weak," Susie said shaking her head as she started across the yard to the big house. As she passed the dining room, she wondered if she should get out some fresh linen so she would be ready when the time came to cover the mirrors. She knew that the master would not recover this time and preparing a house this big for mourning was a daunting task. She had already unpacked Miss Betsy's black bombazine dresses and hung them out to air.

Poor little thing. She'd had to wear them too many times lately, every time she lost another precious baby.

Quietly she opened the great door. In the sick room the windows were closed and the drapes drawn. The air was still, as fresh air was deemed harmful to those suffering from the fever. The room reeked of the turpentine and mercury that Dr. Wilson had ordered to help fight the illness. Henry Rogers lay on the bed, wrapped in heavy blankets to sweat the fever out of him as Betsy dabbed at his face with a cool cloth dipped in the smelly mixture.

Susie placed the cloths on the nightstand and sat down to wait.

While the old man hovered between life and death, the demon struck again. Before dawn, the sound of a weak cough woke Sally, wet nurse to two-year-old Henry Rogers Heard, heir to his dying grandfather's wealth. Rushing to the baby's cradle, she found the blond curls around the boy's face wet with perspiration and his skin fiery hot. Grabbing the child, she ran down the hall to the master's room where she found Betsy asleep in a chair by his bed.

"Miss Betsy, the baby's got the fever!"

They hurriedly poured water from the china pitcher into the large bowl and plunged the whimpering child into the cool water, causing him to gasp for breath. After a few minutes, Betsy wrapped her son in a blanket and held him close. His skin still burned with fever and his body was limp. Instinctively she knew that his ability to withstand the ravages of the disease was minimal.

For three days and nights, Betsy sat in the nursery with the fever-ridden baby, leaving him with Sally just long enough to check on her dying father.

As the sun's light began to fade, she rocked the lethargic infant in the wicker chair her mother had used to rock her. She had spent many happy hours singing to her babies as she rocked them and she had spent too many hours praying that they would thrive. She had sat, too, rocking her babies even after they had gone to be with God. Somehow, she feared again that God was waiting for her child.

In the darkness, she sang once again, this time a song of comfort she often heard the slaves sing as they worked.

> *Oh, I'm a poor wayfarin' stranger,*
> *Travlin' through this world of woe.*
> *Yet there's no toil no sweat or danger,*
> *In that world to which I go.*
>
> *I'm going home to see my lov'd ones,*
> *I'm going home, no more to roam.*
> *I'm just a poor wayfaring stranger,*
> *Going home, just going home.*

Edwin came in and out of the darkened room, but the baby continued to weaken. Betsy clutched her son close to her breast in a futile effort to keep him from harm but he slept fitfully and refused even to nurse. In the shadows, Mama Juba muttered chants and shook her strange charms, trying to find the right spell to drive away the demons that held the child captive.

Down the hall, Susie kept vigil at the old man's bedside. As the first chill of autumn filled the air, Henry Rogers, master of Marsh Oaks, slipped into a coma and died in his sleep. Two days later, his namesake's brief life ended as well.

As the toddler's tiny body succumbed to the ruthless disease, Edwin stood silently by the bed where Betsy was cradling her lifeless son. Without a word of consolation to his distraught wife, he turned toward the door. Seeing his daughter Eliza cowering in the shadows, his anger flared again as he stormed from the room.

For almost two years, he had coddled young Henry, proudly showing off his heir. Now his longed-for heir had succumbed to the fever and, once again, the girl had survived. On this day, he at last became the master of Marsh Oaks, but his ascension came at a bitter price. The epidemic brought with it the realization of his life-long goal, but took with it his hope for the future.

Eliza
1861

As was his habit on Sunday afternoons, Edwin sat at the desk in his office studying his accounts. Although it was October, the warm days of Indian summer lingered. Edwin anticipated another profitable year, especially if the war were prolonged. The long season had made for a very bountiful harvest and, with the war now being waged in Virginia, market prices were high. Both armies would require considerable foodstuffs and, with his family connections in the north, he stood to be in a very lucrative position. Armies also needed leather goods—boots, saddles, holsters—and the Heard family factories in Boston were producing at top capacity. True, no love was lost between the two brothers, but Nathan prided himself on being a very ethical man and religiously sent Edwin's quarterly share of the family business earnings.

As he was congratulating himself on his unique position as an entrepreneur who stood to benefit from the requirements of both the warring factions, he heard the sound of an approaching horse and looked out the window toward the long drive leading to the big house.

"Blast," he muttered as he recognized the youngest son of his neighbor astride a dreadful nag. James Coleman was a tolerable neighbor, hard working and honest, but never quite able to rise above the level Edwin considered a "dirt farmer." Either morally opposed to owning slaves or, more likely, unable to purchase them, he farmed the land himself along with the eight strapping sons his dumpy, working-stock wife had produced. They worked well enough, but since they consumed most of the meager crops the poor ground yielded, Coleman would never be prosperous enough to rise to the level of Edwin's social equal. In truth, Edwin despised the man because of his many sons. He had never overcome the loss of his own sons and the wretched fact that his daughter would be his only heir still aggrieved him.

Nevertheless, against his often expressed wishes, Eliza insisted on maintaining a friendship with the last of the Coleman brood, the interloper now imposing himself into this peaceful afternoon. Intending to speak to Eliza once again about this inappropriate relationship, he frowned and turned back to his books.

Watching from a window in the front parlor, Eliza, too, saw the approaching horse and rider but her reaction was quite different. Throwing open the door, she hurried to the hitching post where Jamie was already tying his horse.

Letting their fingertips touch briefly, they followed the path around the house on the side away from her father's office. When they were out of the view of the parlor windows, they embraced briefly.

"Have you said anything to him?" he asked anxiously. "Does he know why I'm here?"

"No, he wouldn't take me seriously. He thinks I'm just a child."

"Will he be angry? I know he doesn't like me. He doesn't like any of us Colemans."

"I don't know. He really doesn't care that much about me or my happiness anyway, but he just has to give us his approval. I want to be your wife when you go to war," she said her eyes filling with tears.

Eliza knew that her father would most likely be very angry and she feared that he would object and possibly forbid their marriage. She was sure he would say that at fourteen   she was still a child, much too young to marry. But she and Jamie had loved each other since they were children. He was everything to her.

"Don't cry now. Everything will be okay. You just wait and see," Jamie said, hoping his words were convincing. Mr. Heard could be a difficult man. Even if he didn't care much about his daughter, he cared an awful lot about Marsh Oaks and Eliza was his only heir.

Without speaking, they entered the big front door and walked down the wide hall to her father's office. Standing before the imposing door, Eliza squeezed Jamie's hand and smiled. Taking a deep breath, he knocked soundly and waited for a response.

The reflection of the full moon shimmered on the surface of the water, lighting Eliza's path to the bank of the river. The glow was so bright that Eliza stayed in the shadows of the great oaks to avoid being seen. At this hour, everyone on the plantation should be asleep but she couldn't risk discovery. If her father learned she had left the house to meet a young man, there was no telling what he would do. He had a quick temper, and though she was his only child, he didn't hesitate to mete out terrible punishment if she angered him. More than once, she had been confined to her room for days or denied meals for minor transgressions. She didn't even want to imagine what he might do if he caught her tonight and tried to force such thoughts from her mind.

Eliza loved and feared her stern father. She had always known of his disappointment when her twin brother died at birth and she lived. Even as a child, she sensed that her father somehow blamed her for her brother's death. Three years later when Henry was born, he was overjoyed. Little Henry, the center of his father's world, was strong and healthy until the yellow fever epidemic took his life and his grandfather's.

After Henry's death, two other babies died before they were born. Her distraught father became moody and spent hours alone in his office. Eliza wasn't supposed to know about such matters since proper young ladies were kept ignorant of certain aspects of life, but Lucy was privy to the conversations of the slave women as they went about their work. Lucy told her the babies came into the world before they were ready and then Miss Betsy was afraid she couldn't have any more babies.

Lucy had been Eliza's only playmate as a child and her only real friend even now. She had been allowed to play with the young slave since her mother, Susie, was a house servant and lived in the big house. But life for Lucy was very different. Unlike Eliza, she was not excluded from everyday happenings. Among the slaves, the miracle of life and the tragedy of its premature loss were shared by all, even the very young. The house servants knew—and gossiped about—the most intimate details of the family's personal lives. Most of what she knew about her own family Eliza learned from Lucy.

The raucous cry of a Great Blue Heron as he flew out of the marsh startled Eliza from her thoughts. The time passed with agonizing slowness. As Eliza waited, she brushed at the mosquitoes singing around her ears. Once she thought she heard someone, but it was only a foraging raccoon waddling down to the marsh to catch some fiddlers for a midnight feast. She knew that Jamie wouldn't deliberately disappoint her but suppose he couldn't slip away? At last, she heard the water slapping softly on the bow of a boat as, hugging the shore for protection, it glided toward the dock.

Softly she called, "Jamie, I'm here."

Tying the boat to a piling and climbing up on the dock, Jamie crept toward the sound of her voice. When he reached her hiding place, she took his hand and whispered, "This way."

Sheltered by the dense shrubbery, she led him to a stand of ancient trees where the remains of a tabby dwelling stood in a small clearing. Although the roof had long since rotted and one wall had collapsed, the remaining ones shielded visitors from unwanted observers.

Due to both her young age and her mother's diligent attention to the proper upbringing of her only child, Eliza had never been completely alone with a boy before, much less kissed one, until the first time she came to the tabby house with Jamie. That night they had slipped away from her father's birthday party, an affair that included all the neighbors. They had sat on the crumbling wall, watching the moon and talking. He picked a gardenia and put it behind her ear. He told her that she was even prettier than the flower and then kissed her shyly. They had not been alone since that evening.

But tonight was different. He would leave soon to join the Confederate Army. Her father had refused to let them marry and her heart was breaking. Once inside the house, they embraced hungrily. Not knowing how long they would be apart, Jamie kissed her repeatedly as his hands explored her body and she had no desire to stop him. With her heart racing, and in the very place where her ancestors had first put down roots in their quest for a new life, she submitted willingly to the awkward advances of the youthful soldier, an act that would inexorably determine the rest of her life.

Eliza stayed close to Lucy as they made their way by moonlight down the oyster shell path to the slave quarters. She was shivering, not only from the cold night air but also with rising fear of what she was about to do. Eliza had always been very regular in her monthly courses until last month. Lucy, always much wiser than she about women's matters, said that maybe she was just upset after Jamie went to the war. But now, she had not had her flow for over eight weeks and she was frightened. Lucy had told her not to worry and promised that Mama Juba would give her a potion to bring on her time. Eliza was praying that Lucy was right. She and Jamie had talked about the future and the children they would have, but not until after they were married. What would she do if she were going to have a baby? The terrifying thought caused her to stop so suddenly that she almost dropped the piece of cloth filled with raw sugar for the medicine woman, but Lucy grabbed her hand and pulled her forward. *Oh, please let Mama Juba help me!*

A shard of light glowed through the crack around the battered wooden shutter at the window of the old slave cabin. Lucy knocked softly on the dilapidated door.

From inside, a raspy voice called, "Who there?"

"It's Lucy, Mama Juba, Susie's gal. An' Miss Eliza's with me. Can we come in?"

"Come on in and close the door. It's powerful cold out and I'm 'bout outta wood."

Inside, bunches of herbs tied with string hung on every wall. A pile of roots lay drying on the brick hearth and steam rose from a rusty iron kettle suspended from a hook in the fireplace. A gaunt old woman in the garb of her native Africa huddled close to the meager fire. Eliza had never seen a person so old. She remembered seeing the voodoo woman when her baby brother died years ago, but the elderly slave hadn't left her cabin for years now. The woman's eyes peered sightlessly from beneath the red turban tied with care around her head. She had not a single tooth that Eliza could see and her hands were gnarled and bony when she beckoned the girls closer.

"Mama Juba, Miss Eliza is doin' poorly. She hasn't been on the rag for two months and she's scared. I told her you could mix her a potion to bring on her time. You can, can't you?"

"Maybe I can and maybe I can't. Has she been with a man?"

"Just once, Mama. Her daddy won't let her marry him and he went to the war."

"Just takes once, little gal," the old hag cackled. "Just takes once! And the gal pays the price."

Eliza started to fear that the aged slave thought she deserved to be punished.

"Can you help her?" Lucy pleaded.

"I can make her a potion but the spirits will decide if it'll work. I don't make no promises."

"Just help her, please. She's my friend and she's powerful scared."

The old woman pulled a root from the pile on the hearth and picked up a small earthenware pot from the floor beside her chair. "Reach me that bunch of herbs over yonder," she said pointing an almost skeletal finger to a string of dried gray leaves.

Lucy handed her the bunch and the girls watched mesmerized as she rubbed them between her palms, letting them fall into the clay pot. Deftly she poured boiling water over them then broke a piece from the root and dropped it into the brew. She stirred the mixture with a stick.

Its foul smell filled Eliza's nostrils, causing a sudden wave of nausea. She put her hand to her mouth and willed the feeling to pass.

When she was satisfied with the brew, the old woman poured the disgusting concoction into a chipped clay mug and held it out toward the sound of the white girl. Eliza took the warm mug from her but was repulsed by the smell of the dark liquid.

Sensing the girl's hesitation, Mama Juba ordered her, "Drink all of it, missy."

All semblance of class or servitude had fallen away. Eliza was no longer the master's daughter nor the ancient crone at this moment a slave. Eliza was a desperate young woman and Mama Juba was the medicine woman who possessed the power to help her—if she could be helped.

Eliza raised the mug to her mouth but could not force herself to drink. Again, the nausea seized her.

"Drink it, missy!" Mama Juba barked. "It's bitter but so is a woman's lot in life. You're young but not too young to learn that the woman always pays the price even if she does live in the big house."

Eliza held her breath and gulped the mixture down. With all her might, she struggled to keep from throwing it back up as she put the vessel in Mama Juba's hand.

"If the spirits favor you, you'll have your flow in two days; if you got a baby in there, he'll come out, too. If not, you'll be a mama by the time the cotton's ready to be picked."

Eliza hugged her arms close to her stomach in a futile effort to ease her fear. Nothing to do now but wait to see if the disgusting potion worked.

Outside a cold rain made the January afternoon seem colder. Even the roaring fire in the hearth did little to assuage the chill in Edwin Heard's study. Eliza sat rigidly in a large wing chair, snuffling and dabbing at her swollen eyes with her handkerchief. In the matching chair by the fire, Betsy twisted her delicate hands and fiddled with the pearl buttons on the bodice of her dress, averting her tear-filled eyes from her daughter. Edwin strode back and forth across the room between them, the veins on his temple throbbing, his face flushed with anger. His hands were clinched into fists he shook menacingly at Eliza.

"Do you have any idea what you have done? Do you understand how you have embarrassed me?" Edwin roared. Before Eliza could answer, he raged on, "No one in decent society will even speak to me when this news is spread! I'll be a laughing stock!"

The sickening smell of smoke from the cigar smoldering in

an ashtray on the desk filled her nostrils. She fought to keep from gagging, holding her lavender-scented handkerchief beneath her nose.

Eliza had known he would be angry but she had no choice. She had nowhere else to turn. Why had he kept her from marrying Jamie? If they were married, she would be the happiest young woman in Chatham County. But they were not married and she was in a miserable predicament. Even worse, Jamie was far away and perhaps in terrible danger.

A few weeks after their clandestine meeting in the tabby house, Jamie and two of his brothers left to join the Confederate Army. He had assured her the war would not last long. With youthful fervor, he vowed his love for her and marched away to whip the blue bellies. When he returned, she would be older and her father could not prevent their marriage. At first, he wrote often, long letters full of optimism. As the holiday season approached, she spent her days waiting for his letters and dreaming of her wedding. But she had not heard from him since before Christmas. He didn't even know that he had a child on the way.

By late December, Yankee warships were in the Wilmington River and troops seemed poised to come ashore. Rumors spread that the islanders may have to flee to the mainland and abandon their homes. Her father's frequent dark moods became even darker and her mother was visibly worried.

As rare snowflakes dusted the ground in late January, Eliza, although poorly informed in such matters, could no longer deny the reality of her growing fear. Mama Juba's foul potion had not worked. Her flow never started and she could not ignore the gradual changes in her body. The relentless nausea every morning was the most difficult to bear as well as conceal. Only her father's very early departure to oversee his workers prevented his discovering her telltale condition. Since her mother rarely came to the dining room in the morning as the result of the escalation of her debilitating headaches, Eliza's absence was not noticed. Lucy was able to slip up to her room with a tray of tea and dry toast without detection. By noon, she recovered well enough to join them for dinner.

Finally, she could conceal her bulging form no longer and

implored her mother to help her tell her father. Betsy, however, having endured repeated miscarriages and years of ridicule from Edwin for her failure to produce another son, was little support and, as Edwin raved, said nothing to defend or even protect her daughter.

The sound of her father's fist slamming against the table jarred Eliza back to the moment. She fought to control another siege of nausea as the smoke from her father's cigar encircled her.

"Does your paramour know what he has done? Has he vowed to make an "honest" woman of you or did he deny any responsibility?" her father railed at her.

"I wrote to him about the baby but I haven't had a letter yet. He can't always get one to me now."

"Don't delude yourself, Eliza. He won't marry you now. You are 'damaged goods.' No decent man will have you."

"He will marry me! He would have married me before he left but you wouldn't allow it! He wasn't good enough for the master of Marsh Oaks' daughter!"

Whirling to face her, Edwin sneered, "You may have a point. Marrying you even under these circumstances would one day make him a very rich man—most likely the reason for his interest in you from the beginning. The problem remains however, that he is fighting on the front and you will not be able to conceal the fact that you are 'enceinte' without benefit of wedlock much longer. Go to your room! You, too, Betsy. Leave me alone to try to think of a way to handle this fiasco."

Without argument, the two women hurried from the room.

The whole house knew of the family's crisis. The servants moved efficiently through their routines and avoided the master as much as possible. For several days, the tension prevailed until the frosty morning a loud knock at the front door interrupted Lucy as she dusted the tables in the front parlor.

When she opened the door, a tall man in uniform stormed into the hall.

"Where's your master?" he demanded.

As she turned toward the study, he brushed her aside and

rushed to the imposing door. He knocked only briefly as he flung open the door and entered, closing it loudly behind him.

After some time the man emerged from the room with Edwin, bid his host farewell, and rode swiftly down the drive, obviously intent on carrying out his duty.

"Bring your mistress and my daughter to my study! Now!" he bellowed to Lucy as he slammed the door behind him.

When the two women entered the study, he launched into a recounting of the report the messenger had delivered to him.

"Seargeant Jones has just informed me that Federal gunboats lie off the coast of Tybee. It seems our army is incapable of defending all of the offshore islands. The soldiers who have been guarding the river are being withdrawn to Savannah. The bridge to the mainland will then be destroyed to keep the Yankees from easy access to Savannah should they land forces here. Island residents are being given the option to abandon their land now or remain and be marooned."

Betsy began to weep as Eliza, her own eyes swollen from her frequent tears, attempted to comfort her.

Edwin put his hand on his wife's shoulder and said in a low voice, "I have been endeavoring to devise a plan to deal with Eliza's unfortunate circumstances and it seems the army has granted us a fortuitous out.

"We'll go to your cousin Robert's home in Musella. At last report there was no fighting in the area and the railroad is still operating to Macon. We'll determine our next move from there. Robert will be obliged to receive us but he's unlikely to insist that we stay very long. We'll take Susie and Sally with us and leave Jacob to manage the others with the overseer.

"Now, Betsy, see to the packing. We'll need to take most of the silver with us. Your jewelry, too, of course. Well, move along. We'll leave on Thursday."

Eliza stepped with care on the rocky path that led away from Cousin Robert's house to the stream that rushed through the woods beyond the split rail fence. Her bloated body caused her to be unsteady at best and she feared a misstep and resulting fall would harm the baby. Reaching her destination, she carefully sat down on a boulder next to the water, smoothed her shapeless muslin dress, and released a long sigh, tired from the exertion.

How she missed her home. She had only left the island a few times in her life and then just to go to Savannah for a special occasion. The months since she and her family had fled the island and taken refuge at Musella seemed endless and no one knew how much longer the horrible conflict would last.

Below her perch, the soft green ferns carpeted the ground, their delicate fronds waving slightly in the breeze. In this secluded bower where clusters of white rhododendron blossoms scented the air, the war seemed unreal, but she knew that men were dying in a senseless war all over the South. She couldn't be sure where Jamie was, but she sent him a long letter every week when her cousin went to town to get the mail. She hadn't had a letter from him for several months so she often came to this place to pretend he could hear her talk to him about their baby and how much she missed him. Here she could cry without making her father angry. Her father had told her cousin that she and Jamie had been married, against his wishes, just before the young man enlisted. In private, she wasn't even allowed to speak Jamie's name.

She stared wistfully at the churning stream as it hurried past her, hurling itself over the rocks, frantic and uncontrolled in its effort to reach the sea. Even the sound was turbulent, like a strong wind blowing during a storm, drowning out the sound of the birds.

How she longed for the peace of the marshland, the lethargic dance of the river lingering in rivulets when the tide ebbed and flowed as if it had all the time in the world. Her heart ached as she remembered the times she and Jamie sat together on the huge branch of the old oak that leaned out over the water. They had watched the water birds stalking their prey along the edge of the water or laughed as they plummeted below the surface and emerged with a squirming catch. They would dream about the home they would build on the land his father had promised to each of his boys and the children they would have someday.

Was this stream really so different or was it her own

restlessness? Her time was very near and she hoped the baby would come soon. She ached to hold him and tell him about his father.

She knew just how he would look—honey blond curls and clear sea green eyes, just like his father. She had decided she would name him Jamie. Once she would have included her father's name, but not now. She wanted her son to have no connection to her father. When the war was finally over and they returned to the island, she would take her son to live with Jamie and his family and turn her back on her father. She didn't need his house or his money.

After a while, she roused herself with difficulty and started back toward the house. Walking through a meadow filled with wildflowers, she stopped to gather a few for a bouquet to lift her spirits.

As she approached the house, she saw a neighbor's horse tied to a porch rail. Hoping he had been to town and brought the family's mail, she quickened her pace as much as her gravid body would allow. As she went into the front parlor, she saw her family gathered in the room. Her cousin was seated on the sofa with her arm around her tearful mother. Her father and the neighbor, Mr. Davis, were talking in hushed tones at the far end of the room. As she entered, everyone looked at her then averted their eyes. Her heart jumped to her throat.

"What's wrong?" she asked in a trembling voice.

Her cousin Ella rose and came to embrace her.

"Come sit by your mother, dear. Your father has received some news from Jacob."

Her mother began to sob as her cousin continued.

"Your husband and his brother were involved in a battle in Tennessee. It happened several months ago but you know how hard it is to get news these days," she said almost apologetically.

"I'm so sorry, my dear, but Jamie and his brother were both killed."

Eliza stared at her in disbelief as something screamed inside her brain. In one horrible moment, her world fell apart. Her plans to escape from her domineering father crumbled and the dream she and Jamie had shared disappeared like the misty fog in the noonday sun. With an agonized cry, she surrendered to her grief and collapsed into her mother's arms.

The room was dark and close. Somewhere in the haze, she heard the sound of her mother's voice. "Are you awake, Eliza? Do you remember what happened? You've been asleep for hours."

"Yes, I had a nightmare," she muttered as she fought to clear her head. But it wasn't a nightmare. It was real. "He's not coming back, is he?" she cried trying to sit up.

"You must not stir, my love. Lie back."

"Jamie's dead, isn't he? He'll never know his son." She collapsed on the pillow then turned her head to the wall and began to cry. A sharp pain like a hot poker jabbed into her belly causing her to scream then all at once the mattress beneath her was wet. Terrified, she turned back to her mother who was already at the door calling for Susie.

"The baby's coming! Bring the linens and start the water boiling! Quickly!"

All through the long night and into the next day, Eliza struggled to give birth. Bouts of intense pain alternated with brief periods of respite as the noonday sun streamed into the room. Lying drenched in perspiration, she breathed in the cloying fragrance of gardenias blooming outside the open window mingled with the sickening sweet smell of her own blood.

As the sun began to set and Betsy feared her daughter's agony would last another night, Eliza screamed and the baby's head broke through. Susie hurried to finish the birth and allow the weary new mother to rest. Wrapping the infant in the soft blanket, she handed the tiny bundle to Betsy who placed her first grandchild in her daughter's arms.

Weak from her long ordeal, Eliza murmured, "Is he okay?"

Betsy, touching the golden fuzz on the baby's head, whispered, "She's perfect."

Exhausted by the prolonged labor, Eliza's strength was further drained by a lingering fever. For several days she slept fitfully, crying out Jamie's name and sobbing pitifully. During her wakeful moments, she talked with him, seemingly unaware of her circumstances.

Gradually, as Eliza's mind returned to reality, she asked for her baby. The infant, in spite of her prematurity, was thriving in the care of her wet-nurse Sally. Betsy tried to avoid bringing the baby to her daughter with a myriad of excuses. When Eliza became agitated, Betsy instructed the young slave to bring the child. Sally came into the room followed closely by Edwin. After giving her charge to Eliza, she hurried out of the room, closing the door behind her.

Edwin moved to the foot of his daughter's bed. "I had planned to delay this discussion until you were stronger and more rational but you have forced the issue. I have decided that when we return to the island, your mother and I will present the child as ours, born during our forced absence. Your lover's death has removed my concern that he might prove a threat to the subterfuge. With him gone, there's no chance he can ever cause a problem about the child's parentage.

"I had at least hoped your bastard would be a male but it can't be helped now. She has been named Annabeth for Betsy's mother and mine. Now you will return your new sister to her mother," he said as he motioned Betsy to take the child from Eliza. Too stunned to resist, Eliza allowed her mother to take the infant from her arms.

"While we are here, we will continue the ruse that you were married and are now a widow. When we return home, no one will know except Susie and Sally and we will never speak of this again, understood? I wish you a speedy recovery from your bout with the fever."

Nodding stiffly to his wife, he turned and left the room, closing the door firmly behind him.

Eliza struggled to sit up, reaching as she did for her baby. Betsy took a few steps away from the bed.

"Mother, he can't do this," she shrieked. "He can't take my baby! You have to stop him!"

Tears streaked Betsy's face as she turned her back on her distraught daughter and took the sleeping Annabeth from the room.

Annabeth
1865

A loud thud signaled that the ferry had reached the dock at Marsh Oaks and a flurry of activity began on board. As the others gathered their belongings, Eliza remained rooted in her seat. She had been unhappy to leave the plantation but she was even more unhappy to return. Her mother was admonishing everyone to hurry as Susie picked up several bundles and Sally carried a tired Annabeth.

"Come along, Eliza," Betsy called over her shoulder to her willful older daughter. "You know how impatient your father is. Susie, be certain we have everything. Sally, don't let Annabeth get near the edge of the dock."

As Eliza relented and rose to follow her mother, she watched the two black women trail behind their former mistress as they always had. She wondered how life would be now that all the slaves in the defeated South were to be free. She sensed that emancipation, as the politicians called it, would require more that just a piece of paper to change a way of life that had existed for so long. She couldn't imagine Jacob and Susie, or any of her father's other slaves for that matter, just walking away from everything they had ever known.

She had heard stories of cruel masters on other plantations and even seen scars on some of the new slaves, but her father, perhaps a reflection of his early years spent in his father's factory in the North, dealt with his people as valuable workers not slaves. They never wanted for anything and were treated with respect. Why would they want to leave? Still, she expected that things would be different. Yes, things would be different for a lot of reasons.

A pang of sadness gripped her as she watched Annabeth chattering with Sally. This was her daughter's first glimpse of her home. She would never be able to call the golden-haired toddler her daughter out loud. The child was to be known as her little sister, an unexpected blessing to her delighted parents born during their sojourn in Musella to escape the perils of the war. *Such a shame*, Eliza thought bitterly, *that even Edwin Rogers' bastard grandchild was a girl, denying him once again a male heir.* During her pregnancy, Eliza had harbored the hope that the child would be a boy and, through her son, she might gain her father's love. But fate had dealt her another cruel blow and her father, disappointed once again, remained aloof.

Now she would be forced to deny her child and be an unwilling partner in the deceit her father had devised to cover the embarrassment brought on by his errant daughter. How convenient that the army had ordered the evacuation of the island in so timely a manner. They had left before her condition became apparent to anyone on the island and enough time had now passed for no one to suspect a ruse. It really had worked out so well for everyone— everyone except Eliza. How she longed to acknowledge that it was she, not Betsy, who had carried this beautiful, precocious child beneath her heart, loved her even before she felt the first flutter of movement, and endured the long hours of excruciating pain as she came into the world. All this, and she would never know the joy of being called "Mother."

She suspected that her parents had almost forgotten that Annabeth was not their child, even though with her golden curls and sea green eyes, she was the image of Jamie Coleman. Watching her laugh was the most painful for Eliza. She saw her beloved young soldier clearly in his daughter's smiling face.

"I'm so glad to see the house is still all right," Betsy rattled on as she left the boat. "I had nightmares the whole time we were away that something would happen to it. And when that dreadful woman on the train starting talking about how Sherman had burned everything in Atlanta, I just knew our precious Marsh Oaks would be in ashes. Eliza, are you coming or not?"

"Eliza! Come on," Annabeth trilled. "Hurry, we're home."

Yes. We're home but nothing will ever be the same as it was when we left. Forcing a smile, Eliza picked up her portmanteau and started up the path to the big house.

Standing at her bedroom window several days later, Eliza pulled back the delicate lace curtain and watched as Annabeth begged Sally to push her higher in the old swing, her golden curls sparkling in the sunlight. Again she felt the torment of wanting to spend every moment with her child but remembering the pain she invited each time she was forced to deny her motherhood. With tears of love and bitterness, she let the curtain fall, a bit of lace that veiled her daughter from her view, a bit of fragile lace that imprisoned her as surely as if it were bars of iron. Her father had robbed her of her motherhood but he could never rob her of the memory of their last night together in the tabby house, the night their beautiful Annabeth was conceived.

Eliza ignored the sound and continued to dab at the painting on her easel. Gardenias, her favorite flower. She had lost count of the paintings she had done of them over the years. Pure, white, fragrant. They always brought her memories of Jamie. Even after thirty-six years, just to smell them conjured up his smiling face and sea green eyes. She kept a vase of fragrant blossoms in her room as long as they were blooming and, when they were not in season, she scented her room with fragrant potpourri she blended from their petals.

Again, the sound drifted through her window. This time it was louder, faster, more frantic.

She stepped back from the image before her, shrewdly scrutinizing her work. Even though she had created dozens of paintings of the delicate blossoms, she never felt she captured their true beauty. So much of their elegance was conveyed through their heady scent and only God could create that.

She knew the sound was coming from her father's bedroom just down the hall. Bedridden for the past eight years, he still ruled his domain from the massive bed that he had given her mother early in their marriage. Crafted by slaves from oak trees grown on the estate, rice plants spiraled around the elaborate posts that supported the yards of netting required to keep out the ever-present mosquitoes.

Although all of the workers were now free men and women, most of them had once been the property of the master of the plantation and, for many of them, not much had changed in the thirty years since they were emancipated after the war. Generations of living as slaves had proved too powerful to overcome. They had chosen the known over the unknown and life at Marsh Oaks had continued much as it was before the world collapsed around them.

Edwin Heard was in the habit of ringing a silver bell to summon his servants to his bedside. As soon as he rang, Sally would appear when her arthritis allowed or would send her grandson when it didn't.

On this particular afternoon, Sally had asked Eliza to listen for the bell so that she could go down to the old quarters to visit her new great-granddaughter before she started cooking Mr. Edwin's supper. She assured Eliza that the old man would just sleep the rest of the warm summer afternoon and nothing would be required of her.

But today the ringing began shortly after Sally and her grandson left the big house. Eliza had agreed as a favor to Sally, but she had no intention of being her father's house servant. She owed him nothing. Once she had longed for his attention, always seeking to earn his love. But that was decades ago and she now cared nothing for his attention.

After her mother died, she had spent more and more time in her room, eventually ordering that her meals be brought to her there. When on rare occasions she was required to be in his presence, she kept their conversations to a minimum and made excuses to return to her room. Over the years, the adoration she once felt for him had become disdain. As he had paid no heed to her grief when Jamie died or her anguish when he forced her to deny her motherhood, so she took no notice of his persistent ringing of the bell. *Let him wait until Sally returns for whatever he fancies. His relentless desires are no concern of mine.*

Once more, she heard the sound but this time it was very faint and sporadic. Eliza rinsed her brush in the glass of water, placed it upright in the cup with the others, and went into the hall. Opening the door to the master's bedroom, her eyes adjusted to the semi-darkness.

Pulling aside the mosquito net, she looked down at her father's emaciated body. An indolent young dandy when he married the landed heiress, he had developed a muscular body when he became the master and spent hours each day on horseback overseeing his estate. Proud of his strapping form, his wardrobe was tailored to enhance his image as the lord of the manor. Now even his soft linen nightshirt was too large for his gaunt frame. His hair, once thick and dark, lay pale and sparse around his face.

With a malicious smile, Eliza said, "How the once arrogant lord of all he surveyed is now brought low!"

A gurgling sound came from her father's throat, alternating with long periods of silence. His eyes, closed when she first entered the room, opened and in them Eliza saw fear. She had never known her father to be afraid of any man or circumstance. As they had fled from the Yankees, he had been stolid and in control. But even the powerful master of Marsh Oaks was powerless against death.

As her father gasped for air, Eliza stood motionless, making no effort to aid the dying man. Unable to speak and sensing that he was about to die, Edwin's eyes begged his daughter to help him but his wordless pleas failed to move her.

Glaring down at him, she scoffed, "Yes, Father, you are dying. I wish I could truly be concerned but whether you live or die matters not one jot to me. When I was a child, I adored you. I was desperate for your love, but you cared nothing for me. You hated me because the sons you wanted so badly died and I continued to live, healthy and strong like you.

"You punished me first by keeping me from marrying Jamie then by forcing me to deny our child. Your only concern was your precious social standing, not what your own daughter was going through. I was always a disappointment to you. I couldn't even give you a grandson."

Still struggling to breathe, Edwin closed his eyes again as a tear slid down the side of his wrinkled face.

"You've made Annabeth pay for my sins as well. You've been so afraid she might embarrass you, too, that you made her a spinster. You've forced her to care for you when she should be entertaining suitors. Well, my darling Father, she has deceived you, too," Eliza taunted. "You allowed her to spend a few hours at the school the Benedictine priests run for the Negro children. You thought she would be safe from the lurid glances of young men there but you were quite wrong. She has a secret lover and he's a priest! That thought should comfort you as you are preparing to meet your maker," Eliza said, enjoying the anguish she could see in her father's face.

A lifetime of anger found expression as she lashed out at him. "You care for nothing but your own desires. Well, I care nothing for you now. I don't owe you anything and I won't lift a finger to keep you from dying.

"When I wanted to die after you took Annabeth from me, Mother tried to console me in her own naïve way. She told me that what cannot be bested must be borne. Well, I've borne your loathing, the death of my lover, and the loss of my child. I'm sure I will be able to bear your suffering a little longer."

Opening his eyes once more, Edwin gazed at the daughter he had rejected all her life. Through his tears, he saw past the embittered spinster who stood before him to the delicate, frightened child begging for his affection. She felt she had been a failure but he had failed her, too. He had blamed her for not being a boy, the longed-for heir. He had punished her for her transgression and failed to value her for herself. But she had prevailed. All that he owned would now be in her hands.

Without speaking again, Eliza turned and started out of the room. As she crossed to the door, her foot struck the silver bell sending it clattering across the carpet. Ignoring the sound, she closed the heavy door on her dying father and her painful memories.

For almost two days, Eliza watched her daughter writhe in pain as her relentless struggle to give birth dragged on. Eliza was thankful that Stanley Wilson had taken over his father's practice after graduating with honors from Emory School of Medicine in Atlanta. The young doctor had used all his medical skill to free the baby lodged within the laboring woman's agonized body.

In the fetid air of the darkened room, Eliza stood by Annabeth's bed, the stomach-turning smell of blood blended with the musky odor of human sweat filling her nostrils. Again and again she beseeched God to end her daughter's anguish, but she had never been able to protect her child and she was powerless now. She could only watch impotently as she had for all those years.

Then with a spine-chilling cry, Annabeth arched her back in an unnatural fashion and the baby was free. Annabeth collapsed, her body relaxed at last. For a few moments, the infant, covered with her mother's blood and ashen in color, made no sound and Eliza was terrified that she had not survived the ordeal. Then she heard a soft, kitten's mewl and knew her granddaughter was alive, at least for the moment. Whispering a prayer of gratitude that the horrible experience was over, she slipped back to her own room to share the news with Jamie.

In the dim light, Lucy watched with sadness as Miss Eliza crossed the hall to her fantasy world. No one really knew just how far removed the troubled woman was from reality. She had detached herself from the true circumstances of her life, a defensive mechanism she had perfected after Annabeth's birth. She could carry on a conversation long enough to fool strangers and casual acquaintances but she lived in a place that no longer existed, one that in actuality never did. In her mind, her beloved Jamie shared her life. In the mornings, she took long walks along the river or sat for hours in the tabby house. On nice days, she painted near the marsh. But every night, she talked to the lover who died over thirty years before.

With a deep sigh, Lucy went downstairs to tell the good news to the baby's father. Having been barred by propriety from being present during the final stages of the delivery, Patrick Aloysius O'Shea waited in the parlor, tormented by the sound of Annabeth's agonized screams.

Hearing Lucy's footsteps, he rushed to the hall door. "Is it over? How is she?"

"Annabeth is resting and you have a beautiful daughter."

"Thank God! It took so long and her screams were terrible. May I see her now?"

"Dr. Wilson is still with her. You can go up in a few minutes."

"Will you drink a toast with me, Lucy, while I wait?" he said as he poured two glasses of sherry.

"Just a little bit, Mr. Patrick. I still have work to do."

"To my beautiful wife and our precious new daughter," he said with both pride and relief.

Allowing a suitable amount of time for the doctor and Molly to complete their necessary tasks, the two returned to the bedroom.

The scene that greeted them was jolting. Instead of the anticipated sight of the proud mother cradling her newborn child, the woman on the bed bore a greater resemblance to a marble effigy on a tomb than to a living body. Annabeth lay deathly still, her face as pale as the clean white sheets that now replaced the blood-soaked ones and, in the shadows, Molly held the exhausted infant. Lucy gasped and behind her, she heard Patrick's cry of despair. Dr. Wilson came to them, rolling down his shirtsleeves and putting on his coat.

"The baby was breech and became lodged in the birth canal. The long, strenuous labor caused Mrs. O'Shea to bleed internally," Dr. Wilson said, his concern evident in his voice. "She's lost so much blood and is so weakened, I'm afraid she may not recover. The baby, however, may be strong enough to survive, but I suggest you find her a wet nurse as soon as possible. Her mother will most certainly be unable to provide for her. I've done all I can. They are in God's hands now." Picking up his bag, he turned toward the door. "If you should need me, just send one of your boys over to my house."

Lucy sensed in his tone that such an action would most likely be unnecessary. "My Molly is still nursing her boy. She'll take care of the new baby, too."

"I'll take her down to the nursery now," Molly said holding out the baby for her father to see. After kissing his new daughter's forehead, Patrick knelt by his wife's bedside, caressing her hand and weeping.

For two more days, the dying woman lay in a semi-comatose state, seemingly neither dead nor alive, her breathing so shallow that Patrick and Eliza had to place their faces near hers to feel her breath. They left her side only to visit the baby in the nursery.

Elizabeth Kathleen O'Shea readily accepted Molly as her wet nurse. Many years before, Lucy had been Annabeth's wet nurse when breastfeeding was relegated to slave women. Times were different now but Annabeth was Molly's friend and, with her loving care, the infant girl seemed to suffer no ill effects from her turbulent birth.

For her mother, however, the birth was much more injurious. Each time Molly pulled back the bedcovers to change the sheets, Eliza saw the spreading, bright red splotches and knew that her daughter could not possibly recover from the loss of so much blood. The sickening smell triggered a flood of memories of Annabeth's birth—the joy of holding her child followed swiftly by the agony of having the infant taken from her arms, the sting of her father's disappointment that the baby was another girl, and the bitterness of her growing hatred of her father.

In some strange way, Eliza's fear for her daughter's life had strengthened her grip on reality, at least for a while. She left the sanctuary of her own room in order to spend long hours with Annabeth. Finally, at Lucy's insistence, both Eliza and Patrick went downstairs to try to eat a light supper before beginning their hopeless vigil again. Absorbed in her grief, Eliza sat in her usual chair by the hearth but, on this dreadful night, even the roaring fire failed to warm the icy feeling deep within her. Her daughter, her only child, lay upstairs delirious, the life blood slowly draining from her pain-wracked body. Her daughter. She couldn't even call her that to anyone. Not that she cared about the consequences, but she could not expose her daughter, and now her granddaughter, to ridicule. No, Annabeth Heard O'Shea would remain to the world her sister and the infant girl clinging desperately to life would face the world as her niece.

Patrick sat with his head in his hands, his body slumped forward. On the table between them, the bowls of soup remained untouched on the supper tray Lucy had insisted on preparing hours earlier. The grieving husband alternated between bouts of wrenching sobs and outbursts of self-condemnation.

"I don't want to live without her. She's everything to me. My life is meaningless without her. I want to die with her."

"Please, Patrick, don't talk like that. You and Annabeth are all the family I have. I know I'm losing her. I cannot bear to lose you too. And, if the baby lives, she'll need her father."

"I mean no disrespect, Eliza, but you've never been married. You can't possibly understand what it means to lose the one who makes your life worth living. I can't face my life without her."

His words struck her, inflicting pain as real as if he had pierced her chest with a knife. Eliza longed to blurt out the long-denied truth about Annabeth's birth to comfort him and to assuage her own unrelenting despair, but she dared not risk even that. Instead, she sat mute while Patrick railed against his unjust God.

"It's all my fault! God's punishing me for abandoning Him! But why is He taking His anger out on her? I'm the one who left my order and turned my back on everything I'd ever known."

"Patrick, don't say such things. God doesn't punish us that way. Annabeth was never a strong girl and she just couldn't survive the difficult birth. Women die in childbirth every day. They always will." Her words were full of conviction but in her innermost soul, she, too, was distraught. *God is taking Annabeth's life as retribution for my own sin so many years ago,* she rationalized. *God's memory is long and He is very patient.*

"It's my fault she even had to endure childbirth! I made her pregnant. I killed her by my lustful nature!"

And I gave her life by mine, Eliza thought. *One night of love that sealed my fate and hers. Could it possibly have been worth the price so many had to pay?* She could still remember Jamie's youthful passion, still feel his fumbling embrace. *Yes, it was a high price to pay, but, God forgive me, even after all these years, I would do it again.*

Patrick lowered his head again, his body shuddering with sobs.

Eliza looked away, staring into the fire. Why were the women in her family destined to pay so bitterly for loving a man? Her mother had loved her father blindly for years, feeling she deserved his disdain for her failure to give him a son and refusing to acknowledge his nocturnal visits to the slave quarters.

She and Jamie had loved each other chastely from the time

they were children until their one fateful encounter. She had spent the rest of her life living with their sin and mourning him, deprived of his love and their child. And no one shared her grief. Now her child would pay with her life and her grandchild, if she survived, would never know a mother's love.

Eliza still remembered how painful that could be, the feeling of being unwanted and unloved. She had turned to Susie for affection. Nestled in the arms of her mother's slave, she had felt secure. Along with her love, Susie had shared her faith, telling the child stories of Jesus and singing hymns to her. The God who had sustained the slaves in their despair comforted Eliza in her loneliness. When she had felt unloved by her father, Susie had taught her that her heavenly Father loved her very much. *Well, a strange way He has of showing His love!*

And what a cruel sense of humor! Citing Eliza's shameful behavior as a young girl, Edwin Heard had refused to allow his younger "daughter" Annabeth to entertain gentleman callers during his lifetime. He did, however, allow the young woman to volunteer in the school for the children of former slaves that the Benedictine monks ran on the island. Her days were spent in the monastery classroom and her evenings in the parlor reading to her father, an ordered life away from lurid temptations of the flesh.

But in an innocent, unintended act of defiance, the sheltered spinster had fallen in love with a priest. They had kept their attraction a secret from her overbearing father, but when the old man died, Father Patrick left the order to marry the woman he loved. A few months later, Annabeth discovered she was pregnant and it seemed that heaven was smiling on them. Now her life was flowing from her and her husband was in despair.

Suddenly Patrick rose and stood in front of the fire, jarring Eliza from her reverie.

"It's not fair! He's controlled my whole life. I never had a choice about anything. When my dad died, my mum was left with six children and no way to feed them. The village priest persuaded her to send my younger sister to a convent in Dublin and me to the local monastery. The four older boys went with her to work in a factory in a neighboring town. I never saw any of them again.

I heard my mum died not long after that but I don't know what happened to my sister or brothers.

"I grew up washing dishes and scouring the kitchen. No one ever asked me if I thought God had called me to be a priest. I had been given to God in order to save my life. I owed Him. I was lucky, I guess, that one of the monks taught me to read and write. If he hadn't, I wouldn't have been sent to America and I wouldn't have met Annabeth."

Patrick turned toward Eliza, his face distorted with grief. "And I wouldn't have loved her and she wouldn't be dying now! He went to a lot of trouble to bring us together just so He could rip us apart!"

Going to stand next to the anguished young man, Eliza tried to comfort him.

"You can't blame yourself, Patrick. Annabeth loves you with all her heart and she wanted a baby more than anything. She had wanted one all her life. When she was a child, she spent hours playing with her dolls. She always made a fuss over the workers' babies. She worked at the monastery school just to be with the children. You would have devastated her if you had denied her this baby."

Gazing again into the fire, he seemed unmoved by her words.

"Patrick, let's pray together for Annabeth and the baby. God could still grant us a miracle and save them both. Please, Patrick, pray with me."

"Pray to God? Why? God doesn't hear our prayers!"

"Patrick! How can you say that? You were a priest! You must believe in God!"

"Oh, I believe that God exists. He exists all right. He just doesn't give a damn about us! He punishes innocent people to get back at those who dare to disobey Him! I have no need for Him or His Church!" Exhausted, Patrick slumped into his chair again as bitter sobs wracked his body.

Eliza touched his shoulder then left the room, easing the door closed behind her. Her own feelings were in turmoil and she needed to talk with her beloved Jamie.

A steady rain continued as the following day dawned and a chill crept into the bedroom. Before the clouds broke, Annabeth was gone. She never regained consciousness and never even held her beautiful daughter.

The infant, however, appeared to be out of danger. She was strong enough to suckle and slept contentedly, unaware of her motherless state.

Eliza forced herself to function in spite of her grief. She donned the black dress she had last worn when her father was buried. She had felt no remorse at his death, but to have done otherwise would have caused tongues to wag and she had no desire to be the topic of gossip for the other women on the island. Although she had passed her fiftieth birthday, her countenance belied her age. The long walks that had brought solace in her youth had become a lifelong discipline and her slight frame was still trim. The traces of silver in her copper hair were almost undetectable as were the tiny wrinkles on her delicate face, the years of denying her emotions having delayed their encroachment. In her funereal attire, she gave the appearance of a child in a bizarre game of dress up.

The burden of making arrangements for Annabeth's funeral fell to her and Lucy as Patrick, succumbing to grief and guilt, had locked himself in the room he had shared with his wife. The ability to detach herself mentally from her situation had enabled Eliza to deal with the emotional pain that had pervaded her life. On this occasion, however, her skill failed her and she fought to maintain control as she sat in the parlor receiving sympathy calls from family friends as word of her loss spread around the island.

At noon, she went into the dining room to find that Patrick had not come down to dinner. She had hoped to lift the widower's dark mood by keeping to the household routine even though she had no appetite either.

"Has Mr. Patrick been in his room all morning?" Eliza asked as she walked into the kitchen. Platters of fried chicken, heaping bowls of potato salad, and cakes and pies of every kind covered every surface in the kitchen as Lucy worked to find a place for such bounty. In the southern tradition, friends of the grieving family were relying on their food offerings to convey the thoughts their words could not express.

"Yes, ma'am. I sent Annie up with a breakfast tray but he wouldn't open the door. Just hollered for her to go away and leave him be."

"Well, please fix him a dinner tray and take it up yourself. See if you can get him to go see his daughter. She needs to know him."

"Yes, ma'am. I fixed you a plate. Sit down here and eat a little something yourself."

Eliza tried to eat but just had no appetite. Leaving the meal barely touched, she withdrew to the parlor to be alone before more neighbors arrived to pay their respects once the dinner hour was over. Although she would much prefer to retire to her bedroom, the ritual of mourning demanded that she be available to receive her callers.

All afternoon a steady stream of carriages came to the big house at Marsh Oaks. Matrons in black bombazine and gentlemen in black suits filled the parlor with the faint smell of mothballs as they filed past Annabeth's simple coffin in the corner then turned to offer words of consolation to her stoic sister. They sipped gallons of iced tea and sampled the infinite variety of confections that traditionally accompanied funeral visitations on the island.

Eliza was certain that tongues would later wag about the conspicuous absence of the grieving widower. In her presence, they expressed their incredulity that such a tragedy had befallen the young couple and offered inane platitudes about God's inscrutable will and a shortage of angels in heaven. Outside in the hallway, they spoke in hushed voices as they speculated about the probability that God just may have meted out His justice on a priest who had abandoned his vocation for the ways of the flesh.

At last, approaching darkness and the renewal of the drizzling rain brought a welcome close to an endless afternoon. Wearily, Eliza sought refuge in her room, longing to rest before supper. She had considered having Lucy bring up a tray to her room, but again she determined to maintain some semblance of the usual household routine. At supper, she would have an opportunity to discuss with Patrick the plans she had made for the services tomorrow.

But when she came down, Patrick was not in the dining

room.

To Eliza's surprise, Lucy informed her that Patrick had refused the dinner tray but had left his room briefly earlier in the afternoon.

"He didn't come into the parlor and I didn't hear him come down the steps. Did he leave the house? Where did he go?"

"He didn't leave the house. He came down the back stairs and went to his office. He just stayed a few minutes and then went back to his room. He's been there all afternoon. He's still up there."

Eliza felt an unexplainable sense of foreboding. "Send Prince up to his room. Tell him to make Patrick open the door. If he won't, take the skeleton key and open it. Surely he has composed himself by now."

Seeing the anxiety in her face, Lucy hurried to find Prince as Eliza stared out at the now soaking rain.

"Please, Lord, let it stop before tomorrow," she said aloud. "Funerals are even worse in the rain."

Suddenly a loud crack came from the upper floor. She rushed into the hall to see Prince bounding up the last few steps. He pounded on the door but there was no response.

"Mr. Patrick! Mr. Patrick, are you all right? What was that noise?"

Lucy pushed past him with the key. Opening the door, she stepped back as Prince hurried into the room followed by Eliza. The drawers of the huge chest were all open and discarded clothing littered the floor. Patrick lay sprawled on the bed, clutching the dress Annabeth wore at their wedding with his left hand. In his right hand, he held the pistol he kept in his desk drawer and, beneath his body, were the shredded remains of the cassock and chasuble he had worn as a priest. A rivulet of blood trickled down his neck from a single hole in his temple.

Prince leaned close and put his hand on the man's chest. The horror-struck look on his face when he stood up left no doubt that Patrick was dead.

PART FOUR

THE JOURNALS

The Chaplain

An old model dark blue truck was parked in the drive when Liz returned to Marsh Oaks from her visit to the dredging operation with Jack. As she opened the front door, she could hear Olivia talking to someone, but she didn't recognize the man's deep voice.

"I'm back," she called from the front hall.

"Liz, we're in the kitchen. I want you to meet someone," Olivia answered.

Olivia was sitting at the table with a man Liz had not seen before. "This is Reverend Smith, my pastor."

"Ben," the man said as he stood to shake her hand. He was so tall that the striped tie he wore on such a hot day stopped far short of his belt. He had obviously dressed to impress someone. "I'm also a volunteer hospice chaplain and I stop by to see Miss Elizabeth every now and then."

"Every now and then? He comes just about every week," Olivia said.

"I don't know if she's aware of my visits but I talk with her awhile, then read some scripture and pray with her. I think on some level she senses my presence and I hope receives some comfort."

"I don't know if he comforts Miss Elizabeth or not, but he sure comforts me," Olivia said reaching across the table to touch his hand.

His jovial smile lit up his face, especially when he looked at Olivia. Liz was surprised to learn he was the pastor of the small African-American church on the island as he appeared to be well beyond retirement age. His close-cropped hair was sprinkled with gray. His singsong speech pattern marked him as a son of the island and his light complexion hinted at the long ago blending of the blood of slave and master.

"Ben grew up on the island, but he moved away to work in Brunswick. He came back after he retired and became a preacher. We sure are lucky to have him back," Olivia beamed.

Liz couldn't remember anyone by that name, but then realized that as a white child growing up in the segregated South, she would not have had any contact with a young black boy unless he worked for her family. *But I'll bet Olivia knew him,* she thought smiling to herself. "I appreciate your visiting my grandmother. I'm not sure she's aware of anything either, but you're kind to take time to visit her."

"It's a privilege. She was always so kind to me. Used to slip me some money when I'd come home from school. 'A young man needs a little spending money,' she'd say. She was always such a grand lady. Pains me to see her in such sad shape."

Again, such loving words about her grandmother puzzled Liz. "Well, thank you anyway. I do appreciate your concern."

Finishing his coffee, the preacher stood to leave. "I'm glad to come by. Besides, Olivia makes the best coffee on the island. Nice to meet you," he said nodding to Liz, then to Olivia. "See you next week."

When Olivia returned from the front hall, she acknowledged Liz's inquiring look. "He's just a friend. We've known each other since we were kids. His wife died a number of years ago before he came back. I enjoy his visits, that's all."

"He seems very nice. Why don't you invite him for dinner sometime?"

"Maybe I will one day," she laughed as she went back to the kitchen.

As the stifling hot weather continued, Liz decided she might as well stay indoors and begin reading her grandmother's journals. Settling into the huge wing chair in the study, Liz turned to the first page of the journal Elizabeth O'Shea Mathews began in 1915 as a schoolgirl. She stared at the meticulous penmanship that filled the yellowed pages. Such precision was characteristic of a person who accepted nothing short of perfection in herself and in others.

She turned the page and started to read the secret thoughts of the enigmatic woman who had controlled her early life.

In a few short years, the carefree girl had become the wife of a soldier, the mother of two small children, and the manager of a large estate as well as the guardian of an old woman who lived increasingly in the past. Liz could not help feeling admiration for her grandmother as she read of the difficult circumstances of Elizabeth's young womanhood.

Peter's Story
1919-1943

January 12, 1919   At last, Peter will return from the war tomorrow. His ship arrived in Jacksonville today and he will board the train early in the morning. If the train is on time, he will be in Savannah by early afternoon and be home in time for supper. Eli will go with me while Mittie stays with the children. Mittie is planning to cook all of Peter's favorite dishes. She says she knows he's lost weight and will be craving some of her fried chicken and sweet potato pie. The children begged to go with me tomorrow but I persuaded them that he would be home sooner if I went by myself. I selfishly want a little time with him alone. He's been away so long. Mittie promised to bake special cookies with them while I'm gone to appease them. I hope Peter will not be overwhelmed by his homecoming celebration. We've all missed him so much.

January 13, 1919 Peter came home to Marsh Oaks today. He boarded the train early in this morning and traveled all day, arriving in Savannah in the early afternoon. The trip was exhausting for him. My poor darling. I am afraid his homecoming celebration was bewildering for him. The children were full of questions and so excited to have him home. Jonathan just wants to be near him. Beth doesn't remember him but she knows he's someone special. Even Aunt Eliza came down to dinner although she said *very little. Nittie was right; Peter is much thinner and his handsome face is so gaunt and drawn. He tried to eat all the enticing dishes she had cooked for him but he just has no appetite. He is quite obviously weakened by his ordeal, but with time, he should regain his strength. Outwardly, though affected by his terrible experience, he is the same man. But, when I look into his eyes, the husband I love with all my heart is not there. Please, God, have mercy on us. Help him find his way back to us.*

Elizabeth stood on the platform at the Central of Georgia station watching for the 2:15 train from Jacksonville to arrive, while Eli waited a respectful distance back from the white people standing near the tracks. Inside the chilly terminal, the air was hazy and smelled of oil. Negro porters leaned on metal carts, waiting to take the passengers' luggage to waiting cars. Shoeshine boys hurried to finish polishing their customers' shoes in hopes of snagging another taker before the train arrived.

Again, she adjusted her black felt hat with her white-gloved hands. Fiddling with the handle of her handbag, she looked around at the others on the platform. *How many are waiting for loved ones returning from overseas? How many of these women too are wondering as I am whether her husband has changed during the time he's been away?*

Peter had been away for over a year fighting in France. Jonathan was just a toddler when he left and she hadn't learned she was pregnant with Beth until weeks later. She was concerned he would be a stranger to them both but she was even more afraid he would be a stranger to her.

A shrill whistle sounded as the train pulled into the depot. A cloud of steam and dust forced the crowd back from the tracks. The porters positioned the steps and the eager passengers began to spew from the cars. First young men in uniform bounded down the steps to the arms of loved ones amid cries of delight. Then soldiers wearing the marks of their wounds stepped tentatively from the train, their arms in slings or their heads bandaged. Weeping but

185

grateful families hustled them into waiting vehicles and drove away.

Finally, Peter appeared in the door of the car, anxious and confused by the commotion on the platform, his eyes darting from one person to another until Elizabeth waved. A slight smile lit his face for a brief moment then faded as once again the boisterous activity disconcerted him. He pulled back into the shadows, hesitant to disembark from the relative security of the train.

Elizabeth shuddered as she studied the man whose form she knew so well. Once proud of his erect military carriage, he now stood with his shoulders slumped and his head almost bowed, leaning heavily on a cane for support. Usually quick to take charge of a situation, he now looked lost and bewildered. His demeanor bore little resemblance to the self-assured young man who left her only a few months ago.

Elizabeth pressed toward the door to meet Peter. With deliberate caution, he came down the steps, using his cane to steady himself. As he reached the platform, he stumbled and fell against her. Beneath his uniform, she could feel how thin he was, his ribs almost exposed under his skin. Her heart ached as she looked at him.

Putting her arms around his neck, she released the tears she had been holding back. "Darling, I'm so glad to see you. I've missed you so. Let me take your arm. You must be exhausted after such a long trip."

"I haven't slept well since the ship left England. I'll be all right after I have time to rest. You mustn't make a fuss. I'll be okay."

Although he accepted her embrace, his body remained tense. After several moments, he asked in an overly formal tone, "How are you? I've missed you. And the children? How are they?"

Disturbed by his uncharacteristic manner, Elizabeth answered, "I have been well, just lonely without you. The children are fine. Jonathan asks about you constantly and Beth is getting stronger every day. She'll be walking soon."

At that moment, Eli came forward to assist her. "Welcome home, Mister Peter," he said cradling the soldier's elbow in his sturdy hand. "I sure am glad you're home."

Elizabeth and Eli exchanged anxious glances. He too realized that all was not well with the master of Marsh Oaks. With agonizing effort, the little party limped down the rough platform and out into the bright sunlight.

September 20, 1919   Today I accompanied Peter to Dr. Wilson's office. I had hoped that the effects of the gas would fade, but after our visit today, I'm afraid now that the damage may be permanent. Peter's recovery is very slow. He tires easily and still must use his cane to move about the house. He sleeps very little, being plagued by horrible nightmares. He is often awake for hours at night, coughing and trying to breathe. I pray that the winter will not be hard on his poor lungs. In recent weeks, his hands shake when he attempts to hold a cup. He tries to cover his weakness, but each day I watch him decline. Dr. Wilson endeavored to be optimistic in Peter's presence but his words to me when we were alone were less so. He explained that the doctors have not had time to study the long-term effects of this devastating new weapon the military calls mustard gas. With time, he said that Peter could completely recover, but the possibility also exists that the trauma Peter experienced, both physical and mental, may continue to afflict him. Only time can tell. God, please give me the strength to take care of my beloved husband whatever the future may hold for us.

"Mrs. Mathews, I don't want to alarm you without cause, but I'm afraid your husband's prognosis is uncertain at best," Dr. Wilson said to Elizabeth while Peter was getting dressed. "We just haven't had much experience with this gas the jerries used on our boys. Obviously, it's sufficiently powerful to kill instantly in a high enough concentration or progressively if the exposure is prolonged. Lower concentrations or shorter exposures produce blistering of the skin or damage to the eyes or lungs. Captain Mathews suffered a somewhat low-level dose but for an extended time. Our scientists just weren't able to come up with masks that were completely effective against the mustard gas," the doctor said, shaking his head and watching Elizabeth's tortured reaction.

"The immediate physical damage to his body is evident. Those nasty sores will heal with time but I fear his vision at least in his left eye has been lost. I am unable to determine the extent of the internal injury to his lungs, but with your good care and a positive response to the antibiotics, he may be able to regain his strength. I am, however, quite concerned about any psychological impairment. He witnessed some horrible things and he may not be able to erase them from his memory. The nightmares you describe may fade or they may intensify. We'll just have to wait and see."

Elizabeth could see the concern in his kindhearted face. He had been her doctor since she was a young woman, continuing his family's tradition of providing medical care on the island. She sensed that his words were chosen with great care to convey the truth without disclosing his own misgiving.

That night Elizabeth lay awake listening to her husband's ragged breath as he waged his nightly struggle for air. Trying not to wake him as she got out of bed, she went to the window and stared out at the dreamlike vista before her. The water cut a silver path through the sea of grass as the full moon rose on the horizon. She stood transfixed, yearning for the sense of peace she had always felt when she gazed at the marsh, but this night tears coursed down her cheeks as she gave in to the wave of despair that engulfed her.

Doctor Wilson had tried to reassure her but he could not hide his concern. She sensed that Peter's condition would never improve and, she feared, would even worsen. The children were growing up and she worried that their noisy play bothered their father.

Aunt Eliza still spent most of the day in her room as she had for years. An embittered spinster, Eliza had been mentally unstable as long as Elizabeth could remember, but, in recent years, her condition had worsened and she withdrew to her room, passing the days painting and writing poetry. On occasion, she would venture out to sit in the ruins of the old tabby house watching the river. While Peter was away, Elizabeth had tried to persuade her aunt to come down and sit with her, but since his return, she had very little time to devote to the now elderly woman. Even with Mittie's help, running the house, caring for the children, and nursing her husband left her exhausted.

Wiping away the tears, she thought about the words her aunt would say to her when, as a child, she complained about her circumstance, 'What cannot be bested must be borne.' Well, she seemed unable to best the problems in her life now and she wondered how much more she could possibly be required to bear.

Peter's frightened voice broke the silence and she rushed back to his side.

"Here they come. Tommy, get down! Get your mask. Get your mask!" Peter screamed, sitting up in the bed and flailing his arms in panic. "Tommy, wake up! Get your mask on!" he yelled, grabbing Elizabeth as she approached the bed and shaking her violently. "Tommy, why don't you wake up? You've got to put on your mask."

"Peter, darling, wake up! You're dreaming again. It's all right," Elizabeth pleaded. "Please lie down, darling."

"I've got to help Tommy. He won't wake up. He won't put on his mask. He's going to be gassed!" he cried then sank back into the pillows, trembling and soaked in sweat.

Elizabeth held him until he drifted into sleep, then rose and walked again to the window overlooking the marsh. "Dear God, please help us," she whispered as she raised her face to fix her eyes on the moon. "Give me the strength to hold our family together. I've never felt alone because you were with me, but I need to know you are near me now."

From the distance, a waterfowl called mournfully to its mate. The melancholy sound from deep within her beloved marsh eased her fearful spirit. She had always drawn strength from the marsh and she would do so now with God's help.

The next morning Peter was tired and agitated. He ate little at breakfast and seemed withdrawn. Elizabeth went into the sitting room with him and, for a while, they sat without speaking. Then Peter started to talk in a low monotone.

"We were just falling asleep when we heard the sound of artillery coming toward us in the trench. I yelled to the men to put on their gas masks. We had orders to use the masks anytime we were attacked, but some of the men hated them because they were cumbersome and sometimes they would get foggy. A barrage of bullets began as I was putting on my mask. I looked around and I thought Tommy was still asleep. I screamed at him to wake up but he didn't move."

Peter's agitation grew as he continued and leaned toward Elizabeth. "Then I reached over and shook him. As his helmet came off and rolled down into the mud, I saw the hole in his forehead. He never saw the bullet that killed him. I just knelt there and stared at him. We were best friends since we were kids. And there was nothing I could do to save him. He was dead. Just like that. Dead. And I was still alive." Then he buried his face in his hands.

"After the gunfire stopped, I could hear the wounded men crying and cursing. Those who had been slow in getting their masks in place were screaming in pain, the gas burning their eyes and noses like acid. By dawn, huge blisters were forming on their faces. As they waited for the ambulances to take them to the field hospital, they lay on stretchers, crying out in agony."

Peter stopped talking and went to the window, his face contorted with pain as if he could still see them and hear their screams. After a few minutes, he continued his litany of horror seemingly unable to stop. "Some of the men were blinded by the gas but were still able to walk. They formed a human train, each one placing one hand on the shoulder of the man in front of him and using the other to wipe at his eyes that watered constantly, the salt just adding to the pain. They moved around the camp like a giant wounded caterpillar, a few now and then falling helplessly in the mud and begging for someone to stop the pain."

As if he had finished a lengthy recitation, Peter sank back into the chair, exhausted and disturbed, still seeing in his mind the carnage in the muddy trenches of France.

May 10, 1921   Peter has survived another dangerous winter although his recovery from his dreadful battle with pneumonia last month is agonizingly slow. He still suffers terribly from the effects of his ordeal overseas. I grieve to see him suffer so and I worry about the safety of the children. Jonathan idolizes his father but I'm afraid to leave them alone for fear that Peter will have one of his spells. His condition just does not seem to improve.

"Mama! Mama! Daddy's hurting me. Help me!" By the time Elizabeth reached the back door, Mittie was already racing across the yard to the terrified child. Clutching baby Beth in her arms, she was horrified by the scene that greeted her. Her husband's arm was locked around her son's neck as the child kicked ferociously, struggling to free himself. Mittie was attempting to free Jonathan, unsuccessfully trying to ward off his frantic kicks.

"Take Beth, Mittie! I'll try to calm him," she said handing the now screaming baby to her.

"Peter! Peter! It's all right, darling. Let Jonathan go. You're hurting him! Please, let him go," Elizabeth cried as she too tried to separate them.

"I have to subdue him. He's a spy. He's going to warn them. I can't let him get away!" he shouted trying to hold on to the terrified boy.

"No, darling. He's not a German spy. You're hurting your son Jonathan. Please let him go!"

Finally, overcome by exhaustion, he relaxed his grip and collapsed on the grass. Jonathan burst free, sobbing hysterically as he fell into his mother's arms.

"You just don't understand. I've got to stop him. He's trying to kill Tommy," Peter covered his face with his hands and trembled like a pathetic child. "You just don't understand."

"Darling, Tommy is dead. He died in France. The Germans shot him. There was nothing you could have done to save him." Elizabeth bent down and tugged on Peter's arm, urging him to stand. "Let's go in and lie down. Mittie has been cooking all morning making chicken and dumplings just the way you like them. By the time you rest a bit, it should be ready. I have some letters to write while you nap. Where did your cane go? Oh, here it is. There, that's better," she said as she helped him to regain his balance.

Elizabeth kept up the calming banter as they trudged back to the house, but her pulse was racing in terror. If she and Mittie had not reached him in time, he would have strangled Jonathan. The episodes were becoming more frequent and more intense. Peter was convinced that he and his friend were in peril. He had even attempted to attack her during one of his violent nightmares. She found that she now slept very lightly, listening for a change in his breathing pattern to alert her to his dreams. The recovery she had hoped for seemed to be slipping away and so did her husband. *Dear God, would this eternal torment never end?*

As they approached the house, Peter's gait slowed and he climbed the steps with difficulty. After such an outburst, he was usually exhausted and slept for a while without dreaming. She prayed that he could sleep and that she would be able to coax him to eat something. He had no appetite, no matter how Mittie tried to tempt him, and was losing weight again. Each day seemed to bring a new challenge more daunting than the last.

January 4, 1922   Today my darling Peter is finally at peace. His body just was not strong enough to overcome his latest battle with pneumonia. I shall miss him so, but I could not selfishly desire him to continue to suffer as he has these past few years. He had long since ceased to be the husband of my youth, but I still loved just having him near. Yes, I shall miss him terribly. Tomorrow he will be buried beneath the great oak in the family cemetery overlooking the river. Someday I'll rest beside him again in the company of my mother and father, my grandparents, and all of my ancestors all the way back to the first Elizabeth on the island. Dear God, give me strength until that day.

Elizabeth remained with Peter until early evening, sitting in the rocker by his bed as she had so many days during his frequent illnesses. At sunset, Mittie came into the room.

"Miss Elizabeth, you need to leave him now. I'll come back after supper and get him ready for tomorrow. The children are askin' for you and you need to eat somethin'. Come on now, honey. You've done all you can for him. He's gone to a better place and you have to look after his babies. Come on, honey. Let Mittie take care of him now," she said.

"Oh, Mittie. What am I going to do? I can't go on without him. I can't keep up this plantation alone. I'll have to move away."

"Yes you can, chile, 'cause you have to. You're gonna keep on doin' like you've been doin' while he was gone away and since he's been back. You're a strong woman. Besides where would you go? You have Elizabeth Brinson's blood in you. Your roots are in this marsh mud just like hers were—and all the other women in your family for that matter. This island is your home, past and future. And what about Miss Eliza? What would she do? You're gonna be fine. Eli and me are here to help you and we are all gonna be fine," Mittie argued with finality and determination. "Now you go on downstairs and get your supper. Jessie's been keepin' it warm for you."

Giving in to Mittie's insistence, Elizabeth bent down and kissed her husband's ashen face once more. Then she hugged Mittie for a moment, wiped her tears, and went downstairs to her children.

"Miss Elizabeth, Mr. Jones from the bank is here. I showed him into the parlor. Would you like me to bring some coffee?" Mittie said to Elizabeth as she sat in her room responding to messages of sympathy.

"Thank you, Mittie. I'm sure he would appreciate it after his chilly trip. I'll go right down."

Alfred Jones stood warming himself before the fire. A member of a wealthy Savannah family, he had once had eyes for Elizabeth O'Shea when they were quite young. His mother, however, a descendant of one of the most prominent families in Georgia, disapproved of her son's interest in the orphaned heiress of Marsh Oaks. She considered Elizabeth's upbringing unsuitable, the girl having been reared by her dotty aunt following first the death of her mother in childbirth and later her father under very questionable circumstances. Mrs. Jones had persuaded her only son that his own social ambitions would be better served by a union with Mary Hall whose family background was impeccable. Young Alfred had honored his mother's wishes and married Miss Hall. Now president of his father's bank, he and his wife were among the pillars of Savannah society.

"Alfred, so good of you to come to the island for our discussion. I truly appreciate your courtesy," Elizabeth said, as she offered her hand. She had been aware of his attraction to her in their youth and of his mother's objections. She had never thought of Alfred as anything other than a friend and had much preferred the company of the dashing Peter Mathews. She inwardly smiled to see that marriage and prosperity had not been particularly kind to him. His portly form and receding hairline made him look mature beyond his 32 years.

Alfred took her hand in his and held it a few moments longer than necessary. He was pleased for an excuse to call on her at home, even if only to conduct their business. Time had not lessened the affection he felt for her and just being alone with her was exciting to him even now.

"I am more than happy to do all I can to assist you at this difficult time in your life and may I extend my sincere condolences on the loss of your husband. He was a fine man."

"Yes, he was. I miss him terribly but I have our two children to think of now. Please sit there," she said directing him to Peter's wing chair by the fire. She placed a small table between them before taking the other chair.

Mittie entered with the tray of steaming coffee and muffins. "Thought you might like something warm, Mr. Jones," she said as she placed the tray on the table.

"Thank you, Mittie. It's bitter out there today. Rained all the way from my office downtown," he said taking a cup from her.

"If the fire dies down, just call me," she said as she closed the door behind her.

"Mittie's still a fine cook," Alfred said as he reached for a second muffin. He wished his own household were as efficiently run as

Elizabeth's obviously was. His wife was more concerned with her card games and social calls than with the proper supervision of household staff and the operation of Magnolia Hall was inconsistent at best. Brushing crumbs from the creases of his vest, the banker reached for his leather bag.

"Elizabeth, I have the papers here you need to sign," he said as he spread them on the table between them. I know you have been doing the bookkeeping for a good while so you are familiar with your financial situation. I just want to assure you that you have nothing to worry about financially. The plantation is profitable and your income from the family businesses in Boston is more than adequate to cover your expenditures. You don't even have to touch your grandfather's assets. I'm sorry I didn't have the privilege of knowing him. He was an exceptionally savvy investor. Few southern planters came out of the Civil War without losing everything, but he actually increased his wealth."

Alfred's own family would have suffered more had his grandfather not engaged in questionable business activities during that period. His parents had refused to discuss that branch of their family tree and focused instead on their successful banking venture later in the 19th century. Edwin Heard, however, seemed to have made his by his exceptional vision and just plain old horse sense.

"We haven't even discussed the funds that are now yours from Peter's family. You may want to consider placing that money in a trust for your children. But we can explore that possibility at a future date."

Alfred sat back in his chair and gazed at the young widow Mathews. Now in her mid-twenties, she was a magnificent figure of a woman. Even in grief, she was a startlingly beautiful woman. Tall and slender, her black bombazine mourning dress only accentuated her regal demeanor and her auburn hair pulled back in a modest bun drew attention to her swan-like neck.

And, now she was one of the wealthiest women in the Low Country. His own wife Mary's lineage was faultless but her family's wealth was nothing in comparison to Elizabeth's. Moreover, his wife no longer appealed to him. Always a bit plump and never considered a beauty, she did not take an interest in her appearance and, following the births of their three children, she had allowed herself to become quite matronly. For a moment, sitting in the presence of this exceptional woman, he wished he had disregarded his mother's wishes and proposed to Elizabeth all those years ago.

April 22nd, 1939   Aunt Eliza passed away in her sleep last night. When Mittie went up to take her breakfast, she was lying peacefully in her bed. She had long since succumbed to the effects of her illness, but she seemed content to live in her own world with her memories. I never truly understood her. She was always so distant and disturbed. When my parents died, if anyone had realized her state of confusion, I would probably have been taken from her. But since she had always been something of a recluse and Mollie had protected her so well, I don't believe anyone really knew how ill she was. In the past few years, she became increasingly delusional. She would cry inconsolably and finally became bewildered about my relationship to her. She called me her granddaughter and thought my mother was not her sister but her daughter. She raved that she hated her father because he took her baby away from her and even blamed me for her daughter's death. She begged her childhood sweetheart Jamie to come and take her and their baby away. Her hallucinations became ever more frequent and she finally ceased recognizing me at all. She was so pitiful.

I shall truly miss her, especially with Jonathan starting his own life in Atlanta and Beth away at school. Perhaps she's with her beloved Jamie at last. I pray God will give her troubled soul peace.

"Miss Elizabeth, Miss Eliza's in a state again. She's down at the tabby house and I can't get her to budge," Mittie called as she ran into the house. "Come quick!"

"Mittie, fetch the smelling salts. I may need it," Elizabeth said as she started down the path. The fading sun was casting an orange glow over the river when she found Eliza sitting on the remains of a tabby wall. She stood watching her for a while before she approached her.

Her aunt's once copper-colored hair was now completely white and she wore it in a long braid wrapped around her head. Her small frame had become stooped with her advancing years, requiring her to use a cane to walk. Her delicate hands had long been so gnarled with arthritis that she could not hold a pen or paintbrush, so she spent her days sitting by the window just staring out at the marsh. On rare occasions, she tottered down to the tabby house where she sat for hours until Mittie walked her back to the house for supper.

Today the tiny woman sat immobile, lost in reverie. The late afternoons were hard for her. She became even more anxious and confused as the sun set.

"Jamie, where are you? I'm waiting for you. Why don't you come for me?" Her words were raspy, barely audible but Elizabeth had heard them before. Her aunt was calling the boy she had loved as a girl to come to her. She had never stopped believing that he would return.

The pain in her voice stung Elizabeth's heart. She touched her shoulder, hoping to comfort her. "Aunt Eliza, it's getting chilly. Let's go up to the house and have some tea."

The old woman stared at her without recognition then turned her eyes back to the marsh. "Did you hear something? It's Jamie. He's coming for me in his boat," her manner becoming agitated. "Do you see him?"

"I think he's coming in the buggy, Aunt Eliza," she said as tears formed in her eyes. "Come with me to the house and we'll wait for him there."

Together they made their way back to the house and climbed the stairs to Eliza's room. Elizabeth sat with her until she was calm again. Later Mittie brought her a tray but could not persuade her to eat. She just kept asking if Jamie had arrived. During the night, Jamie came for his long lost love.

Liz let the journal rest open on her lap. She had no idea that her grandmother's life had been anything more than that of a pampered rich woman. She knew that she had lost her husband and her children but she never mentioned them and, from the way she conducted herself, the youthful Liz had wondered if she really missed them.

After losing her own baby and the two men in her life that mattered, Liz understood just how deep the pain can be and that for some the only way to cope is to suppress. She never kidded herself about her motives for making her career her life for so many years. At least she'd had a choice. Elizabeth Mathews' fate was dealt to her and apparently the only way she knew to survive was to withdraw.

She thought again of that phrase from her childhood, *If it can't be bested, it must be borne.* Her grandmother had borne her grief in solitude and she had borne hers in denial. They had both lost so much, even each other. How she wished they could have shared their grief.

Stretching her stiff muscles, she climbed the stairs and opened the door to the bedroom. The room was bright with sunlight, but her grandmother was sleeping as usual.

Liz pulled the chair up to the bed and took her hand. "Grandmother, I'm sorry I didn't know about all the pain in your life. It must have been so hard to care for your husband, your children, and crazy old Aunt Eliza and have all the responsibility for this place too. I always thought you had a life of luxury.

"You never knew that I lost my child too. I never told you about Jeff and our baby. I was so alone when they died. We've both had to bear so much. I'm sorry we couldn't help each other."

The old woman made no response. Liz watched her steady but shallow breathing then placed her grandmother's hand back on the silk coverlet. Closing the door softly, she went back downstairs to join Olivia for lunch.

Copper Curls and Sea Green Eyes

Sitting across from Olivia at the kitchen table, Liz said, "Boy! This lunch takes me back. I loved nothing better as a kid than sitting on the dock on a hot summer day with a picnic basket full of Mittie's pimiento cheese sandwiches and syrupy-sweet iced tea. Remember?"

Olivia nodded. Liz stared down at the sandwich made with good old white bread. With an unexpected lump in her throat, she continued. "She was so special to me. After my parents died, she was my safe harbor. I really needed her and she loved me no matter what I did."

Olivia smiled. "She was my harbor too, especially after Mama moved to Chicago. It was hard for her to leave me here but my stepfather got work up there and jobs around here were scarce as hen's teeth."

"I haven't heard that expression in years," Liz laughed. "I'm beginning to realize how I've buried so many memories and just being here brings them back." Liz glanced at Olivia. A shared memory of the woman whose love and faith had shaped them both filled the space between the two women and melted away the years of separation. They were young girls again, best friends who vowed nothing would ever keep them apart. Her life had taken her far from this island and those who had loved her. Now she was beginning to realize that she had a strange longing to experience that unconditional love again.

Changing the subject, Liz said, "I'm learning a lot about that old lady upstairs from those journals. I never really knew much about her role as caregiver to my grandfather through the harrowing years of his illness and then later to her Aunt Eliza as she succumbed to dementia.

"She must have been a really strong woman to keep it together the way she did. She certainly had to overcome more than her share of heartache. She lost both of her parents, then her young husband, then the woman who reared her, then her son. I haven't even gotten to my birth or the death of her daughter, but I already know that's coming. I want to understand her feelings, but I dread reading that part in a way. It's funny, but I barely remember my mother. Must be more memories that I blocked out," Liz mused.

"Let me know if you find out anything good—or bad—about my family," Olivia laughed.

"I will. I think I can get through the rest of them this afternoon if I stick to it. You ought to read them too one day. She was very meticulous in recording the events of her life. I guess that's no surprise, huh?"

After a large bowl of banana pudding, Liz returned to the sitting room to finish her task. Thomas wedged his plump body beside her as she settled into the big wing chair again. She had just started to read when she heard the sound of a car on the crushed shell driveway. *No chance of someone sneaking up on this house.* Going to the window, she saw a silver Cadillac pulling up in front. She watched as a corpulent man in a dark suit got out, adjusted his jacket, and walked toward the door.

"Who can that be?" she muttered, a little irritated at being interrupted from her reading. She certainly didn't want to be bothered by some salesman.

Olivia answered the door, then came into the sitting room. "It's a Mr. Smith. He says he went to school with you," she said handing Liz his card. "Should I show him in here?"

"Randall Smith? Yes, please, Olivia. Thank you." Liz was a little uncomfortable when Olivia stepped into the role of housekeeper. She saw herself as her friend not her employer.

"Liz, it's so good to see you after all these years," Randall said as he strode into the room. "You look terrific!"

Liz quickly extended her hand to avoid an awkward hug that so many islanders felt obligatory when greeting each other. Randall's appearance reflected his obvious success, but he must have put on fifty pounds since she had last seen him. The short walk from his air-conditioned car to the coolness of the house had produced a sweat and the front of his shirt was soaked with perspiration. *Please let me avoid the required embrace when he leaves.*

"I hope you don't mind my droppin' in on you without callin' first, but I saw Jack Coleman at lunch and he told me you were here. Said you'd been here for a while now takin' care of Miss Elizabeth. How's she doin'? She must be gettin' on up there."

"Yes, she's quite elderly now but she's hanging in there. She has Alzheimer's disease and is bed-ridden but otherwise she's in good health."

Liz thought she detected a fleeting expression of disappointment on her visitor's face. He pulled out a linen handkerchief and mopped his damp brow.

"I hope while you're here you'll have time to have dinner with Roseanne and me at the club. You remember Roseanne Davis, don't you? We got married right after college and we've been together ever since. Got four kids, three boys and a girl and eleven grandkids. Most of them live nearby. We've been real blessed. Grandkids are more fun than anythin'. They come out for supper on the weekends, but then they go home. Glad to see 'em come; glad to see 'em go, if you know what I mean," he chuckled.

Taking another swipe at his brow, he continued, "Since Miss Elizabeth hasn't gotten out much in recent years, I haven't kept up with what you've been doin'. Where do you live these days? You married? Kids? Grandkids?"

Olivia came into the room with a tray of iced tea. "Thought something cool might be welcome," she said setting the tray on the stool in front of Liz.

"Thank you," Liz said exchanging a surreptitious look with her. Both women were curious about the purpose for the impromptu call. As Olivia left, Randall continued his inquisition.

"You still workin' or are you a lady of leisure?"

"I'm still working in Atlanta. I'm an attorney. I'm a widow and no kids, no grandkids. Does that cover it?"

Oblivious to Liz's growing discomfort, Randall continued to probe her for information about her reason for returning to Marsh

Oaks after so many years. His developer's sixth sense told him that the coveted property may soon be on the block and he wanted to be sure he had the inside track when it became available. He'd been lusting over the prime waterfront location for years and he couldn't bear the thought that it might go to someone else. He could just see in his mind's eye the extensive dock, the hi-rise condos and the five-star restaurant he could build overlooking the river and the considerable expanse of marsh. *A primo development for discriminating clients.* He salivated just thinking about the possibilities.

Shaking the vision from his mind, he persisted. "You didn't say how long you would be here."

"Oh, I don't know. I haven't made up my mind." Liz was beginning to see the point of his visit. He had heard that her grandmother was dying and knew that she would be the new owner of Marsh Oaks. He was trying to insure his place at the head of the line when she listed the property for sale.

"You thinkin' you might come back here someday to live?" he said, anxious to know her plans. With each parry, he leaned forward in his chair a little more until he was almost on the edge.

Liz was enjoying keeping him wondering. She dangled the bait before him, giving him no satisfaction. "I can't decide. I can retire anytime I want to but I just haven't decided whether I would come back here or stay in Atlanta. I have so many friends that it would be hard to leave."

A wide grin spread over the man's face. *If she stays in Atlanta, she'll sell the place for sure.* "Well, you know Marsh Oaks is a very desirable piece of land and waterfront sites are much in demand these days. I could get you a tidy sum for this property should you ever decide to sell," he said amiably. Then realizing his *faux pas*, he added with obvious discomfort, "You *and* Miss Elizabeth, I mean."

"Actually, Olivia keeps trying to persuade me to come back here permanently," Liz said watching his broad smile fade. Relishing his uneasiness, she said, "I'll just have to wait and see." She flashed him her most charming smile and stood up, signaling the end of his visit.

"Well, Roseanne and I would love to have dinner with you while you're here."

"Thank you. That would be nice," she said non-committally as she showed him to the door.

As she watched him drive away, she pondered why she had been so rude. Wasn't it part of her plan to sell Marsh Oaks as soon as she became the legal owner? Why did she resent his broaching the subject? She would never live here again—or would she? She wasn't minding her stay here as much as she had thought she would. She was actually enjoying spending time with Olivia and renewing her friendship with Jack. Could she ever adjust to the slow-paced island way after years of the rat race in Atlanta?

"Do you think you could adjust to living here, Thomas?" she said to the cat as he stretched out in the now-vacated wing chair. Shaking her head to clear her thoughts, she went to the kitchen to fill Olivia in on Randall's spiel over a glass of lemonade and a cookie.

After dinner that night, Liz returned to the study to continue her reading. She placed her glass of Merlot on the low table beside her chair, reopened the leather bound journal, and began to relive her childhood through the words of her loving grandmother.

The Christening Dress
1943-1947

June 26, 1943   My first grandchild was born today at 2:19 a.m. in the same room where her ancestors have been born for almost 200 years. For the first time since Peter died, I am looking forward to the future. She will be christened Elizabeth Brinson Briggs after the first woman in our family to live on this island. Her tiny little head is covered with copper—colored fuzz. The first Elizabeth was a strong, courageous woman. I pray that our little Elizabeth will grow up to be the same.

"Oh, Mother, this christening dress is exquisite. It must have cost a fortune! How did you ever find someone to make it? It's so like the one in the portraits," Beth said as she lifted the delicate gown from the tissue. I don't know how to thank you. Liz will be beautiful in it."

Elizabeth smiled as she held the tiny infant. "It's exactly like the original, my dear. I had it made in London in a shop that has been family-operated for over three hundred years. They might actually have made the first dress. I would have loved for her to wear the heirloom one but it's just too tattered now. I sent them a photograph and a swatch of the fabric and they created it, silk roses and all. With her copper curls and sea green eyes, Elizabeth will look like her namesake must have when she was christened in 1718 in Clovelly. I hope you and Ralston are pleased."

"You know what a traditionalist Ralston is. He'll be thrilled."

"Well, I wanted to do something very special for you. I know you came here for her birth just to please me and it meant so much.

This house is so precious to me. All my memories are here, but most of them are colored with sadness. Her birth is the beginning of a new era of joy for Marsh Oaks. I so want her to know her heritage and I couldn't think of a better way to begin."

Elizabeth had forgotten how much one could love a baby. The stress of caring for Peter during Beth's early life had blocked even the pleasant memories. She vowed not to let anything keep her from treasuring every moment of her grandchild's life and teaching her about her wonderful family history.

"I just wish her Uncle Jonathan could be here for her christening but he does hope to be home for Christmas if his commander will give him leave. Anyway, I can't wait to see her in the dress," she said as she placed the sleeping baby in her daughter's arms.

"What were you humming to her, Mother?" Beth said taking the child.

"'Wayfaring Stranger'," Elizabeth whispered. "You remember the song Mittie used to sing to you, don't you?"

"Yes, but I hadn't thought about it in years. That really takes me back."

"Me, too," Elizabeth said blowing Beth a kiss as she left the room.

June 26, 1947 Elizabeth is four years old today. We invited all of the little girls on the island and their mothers to a tea party. They arrived wearing their best dresses and little white gloves. We sat at little tables under the oak trees and sipped tea from the delicate china cups that my great-grandmother bought in Paris on her honeymoon. Elizabeth—I dislike Liz, as Beth calls her—was the perfect little hostess. My granddaughter loves to play dress up and have me tell her stories about her namesake. For her birthday, I gave her the wonderful dress I had made for her in London, an exact copy of the exquisite green velvet gown Elizabeth Brinson wore in the portrait in the locket. When she put on the dress, she looked for all the world like the ghost of the first Elizabeth. I *have commissioned an artist from Atlanta to paint her portrait posed as the girl in the locket. How beautiful she will be!*

Beth and Ralston are still in Europe but they sent her a new doll dressed in the national costume of Italy where they are traveling. She misses them terribly but I promised her another party when they return and she went to bed smiling. I feel guilty that I have been glad to have her to myself for these weeks. She gives me such joy!

I have finally overcome my anxiety about Beth's trip. I cannot imagine why I felt so apprehensive. Elizabeth and I are having a wonderful summer and her parents are enjoying their sabbatical. Ralston is writing everyday and Beth has taken up painting.

I am sure my friends think I am too extravagant where Elizabeth is concerned. I have lost so much in my life and spent so many years taking care of others that I relish the joy of spoiling her. Somehow, her love eases the old pain of losing Peter and Jonathan too soon.

"Oh, Mother, it's going to be so wonderful, just like a second honeymoon," Beth said pausing as she placed her folded clothes into her suitcase. "A whole summer in romantic villas in Italy, housekeepers and gardeners to care for us, and long sunny days to spend together, just the two of us, visiting some of the places I've always dreamed of seeing. I'm not being selfish, am I? I mean Liz will have a wonderful time here with you."

Elizabeth knew her daughter was looking forward to the summer in Tuscany with her husband while he did research for his book on Italian literature during the Renaissance. She could not imagine that anyone would actually be interested in such a work, but university professors were expected to publish their work periodically. Ralston felt that their grueling itinerary through the remote Italian countryside was no place for a child and Elizabeth had agreed to entertain her while they were abroad. She questioned the wisdom of leaving the child for so long at her young age, but as usual, she could deny her daughter nothing.

She found it hard to believe that they had been married six years. Their courtship had been brief. Dr. Ralston Briggs had been a visiting professor from Cambridge when Beth enrolled in his literature class. At the end of the term, Dr. Briggs had secured a position on the faculty of Agnes Scott College. In July, the society page of the *Savannah Morning News* had detailed at length the wedding of the beautiful debutante Miss Elizabeth Mathews of Marsh Oaks Plantation to Dr. Ralston Briggs of Cambridge and Atlanta. She remembered as if it were yesterday, the young couple saying their vows on the veranda and receiving their guests alfresco under the ancient oaks. Following an extended honeymoon in England, Beth left with her dashing new husband to make their home in Atlanta, only returning to the island for brief visits.

"I've planned several excursions while you are gone that I think Elizabeth will enjoy," she said. "I hope she'll be too busy to miss you very much. I've promised her a birthday party, too. Just some of the other little girls on the island and their mothers for tea. Mittie is already looking forward to making a very special birthday cake. Before we know it the summer will be over," she said with more enthusiasm than she truly felt.

She was delighted to have Elizabeth with her for such an extended time and she knew the arrangement was best for the child, but, for some unexplained reason, she still felt anxious. "You will wire whenever you can, won't you? I know she will want to hear from you often."

Elizabeth smiled as Beth came over to kiss her on the forehead before she turned back to repacking the suitcase she had brought with her for the few days on the island.

"Mother, you know I will and don't worry so. Ralston and I will be back by the middle of August. Liz loves being here with you and Mittie will help look after her. I know you love having her with you. You'll both be fine."

"You know how mothers worry, dear. Still I'm glad you and Ralston will have this trip and Elizabeth and I will have a wonderful time while you are gone. I could never have enough time with my precious little girl."

Osprey Freedom

The clock in the hall struck midnight. Liz let the book rest in her lap and rubbed her tired eyes. Elizabeth Mathews had written in her journal every day of her adult life, recording in painstaking detail all the events that filled her days, the joys as well as the sorrows. Every phase of Liz's childhood had been documented with care—her first words, her favorite foods, even the songs they sang together.

The words were so hard to absorb. The grandmother she remembered as aloof and disinterested had been overjoyed by her birth, especially with her bright red curls. She had even chosen her name—Elizabeth Brinson after the first woman in her family to come to Skidaway. She had doted on her, insisting on frequent visits by her daughter so she could be with her precious grandchild. She had showered her with expensive gifts, outfitted her in elaborate clothes, and showed her with unabashed pride to the other matrons on the island.

Liz was awed by the obvious care her grandmother had taken to acquire an exact copy of the first Elizabeth's elaborate christening gown she had discovered stored with care in the antique chest. The ceremony followed by a reception for everyone on the island must have been quite an elegant affair.

As she grew older, her copper curls and sea green eyes must have heightened her resemblance to her revered ancestor even more and, in a curious way, strengthened the growing bond with her grandmother. But most amazing of all, her grandmother had loved her. She hadn't rejected her or found her unlovable. Quite the opposite, the emotionless disciplinarian of her childhood recollections had adored her.

Yawning, Liz looked away from the journal, gazing out the

window into the eerie silence. The moon reflected on the surface of the high tide, a quivering shard of light that stretched almost to the horizon then disappeared into the tall grass. The surreal beauty of the marsh touched the innermost part of her being. Somewhere within her, a memory stirred of sitting on the dock, her feet dangling in the water as her grandmother told her imaginative stories about the way the island was when Elizabeth Brinson lived here.

The details of the stories eluded her now but from deep in her memory came a feeling of warmth and closeness as her grandmother held her near and spoke in a soft, musical voice just to her. She could almost smell the lavender fragrance her grandmother always wore mingled with the pungent scent of the marsh. She recalled the sense of pride in who she was that her grandmother had instilled in her. But for some reason, she had blocked those memories from her consciousness. Until now, Liz's earliest recollections of her legal guardian were filled with indifference and stern discipline.

But if her grandmother had loved her so much in her early years, why had she turned against her? Had she blamed her granddaughter for her daughter's death? Or even worse, could the story of a fiery crash in Europe have been a lie? Could she possibly have been involved in her own parents' death?

She was compelled to continue reading, but her thoughts were reeling and her head ached. The answer to her quandary must be somewhere in the journal but it would have to wait until tomorrow. She could read no more tonight.

The next morning, Liz struggled to tell Olivia what she had learned from the journal about her grandmother's all-consuming love, the extravagant gifts, and special parties. "It just doesn't make sense. It's obvious that we were very close but somehow I've just blocked it out of my conscious memory and replaced it with feelings of rejection. But why would I do that?"

Olivia listened intently while she prepared breakfast. "Maybe you were just too young to remember. Have you finished the book?"

"No, it's very slow going. I have to stop and think so much that I don't get very far. I've only read as far as my fourth birthday, but if what she wrote is true, she adored me then. She doted on me and showered me with affection. I don't know why she changed so. I'm hoping that she wrote about what happened." Taking her mug of coffee to the table, she said, "I wanted to finish last night but it's so intense that my head was throbbing by the time I gave up about midnight. As soon as this caffeine kicks in, I'm going to hit it again."

After breakfast, Liz took the journal and headed for the dock to sit in the sun, determined to finish it before lunch. Beneath her huge straw hat, she smeared a heavy layer of sunscreen on her face. Stretching out in a chair, she glanced across the marsh to an untidy pile of sticks atop a piling that marked the channel in the river. As she watched, a female osprey emerged from the nest. After circling several times, she swooped down and landed on the surface of the water. Maneuvering her wings in an awkward fashion, she moved a few feet across the surface then took to the air again, calling in a shrill voice as she rose. Shaking the water from her feathers, she circled over the marsh once more then repeated her strange behavior.

Liz laughed but wondered why a bird so obviously out of place in the water would act in such an extraordinary manner. At first, she thought the bird might be injured, but after witnessing several dives, she decided the creature was playing.

Earlier she had been fascinated by the mating pair as they conducted their courtship, soaring high over the river then diving just below the surface to catch their prey. After building their nest, they spent many weeks incubating the eggs then tending the voracious chicks. Liz speculated that the long period of caring for her brood must have taken a toll on the female and this uncharacteristic display was her way of letting off steam.

"Go for it, girl! You deserve to kick up your heels," Liz called to the cavorting bird now positioning herself for another dive. In an odd way she envied the osprey her moment of frivolity. Her own emotions were so controlled; her first concern was always how her actions would appear to others. Acting on impulse only led to problems. She had been impulsive when she moved in with Jeff but she was very young and a bit rebellious. *It was the 60's, for heaven's sake. Everyone was rebellious.* A moment of passion, a lifetime of regret. No, she didn't regret her ill-fated love for Jeff and their baby, but since then she had been much more cautious in managing her life, a life that now seemed to be racing ahead of her at too fast a pace. Maybe it was time for her to loosen up too.

Rising from the water, the bird shook her feathers once more, then returned to her nest, the flight of fancy over and the duties of motherhood again her first concern. "Break's over, huh? Back to the real world," Liz said, sorry that the strange spectacle was over and feeling a little unnerved by her own unexpected response. *Well, my break's over too. Time to get back to work and finish this journal.*

Thankful for the hint of a breeze, she opened the book and once again was transported to a time over 50 years before.

PART FIVE

THE WAYFARING STRANGER

Alone With Memories
July 16, 1947

July 16, 1947   This is the last day of my life. I can endure no more pain. Through all of the trials I have been forced to endure, I trusted God to give me the strength to persevere. I held to my belief that my misfortune was the result of unavoidable circumstances but I have now come to believe that God is punishing me. I was cursed from my birth and that curse extends to all I hold dear. My mother died giving me life and my father died from his grief. My only relative Eliza lost her mind and ended her life blaming me for my mother's death. War took my beloved Peter and our son. I have buried them all under the oak tree. Now my only daughter has been wrenched from me, too. And I am to be denied even the privilege of burying my daughter, but I will erect a memorial for Beth and Ralston near the others. And still I survive. All I have left is my precious granddaughter. I have no choice but to send her away before my toxic love condemns her as well. I cannot bear to bury her, too. I can love her no more.

"Grandma, tell me about the other Elizabeth again. About how she came over on the big boat," Liz begged as she sat on the dock, dangling her feet in the cool water lapping against the ladder. Her grandmother sat in a beach chair, reading a book and holding a huge umbrella to protect her flawless skin from the midday sun.

Putting down her book, Elizabeth laughed. "Let's go up to the house and get out of this hot sun. You are going to have freckles all over your face and no well brought-up young lady has freckles. Mittie will have your lunch ready, I'm sure. After lunch, you can lie down and rest and I'll tell you all about Elizabeth. Maybe we'll have another postcard from your mother and father. They should be in Tuscany by now."

Liz took her grandmother's hand as they walked down the long wooden dock, the heat of the sun-baked boards stinging her bare feet.

"Ouch! Ouch!" she squealed, hopping from one foot to the other. "My feet are burning! Ouch!"

"Darling, let me carry you. I should have reminded you to bring your sandals when we came out. You hold on to the umbrella."

As her grandmother lifted her into her arms, Liz could smell the familiar lavender scent she always wore. Tired and hungry, she snuggled happily against her. "Sing about the stranger again, Grandma."

Laughing, Elizabeth began the familiar refrain as the child joined in and sang it several more times until they reached the porch.

After lunch, Liz fell asleep as her grandmother retold the familiar story of a brave young woman in an alien land. Elizabeth held the sleeping child for a few minutes longer, treasuring the exquisite contentment of having her precious granddaughter in her arms. When Jonathan and Beth were small, she had not had the luxury of time to spend reading to them or just enjoying their childhood. She had been required to run the estate while Peter was overseas. Then, when he returned, she not only continued in that role but also became caregiver to him as his condition deteriorated. By the time they were teenagers, Eliza had become more withdrawn as her dementia increased and she became almost bed-ridden. And then they were gone, busy with their own lives. Surely, no one could fault her for lavishing her love on her only grandchild. She had waited a long time for this pleasure. Settling her under the cover, she touched her lips to the child's forehead, then slipped from the room.

Deciding to take a short nap herself, Elizabeth went to the

bedroom window to draw the drapes against the bright midday sun. She was still standing at the window savoring the beauty of the marsh when she heard the unexpected sound of a car approaching on the crushed shell drive. *Odd, to have a visitor this time of day. I'm not expecting anyone.* People only came to the island when they were invited or they had official business. Going to the top of the stairs, she watched Mittie open the heavy door to Sheriff Price and one of his deputies. An ominous sensation passed through her body. Her sense of foreboding was immediately confirmed when she looked at the men's faces as they removed their hats and stepped into the foyer.

"Show the officers into the parlor, Mittie," she said, willing herself to descend the stairs at her normal pace. "And bring us some iced tea, please. I'm sure the gentlemen must be parched," she called after her as if she were entertaining invited and welcome guests.

With regal poise, she entered the sitting room and crossed with deliberate ease to her usual chair near the fireplace. Although the temperature was in the nineties outside, Elizabeth felt a chill as she motioned the men to two large chairs across from hers. With a steady voice that belied the turmoil within her, she addressed the uneasy men. "Gentlemen, I'm a little surprised by your visit. I cannot imagine that you have come out here just to be sociable. I fear you are here to deliver news I do not wish to hear, so please proceed."

"Yes, ma'am, we're here on official business. We're truly sorry to have to tell you, Mrs. Mathews," the sheriff began, "but we've just had a message from the Italian police. Accordin' to them," he said reading from a worn notepad, "your daughter, Elizabeth Briggs and her husband, Dr. Ralston Briggs, have been in an automobile accident in Northern Italy. Seems they'd been staying on a lake in the mountains and were headed to Florence." He paused to give the stricken woman time to grasp the meaning of his words. "They were drivin' one of those fancy little sports cars and I guess they just didn't realize how treacherous those twisty roads can be." He elected not to tell her the report said they were traveling at a high rate of speed. She didn't need to hear all the gory details. "The car went off the road and they were both killed. I hate to be so direct but I know you like to have the whole story."

Sheriff William Price, called Bubba by the islanders, knew Elizabeth Mathews very well in fact. He and her son Jonathan had been inseparable growing up. They had gotten into some minor scrapes as most boys do, nothing serious, but enough to warrant parental disapproval. Bubba had always tried to manipulate the truth with his folks and sometimes managed to avoid punishment but Jonathan took a different tact. His best shot, he said, was to 'fess up as soon as they were found out. His mother would tolerate almost anything but a lie. Yep, the news was horrible but he figured she wanted the straight truth no matter how hard it was to bear.

He watched her as she fought to control her emotions. She would never let them see her break down. Her usual erect posture intensified as she straightened her shoulders. Rising from her chair, she seemed to steady herself before she spoke, addressing the sheriff in a flat tone. "I assume I will need to complete some paperwork to have their bodies returned for burial."

Bubba leaned toward her as he said, "Miss Elizabeth, I'm afraid I didn't make myself clear. Accordin' to the report, when the car hit the bottom of the ravine, it burst into flames and they were unable to escape. There won't be bodies to bury. I'm just awful sorry 'bout this."

Elizabeth willed her body to remain upright as her head began to whirl. Steeling herself, she said, "Gentlemen, if you will excuse me, I think I would like to lie down. Mittie will be right in with your iced tea. Please make yourselves comfortable. William, thank you for your promptness and your candor in bringing me this dreadful news. Good day, Officers."

The men stood as she left the room, helpless to say or do anything to ease her grief. "Her heart's broken," Bubba said to his deputy, "but she'll never let anyone see her pain. They don't make women like her anymore. She's one grand lady, she is."

Climbing the long staircase with slow, deliberate steps, Elizabeth had just closed her bedroom door when she felt the room begin to spin. Collapsing on her bed, she surrendered to her anguish.

She had been at her window looking out at the marsh that day too when she heard the car on the crushed shell drive. Those two men had worn Army uniforms but their faces, too, had revealed the unpleasant nature of their visit. She knew before they spoke why they had come. Military officers did not pay social calls to the mothers of soldiers, particularly during wartime.

Standing before her in the parlor, one of the officers had said simply, "We're sorry to have to inform you, Mrs. Mathews, but Captain Jonathan Mathews' plane took enemy fire over Romania on 1 August, 1943. His plane went down and both he and his co-pilot were lost." With hesitation, he held out to her the folded flag he carried. "The President wishes us to convey his sincere condolences."

With so few words, the life of her son was extinguished. All her hopes for his future snuffed out in an instant, thousands of miles from his island home and safety.

Before Elizabeth's eyes flashed an image of her dashing son when he came home during his last leave sporting his uniform. Always popular as a youth, he had been irresistible to the young ladies as a war hero. As a child, he had been fascinated by the tales of the First World War his father told during his rare lucid moments. The young Jonathan had collected model airplanes and told everyone that he would be a pilot when he grew up. He had realized his dream, but it had cost him his life.

And now her daughter was gone, too. Now she was childless.

When she left the house, Elizabeth had no thought of where she was going. Her only objective was to flee from her excruciating pain. Oblivious to the beauty of a perfect summer day, she found herself at the old tabby house, staring out across the marsh as she had done so many times before. Decades of wind and driving rains had reduced the tiny structure to little more than ruins but she still found solace within its crumbling walls. Tears streamed down her face as she collapsed against the crumbling wall, longing to surrender her grief to the healing presence of the marsh and her memories.

"This is a cruel joke!" she screamed at the heavens as she railed against God. "It's unnatural to outlive your children! They're supposed to bring you joy and make you proud of their accomplishments, take care of you in your old age then go on to live their lives. A mother should not have to bury her babies! This was not part of the bargain," she sobbed as she sank down onto the wooden bench.

Suddenly a large orange cat jumped into her lap, rubbing its chin against hers and purring softly. "Samson, what am I going to do?"

As she stroked the cat's fur, the soothing rhythm and the warmth of the sun started to melt the tension in her body. Across the river, a marsh hen called to its mate and a gentle breeze signaled the turning of the tide. As her long delicate fingers relaxed, a postcard slipped from her hand and fluttered to the dirt floor.

The sun was setting when Mittie reached the ruins of the tabby house. Her footsteps on the path were so soft and the other woman so lost in her thoughts that she stood for a long time before disturbing the woman's grief.

"Miss Elizabeth, you need to come back to the house now," she said as she draped a sweater around Elizabeth's sagging shoulders. "Supper's ready and you need to eat something. You've been out here all afternoon. I gave Liz her supper and she's ready for bed, but she's asking for you. You need to see her before she goes to sleep."

"Mittie, I can't. I just can't. I wouldn't do her any good the way I am."

"Miss Elizabeth, you have to. That child has no one on this earth now but you. You have to be her mama and her daddy, too. She's only four years old and she needs you to help her get through this. You've got to think of her now."

"I can't! I'm too old to rear a child. I'm too tired. I'll make sure she's well cared-for but I just can't do it myself. I cared for Aunt Eliza and when Peter was away in the war, I ran the plantation and reared two small children by myself. I did my part. I was a good mother. You know Peter was never right when he came home from the war. He couldn't help his rages, but he frightened the children so. He sank deeper and deeper into his madness and I had to watch him every moment so he wouldn't hurt them. I never let them know how sick he was. I felt like a widow long before he died, but the children never suffered.

"I kept our heads above water during the depression and another war. Now I've outlived both of my children. What more should a woman have to bear? I'm tired and I want to be left alone with my memories."

"But you're not alone! You have a granddaughter and she has only you. She needs your love now."

"But, Mittie, I can't love her—I can't destroy her life, too. I'm cursed! Everyone I've ever loved died a horrible death. My birth killed my mother and my father's grief killed him. Even Aunt Eliza blamed me. War took Peter and my son and now my daughter is dead, too," she sobbed covering her face with her hands. "I caused their deaths, you know. God is punishing me. I don't know why, but he is. He takes all my loved ones from me."

"Miss Elizabeth, don't say that! God don't punish His people like that just for meanness. He didn't take your folks from you. People just die. They get sick. They have accidents. That's just the way the world is. God don't act like that. He loves us too much to hurt us on purpose. You know I believe He's real sad too that your precious daughter and her husband died. Please don't blame Him," Mittie pleaded. "He still loves you and He'll take care of you."

"Mittie, I wish I could believe that, but I've had too much tragedy in my life. I'm not even sure God ever did really love me, but He must love Elizabeth. How could He not love her? But if I let myself love her, she'll die, too, and I can't bear to bury my only grandchild. The only way to protect her is to turn away from her. I'll send her to the best school I can find."

"Miss Elizabeth, don't send her just yet. She's still a baby. Let me take care of her for a while. I just can't stand for her to be alone in a strange place. She just lost both her parents and she don't understand. She feels abandoned. Please don't let her think you're abandoning her, too. Don't send her away. She won't interfere with my work and she can play with my granddaughter Olivia. I won't let her bother you."

Elizabeth rose, weighing her own grief against the welfare of the child, and turned toward the woman who had been her companion since she was a child herself. "Oh, Mittie, what am I going to do? It just hurts so much," she moaned as she sank into the black woman's strong arms.

Nightmare Becomes a Daydream

The flowing script stopped abruptly on July 16, 1947. Liz turned several more pages but all were blank. For Elizabeth O'Shea Mathews, life had ended on that day and she recorded no more in her journal. Liz was stunned. At last, she understood that the devastated woman had withdrawn from her orphaned granddaughter not because she no longer loved her, but because she loved her so very much. She had sacrificed her own happiness to protect the one she loved most in the world.

The sun was low in the sky and her flushed skin was tingling. She had spent most of the day on the dock in the blazing sun as she finished the journal, stopping only to return to the house for lunch. Liz grabbed her flip-flops and hurried across the warm boards of the dock in her bare feet. As she reached the veranda, Thomas met her, inquiring in a loud voice about her day. She scooped him up and carried him into the cool darkness of the hall.

She could hear Olivia humming as she prepared the usual glass of drinking custard. In a little while, she would try once again to coax her charge to eat something before settling her for the night.

Having at last uncovered the reason for her grandmother's rejection, Liz longed to go to her, embrace her, and tell her how much she had always loved her, but would the confused elderly woman understand her or even know who she was?

Depositing Thomas in the wing chair and dropping the journal on the table by the door, Liz went upstairs to shower and change clothes. When she came back downstairs, she called to Olivia, "Would you mind if I took the tray up to Grandmother? I'd like to see her. She may not eat for me, but I would like to try. I want to spend some time with her."

Olivia gave her curious look. After her first visit, Liz had made every effort to avoid her grandmother's room. Why did she want to see her now?

"I know," Liz said when she saw the questions in Olivia's eyes. "I'll explain to you when I come down. How about opening a good bottle of wine? We're both going to need it," she called over her shoulder as she headed toward the stairs.

Knocking before she opened the door, Liz took a deep breath, straightened her shoulders, and entered the shadowy world of her grandmother's bedroom. The frail old woman lay beneath the silk coverlet, propped on huge down pillows with her eyes closed in the fading light of early evening. Placing the tray on the nightstand, she leaned down toward the bed.

"Grandmother, it's Liz. I've brought your custard. Olivia just made it for you."

The woman did not respond. Only the slightest movement of her satin bed jacket indicated that she was still breathing. Sitting in the delicate French chair by the bed, Liz touched a spoonful of the custard to her grandmother's lips. Like a baby bird, the old lady's mouth opened a slight bit but her eyes remained closed tight and soon she no longer responded. With resignation, Liz placed the glass again on the tray and turned back to the bed.

"I love you, Grandmother. I know now that you loved me, too, that you didn't reject me. I can remember now how close we were when I came to visit you. When my parents died, I thought that you were angry with me because I had somehow caused their deaths. I didn't understand that you felt you had to push me away in order to protect me."

Stopping to dry her tears, Liz sensed that, although she had not opened her eyes, her grandmother's breathing appeared to quicken.

"I'm so sorry that I wasn't here for you all those years after I left the island. I realize now how much it must have hurt you to let me go. But I'm here now and I won't leave you again."

Her grandmother's hands rested on the coverlet. She had been once so proud of her elegant hands and long slender fingers. Now her hands were merely bones with a maze of blue veins beneath almost transparent skin but they were still smooth and soft. Liz took the frail hand in hers, breathing in the comforting scent of lavender as she did.

A vague memory came to her mind. She was sitting on the bed as her grandmother smoothed lavender-scented cream on her small, childish hands. *"You must take very good care of your hands, Elizabeth,"* her grandmother was saying. *"You can always tell a lady by her hands."*

"And you are still a fine lady, Elizabeth Mathews," Liz said, smiling as she tucked her grandmother's delicate hands beneath the cover then kissed her forehead.

Taking the tray, she turned down the light. Starting down the stairs, she could hear the sound of Ben's laughter as he shared an anecdote about his day with Olivia.

"How 'bout another piece of fish or some more cheese grits, Ben? We still have plenty of both," Olivia said as she started to clear the dishes from the dining room table.

"Thanks, Olivia, but I couldn't eat another bite. That was delicious. You sure haven't lost your touch," Ben said pushing his plate away.

"I hope you saved room for lemon pie. The coffee's almost ready," she said removing his plate.

"I'll help you," Liz said, starting to push her chair back.

"No need. You entertain our guest," she said, as she headed toward the kitchen.

"I'm afraid I don't have a repertoire of after-dinner jokes, Ben. Not my style," Liz said.

"Mine either. I never could tell a joke right."

"I'll bet that's a problem for a preacher. Aren't all sermons three points, two jokes, and a tear-jerker?"

Ben laughed—a deep, resonant sound that revealed how much he liked doing so. "Do I detect a note of cynicism in that comment or do you just dislike preachers?"

"I don't have anything against them. I can't say I've known enough of them to form an opinion," Liz quipped, then in a more serious tone continued, "I suppose it's with their boss I have a problem."

Ben leaned forward, propping his elbows on the dark mahogany table. "You mean you have a problem with God?"

Liz waited a moment then said, "I've been reading my grandmother's journals. I'm sure you know that we had a very difficult relationship as I was growing up. I always thought she blamed me for my parent's death or even that I might have been responsible in some way. I've learned from her journals that she didn't blame me; she blamed herself."

"What do you mean? They were killed in an accident in Europe. I remember the story very well."

"That's not what she meant. She felt that for some reason God was punishing her by sending everyone she loved to an early grave. Her parents, her husband, her son, finally her daughter, all died young. She decided that her love was lethal and the only way to protect me was to push me away."

In his profession, Ben had spent many hours listening to people as they poured out their innermost thoughts. Each time he grasped for something to say that would ease their pain. He had learned that very little he could say would give them peace, but just letting them talk sometimes helped.

"But that doesn't explain your problem with God," he said.

Liz toyed with her spoon, drawing invisible circles on the damask tablecloth and avoiding his eyes. "I lost my fiancé and our unborn baby when he was shot down in Viet Nam. The pain was awful and I swore I would never risk such pain again. Years later, I allowed myself to fall in love once more and I married a wonderful man. We had five marvelous years together and then six months of hell as I watched him slip away from me. If God is love as the televangelists profess," Liz said as her voice rose and became strident, "then why does He hate people who love each other?" Embarrassed by her own outburst, she stared down at her hands. "I'm sorry. I'm not quite sure where that came from! I've never put those feelings in words before."

"Then maybe it's time you did. You've carried that pain for a long time."

Olivia heard the anger in Liz's voice as she brought the tray of dessert into the dining room. "What's wrong, Liz? Are you okay?"

"Liz is being truthful about some feelings she's kept inside for a long time. I don't blame you for being angry, Liz," Ben said.

Olivia handed them huge slices of quivering lemon filling topped with mounds of fluffy meringue, finished pouring the steaming coffee into the delicate porcelain cups, then sat down again without a word, waiting for someone to explain why her friend was so upset.

"Liz is wondering whether God caused the grief that both she and her grandmother have had to face. It's hard to lose folks we love and sometimes we just have to hold someone accountable," Ben continued. "But I believe that God doesn't cause the bad things that come into our lives. When God gave us free will, He took a big chance. For thousands of years, we've been doing things that grieve Him and cause us pain. Your family has had a lot of grief, but I don't believe God caused it. In fact, I believe that when we suffer, God suffers with us and together we just get through it. I don't expect you to be convinced of what I've said, but think about it and, if you like, we'll talk about it again one day."

"Thanks, Ben. I appreciate your concern, but I'll have to think about what you've said. Right now, I think I'll walk down to the dock for a while," she said as she stood. "Sorry, Olivia. I'll have to eat my pie later. Good night, Ben. Please come again soon."

Later when Liz returned to the house, Ben was gone and Olivia was finishing the dishes.

"I didn't mean to skip out on you but I just needed some time to think," Liz apologized.

"So tell me what happened today. You've been in a fog all evening."

"You know me too well. Grab the rest of that bottle of wine and let's go out on the veranda."

They sat in the encompassing darkness on the back porch sipping their wine. The air was still and humid. Overhead the ceiling fan whirred. From the woods, a whippoorwill called.

"I finished the journal this afternoon," Liz said and began to tell her childhood friend the incredible story.

Olivia remained silent as the details of two unhappy lives

unfolded. Years of wasted opportunities to share their days and comfort each other in their mutual grief.

"I couldn't understand how the icy woman who didn't want her own grandchild in her presence could be the generous benefactor to the granddaughter of her housekeeper, much less be so charitable to a young black boy she hardly knew. She just couldn't be that different."

Liz stared at her wine glass. She wasn't sure she knew how to explain a lifetime of conflicted feelings.

"When I look back over the years, I realize that the memory of our loving relationship never died. It just sort of faded into the background for a while—a long while," she said. "All my life, the scent of lavender or even warm sun on my face would stir a deep sense of longing in me that just came from nowhere. I would be so melancholic, I would start to cry. I never understood why I suddenly felt so sad.

"I suppose when I was a child I suppressed the memory of the time before my parents died because it was too painful to accept that I had been abandoned by everyone I loved without any explanation. I even feared I might somehow be responsible."

Before tonight, Liz had never admitted her deepest feelings to anyone. To be rejected by the one who was supposed to love you unconditionally was bad enough, but to believe that you were to blame was even worse.

"I still remember crying myself to sleep after Mittie turned out the light. I thought that Grandmother blamed me because my mother never came home from her trip, that she was having a good time and didn't want to come back and take care of me. I felt so guilty."

"I never knew you had those feelings. I'm so sorry. Did Grannie know how you felt?" Olivia asked as tears filled her eyes.

"No. I never told anyone at all. Just kept it inside. All those years," she said choking back the flood of tears that threatened to halt her story. Olivia reached for her hand but remained silent as Liz fought to regain her composure.

"I suppose in my child's mind it was the only explanation for my grandmother abandoning me. As I got older, I started to wonder if the story of the accident had been a lie. I even had nightmares that I had somehow caused their deaths and blocked out the memory. Of course, as an adult, I realized that I had nothing to do with their deaths, but as a kid, I really believed it.

"Reading in her own words about her love for me, and her fear that something horrible might happen to me because of that love, made me realize how terrible her life has been. She really felt God was punishing her. I only wish I had known the truth years ago. We spent so many years apart when we could have been helping each other," Liz said, her voice trailing off to a whisper.

When she spoke again, her voice was filled with emotion. "I know enough about Alzheimer's disease to recognize the signs. I've been involved with so many clients who were battling with the devastating effect it has on families that I decided to learn something about it. She's probably had the disease for years, but I suppose that's to be expected at her age. I don't really think that she will ever be able to communicate with me, but I wish I felt that she could even understand how much I've always loved her. I'm just so sorry that we wasted all those years."

Liz and Olivia continued rocking without speaking, each one lost in thought. A gentle breeze from the incoming tide cooled the evening air as night birds called hauntingly from the marsh and darkness overtook the fading light.

An Invitation From Jack

The next morning as Liz sipped her coffee and Olivia poured eggs into the frying pan, they heard the sound of a boat horn coming from the river. From the window, Liz saw Jack climbing up the ladder to the dock.

"It's Jack. He's coming up."

"What a surprise," Olivia teased.

Jack had begun stopping by on his way to or from the park. He was a now frequent guest at dinner and often stayed to sit and talk for hours about both the past and the future of Skidaway. Olivia had noticed that his obvious love for the island was having an effect on her friend. When Liz first returned to Marsh Oaks, she was very clear that she was just staying no longer than necessary to get things in order. As the weeks passed, her attitude changed. Her departure was mentioned less often and she talked less about her life in Atlanta. Olivia decided that Jack Coleman, or at least his influence, could be part of the change.

"We're just old friends," Liz said straightening her shirt and smoothing her hair as she went to open the door.

Olivia broke three more eggs, took out another plate, and filled an over-sized mug with steaming coffee.

"I was on my way over to Ossabaw to check on some turtle nests and thought you might like to ride with me," Jack was saying as he entered the kitchen. "Mornin', Olivia. Thanks," he said as he took the mug she held out to him.

"I hope you haven't had breakfast yet. I just put in a few more eggs," Olivia said.

"Thanks. That would be great. I usually don't bother with a real breakfast. Just grab a bagel or something as I head out the door. It doesn't seem worth the effort to cook for just me."

Liz had been watching with amusement as he settled his muscular frame onto one of the delicate antique chairs at the table. He was obviously more at home in a rustic cabin than in a Victorian parlor. *Bet his place is full of overstuffed chairs and tables covered with white rings and scratches. His kitchen is probably a mess and his fridge is full of beer and hot dogs.* She wondered if he cooked much at all. The divorced men she knew ate every meal out. But that was in the city. Maybe Jack had to cook or starve on the island. *Maybe I'll be invited to find out,* she mused.

"What do you do with the turtle nests?" Liz asked.

"I don't do anything except make sure they're still safe. We put a fence around them and volunteers keep watch until time for the eggs to hatch. I just check on them from time to time. They should be hatching soon," Jack explained. He stared at his mug as he continued, "I thought we might ride over, then grab some lunch at the marina. That is, if Olivia can spare you."

"I'll manage just fine. You two young folks go ahead," she laughed as she placed the brimming plate of scrambled eggs and country ham on the table. "The biscuits are almost done."

"Thank you, Olivia. This sure looks good. I haven't had a home-cooked breakfast since . . ." He looked away for a moment before he continued. "Well, for a good while now."

Liz knew he was thinking about his ex-wife. *At least that answers the question about the cooking. Definitely fast food lunches and take-out dinners. He had probably never adjusted to living alone.*

Finishing the last biscuit, Jack leaned back contentedly. "Well, are you going to come with me?" he asked.

"Let me get a jacket," Liz said glancing at Olivia, who gave her a knowing wink.

"It's going to be a beautiful day. Why don't you take some sandwiches and make a day of it?" Olivia suggested. "I know Jack likes my pimiento cheese and there's plenty of ham."

"Are you sure you don't mind?" Liz asked.

"Heavens, no. And you could use a day on the beach. Now make this man some lunch while I go check on Miss Elizabeth."

A Change of Heart

The day was bright and clear. The noise of the boat's motor made conversation difficult, so Liz propped against the rail, drinking in the beauty of the marsh as she inhaled the salt air. Without warning, an old memory flashed through her mind—a young couple running on a deserted beach, their bodies tanned and lean, their whole lives stretching out before them. Was it really over forty years? It seemed like yesterday.

Jack guided the boat toward the island and dropped the anchor. On the narrow beach, frantic fiddler crabs scurried in every direction, disappearing into tiny holes in the sand to escape the invaders. Kicking off his boat shoes, Jack jumped into the shallow water.

"Sorry I can't take you to dry land but the propeller will drag the bottom. Just leave your shoes on the boat. I'll carry you to the beach so you won't get your clothes wet," Jack said laughing. "Just like I used to. Remember?"

"Oh, I do remember. I just don't think you realize that we are a lot older and I'm a lot heavier than I was then," Liz joked as she slipped over the side of the boat and into his waiting arms.

She remembered very well. They had spent most of their summers exploring the barrier islands in Jack's boat, an old Chris-Craft his grandfather left him. That last summer, they had sought the most isolated beaches to spend time alone. They had pretended that they were shipwrecked on a desert island and had made love for the first time on the warm sand. Now in his arms, she recalled their youthful passion and felt a sensation of tenderness that she had not known in a long time.

Jack carried her a little farther above the waterline than necessary, reluctant to release her. Memories were racing through his head as well. Since he first saw her again on the dock, he had spent many hours remembering how much he had loved her so many years ago. He had resisted admitting even to himself that the feelings he once had for her still haunted him. It had taken years to recover from the pain of losing her the first time. This time, she had made it clear from the start that she intended to go back to her life in Atlanta, a life that would never include him. Did he dare risk loving her again?

Pushing such thoughts from his mind, he put Liz down and headed toward a marked area at the edge of the dunes. They spent the morning checking on all the nests. At mid-day, they found a shady spot under a windswept pine tree and devoured their sandwiches with gusto. Later they strolled down the otherwise deserted beach, disturbing the sandpipers, probing the damp sand with diligence in search of tiny organisms.

As they walked, Jack took her hand and they strolled contentedly along the shoreline. Liz felt as if the years had been peeled away and they were love-struck teenagers again.

"You know, this island must still look as it did when the first settlers came to this area. Virgin beaches, wind-swept trees, abundant wildlife. I walked this beach hundreds of times as a kid, but I don't think I ever appreciated its beauty until now. It's so primitive. I feel like my ancestor Elizabeth Brinson must have when she saw Georgia for the first time," Liz said with a dreamy quality in her voice.

She realized that Jack was looking at her and felt foolish for letting her imagination run away with her. This place was beginning to have a strange effect on her.

"Guess I've been spending too much time in the past, reading Grandmother's journal and rummaging through her old treasures. The ghosts are starting to get to me," Liz laughed and picked up the pace to avoid saying anything else.

Jack smiled at her, then looked out to sea as they continued walking.

"So how long do you think you can be away from your firm?" Jack asked after a long period of silence.

"Oh, I don't know. I turned over all my pending cases to the other partners before I left, so nothing is urgent. I really don't have to be back at any particular time. I didn't realize I would be here this long but it doesn't really matter." They walked for a few more minutes before she spoke again. "In fact, I'm not sure I'm going back."

Jack stopped abruptly. He couldn't believe what he was hearing. *Is she kidding?*

Seeing his startled response, Liz continued. "I told you that I was reading my grandmother's journal. It's been very revealing and confusing. All these years I've believed that she didn't love me but her journal is filled with stories of her love for me. Her attitude toward me changed when my parents were killed, but not for the reason I believed. In her own words, she wrote that she withdrew from me to protect me. She felt that her love was toxic, that she had somehow killed everyone she loved and that her love would in time kill me. It must have been agonizing for her to turn away from her only grandchild without explaining why."

She could see concern in Jack's face as he tried to make sense of her disturbing revelation.

"Anyway, it's caused me to think about staying with her as long as she's alive. I'm not sure she knows me or even realizes I'm there, but *I know* and somehow I'm beginning to have a different feeling toward her. I'm sure that sounds crazy and I can't explain my feelings. I just know I don't want to leave her now."

Jack didn't respond, but he was glad for any reason to delay her return. He knew he was setting himself up for disappointment again but he couldn't help wishing she would stay.

They spent the rest of the afternoon conjecturing about the troubling turnabout in Liz and Elizabeth's relationship. It was late afternoon when they waded into the surf to climb back onto the boat.

"I don't know when I've spent a day doing nothing and felt so relaxed," Liz said as she dodged the breaking waves.

"Doing nothing, huh? Thanks for the compliment."

"You know what I mean," she laughed.

"I do, and actually I do consider it a compliment."

"You should. You've been the perfect partner today." They

had grown very close in the past few weeks, sharing the laidback pace of life on the island and just enjoying each other's presence. Could her feelings for Jack be part of her reason for wanting to stay? *Get a grip, ol' girl. You're a post-middle-aged woman, not a silly teenager.*

As Liz was trying to push away such thoughts, Jack took her in his arms to help her into the boat. His face was very close to hers. He could restrain his impulses no longer and he kissed her—very gently but with deep emotion. For a moment, she looked at him, the glow of the sun setting on the water bathing his ruddy face with golden light.

Careful, ol' girl, she told herself. *Don't let this romance novel setting overpower your good sense.*

Then Jack kissed her again, this time with obvious passion and she didn't turn away.

Without a word, Jack turned and walked back to a dry spot on the beach. Putting her down, he took the blanket from the picnic basket and spread it again on the sand. Stretching out, he took her hand and pulled her down beside him.

At first, she was hesitant. It had been years since she had she been involved with anyone, much less made love. Did you ever forget how or did it come back to you like riding a bicycle? *Not a good comparison,* she thought remembering the difficulty she had the first time she borrowed Olivia's bike to go to the marina. *And what will he think about my body? I work out like an addict but I still have a sixty-plus chassis.*

Sensing her uncertainty, he kissed her hair and held her against his chest. She realized that although his active life had kept him fit, he too had a sixty-plus chassis but his arms still felt like her safe harbor.

When his lips brushed her cheek, she responded with the same eagerness she had felt as a young girl. Then he kissed her again as if the more than forty years since their last embrace had never happened.

With the fading sun painting the sky in shades of copper and gold, two post-middle-aged lovers put aside the years and remembered how much they once loved each other.

Fastened to the Marsh II

Thomas was already lapping up the bowl of milk Olivia gave him each morning when Liz came into the kitchen.

"Good morning," Olivia trilled as she continued arranging colorful zinnias in a crystal vase. "Coffee's still hot and you look like you need it. I didn't hear you come in last night. Good day, huh?"

Liz nodded. Leaning on the countertop, she sipped the hot coffee as she went over in her mind the events of yesterday. In her usual analytical manner, she was trying to be objective in evaluating her disturbing emotions. As a young woman, she had thought her feeling for Jack was just a combination of youthful affection and raging hormones, not enough to build a lasting relationship on. Over the years, when she reflected on her time with him, she became convinced that she had tried to force herself to love him in a romantic way. Now she wasn't sure. She had been very comfortable in his embrace on the beach, but was it real emotion or just the dizzying effect of the moonlight?

As Olivia stepped back to evaluate her creation, Liz blurted out almost without intending to, "Last night, Jack and I made love on the beach."

Olivia held a fuchsia bloom in midair. "Oh," she said, then added it to the bouquet, waiting for Liz to continue.

"He says he still loves me."

"And how do you feel about him?"

"You'll think I'm crazy but I'm almost afraid to care for him. Remember I told you about the other two men in my life and how their deaths almost destroyed me? Even though I realize now that Grandmother thought she was cursed and sacrificed her own happiness because of her love for me, all those years of feeling unloved and rejected took a toll on me. Every time I let myself become involved with a man, he died. I began to feel that God was punishing me, and wanted me to be unhappy. Grandmother would probably have said that I was cursed, too," she said with a sarcastic laugh.

"I don't think I ever considered it was a curse; I just thought I wasn't worthy of being loved. I thought that my own Grandmother didn't love me. And neither did God, for that matter. Do you remember how as kids we both had to go to church every Sunday with Mittie? Well, when I left the island, I gave up all pretense of religion. God and I have continued to be on opposite sides since then."

"I know you've had a bad time, but I wish you didn't blame God for all your suffering. Grannie taught me that God doesn't pick on us or punish us by causing us deliberate pain. Bad things just happen to everybody whether we believe in God or not. Believing just helps us get through the rough spots. He's always been there for me when I'm struggling. After Grannie died, I felt so alone, but God pulled me through. He'd help you too if you'd let Him," Olivia said.

"It's probably a little late now to try to convert me, Liv. Too much water under the bridge as they say, but I've given some thought to what Ben said the other night. I'm not sure how God feels about Johnny-come-latelys but maybe we'll continue the conversation sometime. Anyway, I'm feeling better about everything, now that I understand. Grandmother suffered as much as I did. I'm just sorry she felt she had no other choice. We would both have been spared so much pain."

"So anyway, what about Jack?"

"I don't know. I feel very close to him, almost as if we had not been separated for over forty years. I just don't know if I want to get involved again and I don't want to lead him on. I'm not sure what to do."

"Well, Jack's been managing just fine before you came back. His lifestyle suits him and he seems content. I imagine he'll muddle on with you or without you but I have a strong feeling that he'd prefer *with*. Just don't string him on. He's too nice a guy."

"I understand, and I don't intend to hurt him again. I have

enough guilt about him from before." Refilling her coffee mug, Liz said, "I'm going in the sitting room to attack Grandmother's records again. I can only cope with so much at a time. Call me if you need me."

Satisfied that he had licked every drop of milk from his bowl, Thomas padded after Liz to the sitting room and curled up in the wing chair for his first nap of the morning.

Weeks later, Liz sat on the porch with Olivia and Jack, rocking in rhythm in the old cane rockers.

"Olivia, that was another mighty fine meal," Jack said.

"Jack, you don't have to flatter me. You're welcome at my table anytime," Olivia laughed.

"I'm serious. You are one great cook."

"Well, I don't think Paula Deen is worried, not yet at least."

"You know, in my time I've eaten in some pretty good restaurants but not one of them can hold a candle to your cooking. Did you ever think of opening a restaurant?"

Liz and Olivia exchanged a glance.

"Jack's right, Olivia. You really are a wonderful cook. In fact, I want to talk to you about an idea I've been tossing around. Jack, it involves you too."

"That sounds sinister," Jack joked, propping his feet up on the railing.

"When we were kids and Liz had an idea, I usually got in trouble," Olivia added. "What is it this time?"

Liz walked over to the railing and stood facing her friends.

"You are both so special to me. For weeks you've listened to me agonize over my relationship with my grandmother and vacillate over what to do. It's taken me awhile, but I've made a decision. I'm going to call my firm and tell them I will not be coming back."

Jack stopped rocking and stared at Liz.

"I realize that Grandmother doesn't even know who I am, but I just can't leave her again. She can't live much longer but I want to be with her as long as she is here."

Liz watched their faces. They were both listening with rapt attention for the rest of her idea.

"There's something else, too. Olivia. Do you remember how Mittie used to say that Grandmother and all the women in this family were fastened to the marsh? Well, maybe she was right. Since I've been here, I've watched how content you are with your life. You're fastened to this place and to this marsh. I've struggled all my adult life, just trying to belong somewhere—anywhere. I've come to believe that maybe that place is here. I never realized how much I've missed this island until I came back. Maybe Mittie was right. Maybe I'm fastened to that marsh out there too."

Liz turned and gazed out at the river glimmering in the moonlight. Breathing in the smell of the saltwater, she continued, "Grandmother's will leaves the estate to me but she made generous provision for you, Olivia. Since I've not even been on the property for years, I'm sure she assumed I would sell it and give you first right of refusal. My plan when I came back was to sell as soon as possible and head back to Atlanta, but I didn't understand then what this place means to you and I had no clue what it truly means to me. Everything is so different now. I never want to be out of sight of the marsh again."

Jack and Olivia exchanged a quick glance then looked back at Liz who continued to lay out her plan.

"How would you both feel about turning this place into a Bed and Breakfast Inn? I know it has six bedrooms and only three baths but more baths could be added. Most B and B's just have a few rooms anyway. That's what makes them cozy and appealing. We could even offer intimate gourmet dinners—southern-style, of course. We would be partners. What do you think?"

Olivia hesitated but Jack responded, "That sounds great, but how does a B and B involve me? I'm not really crazy about waiting tables or changing sheets."

"Jack, who knows these islands and the marshes like you do? Who tells a better tale than you? We could offer a taste of the Old South beginning with the founding of the island. We take guests on a picnic cruise to one of the uninhabited islands, tell them the story of the first settlers and the Civil War tales, treat them to Olivia's southern specialties, and then bed them down in antebellum suites. I think it would fly," Liz finished with excitement.

Jack was still too dumbfounded to answer. He couldn't believe his ears. Since the afternoon on the beach, he had been tangled in Liz's spell again. It had taken years to put her out of his mind and now thoughts of her consumed him. He had been grateful that Miss Elizabeth had continued to hold on to life. He felt guilty about that but he hadn't dared hope that Liz would stay once her grandmother died. He was ecstatic to think that she was even considering moving back.

"Well?" Liz said.

He realized that she was staring at him, waiting for his assessment of her idea.

"I think that's the best idea I've heard in ages."

Liz turned to Olivia. "What do you think, Olivia? You'd have your restaurant without having to leave the island."

"I'm stunned. I've wished so many times that I could buy Marsh Oaks and do exactly what you're suggesting, but I didn't think I could manage it by myself. And I didn't envision your wonderful plan for offering such a complete experience. You always were so imaginative! I think it's great," Olivia said as she rose to hug Liz.

"You don't think I'm crazy or that it's too big an undertaking?"

"It will take a lot of work but I do like to stay busy. I was starting to worry a little about what I would do when the Lord calls Miss Elizabeth home. Sounds like that's been taken care of. I'll have plenty to do and I can continue to live here. It's really the only home I've ever known," Olivia said as tears ran down her cheeks.

As they embraced, Liz felt her own tears start to flow.

"Cut that out or you'll have me blubbering," Jack said, putting his arms around the two women as they sobbed happily.

Wiping at the tears on her cheeks, Liz said, "I think this calls for a toast. Let's break open Grandmother's best bottle of brandy. I'm sure there's still some good stuff in the liquor cabinet."

"I'll get it. I know exactly which one," Olivia said, already heading inside the house.

"And bring the best crystal glasses, the ones that Great-great-grandmother Betsy brought back from France. Marsh Oaks Inn deserves the best."

Just then the doorbell rang.

"Who can that be at this time of night?" Olivia said as she turned toward the front door.

"You do approve of the name don't you?" Liz chirped as she threw her arms around Jack in excitement.

"I can't think of a better one." He held her close and kissed her. "Welcome home, Liz. I'm so happy about your decision to come back. I've missed you so." He held her at arm's length so he could see her face. "I know it's too soon to say this but I've never stopped loving you. Do you think you could ever consider marrying again? I'm in on the venture either way, but I love you, Liz, even more than I did when we were kids. You told me then you just weren't ready to marry me. I still want you to be my wife. Do you think you're ready yet?"

Startled by his unexpected proposal, Liz laughed. She too had felt a renewed affection since that day together, but she had been so involved in trying to reach her grandmother and deciding whether to sever her connections with her law firm that she had not allowed herself to consider where their relationship might lead.

But in the moonlight with the heady scent of the marsh in her nostrils, Jack's arms felt like home.

Pulling his face close to hers, she whispered, "Yes, Jack, I think I'm ready now."

They were still in each other's arms when Olivia returned with the brandy and Ben Smith.

Releasing Liz, Jack laughed. "You caught us smooching. Just like you did when we were kids."

"Good evening, Ben," Liz said, blushing. "It's good to see you but it's a little late for a pastoral visit, isn't it?"

"Well, actually I was making an official visit down the road, but this is purely a social call. I come to see Miss Elizabeth as a chaplain, but I come to visit Olivia as a friend."

Olivia was smiling as she busied herself with the tray of glasses. "I told Ben about the new venture while we were getting the brandy. He thinks it's great."

"In that case, share a toast with us," Jack said, noticing that the silver tray held four glasses.

Opening the bottle, he poured the dark liquor into the exquisite glasses and handed one to each of the women then to Ben. Raising his, he said, "We were about to drink to the future Marsh Oaks Inn. But Olivia, while you were gone, another occasion for a toast developed. After only 45 years, Miss Elizabeth Briggs is finally ready to become my wife. You two are the first to know."

Olivia shrieked and threw her arms around them both. "I just knew it would happen."

As Ben shook hands with Jack, Olivia hugged Liz. "I knew you always loved Jack but you just had to get a taste of the world. I watched him after you left and saw how brokenhearted he was. And I've watched you both since you came back, both of you thinking that you were too old for romance. Ben and I just prayed that the two of you would see the light. You've wasted all those years, but you can make up for it now. Congratulations to you both! The Lord does work in mysterious ways, doesn't He?"

"I guess it's never too late as long as we're still breathing," Liz said remembering her words to Olivia earlier. "And Ben, I think I'm ready to continue our discussion when you have some time."

"I'll make time for that, Liz."

Setting down his glass, Jack took Liz's hand. "How about we stroll down to the dock and watch the submarine races?" he said, repeating one of the lines he used as a teenager to get a girl alone.

"Do you think I'm still naïve enough to fall for that?" Liz replied.

"I hope so," he said with a big boyish grin.

"You kids have fun," Ben laughed, putting his arm around Olivia's shoulder. "I have something to talk over with this pretty lady too."

Fastened to the Marsh At Last

The next morning Olivia told Liz that she and Ben were also considering marriage. "It's a little scary," Olivia confessed. "I had a big crush on Ben as a girl but I thought it was one-sided. I've never even had a really serious relationship and now I'm thinking about marriage, at my age."

Liz started to speak but Olivia interrupted, "I know. It's never too late."

In the following weeks, Liz continued her efforts to reach her grandmother, to penetrate the fog that surrounded her demented mind. Olivia watched without comment as her friend became more frustrated with her inability to coax a response from the almost comatose woman. But Elizabeth Mathews remained unresponsive.

On a warm late summer evening, Liz tried once again to tell her grandmother of her love and forgiveness. After emptying the crystal goblet one slow teaspoon at a time, she placed the glass on the table and walked to the window already open to the gentle breeze from the water.

God was directing the regular late afternoon show across the river. The huge orange ball was hanging just over the marsh, bathing the horizon with a golden glow. Overhead gulls screeched as they rode the air currents in aimless spirals looking for prey. A Great Blue Heron strolled along the water's edge, stalking the small fish just below the surface as they chased even smaller species. The same drama had played out unchanged for millions of years, the drama that controlled the rhythms of her life, just as it controlled the setting sun and the wildlife.

Before returning the tray to the kitchen, she settled back in the chair, discouraged and becoming convinced that she would never be able to reach to her grandmother.

"How I wish you could understand me, Grandmother. I want so much for you to know that I love you, and I know you love me. I remember now how close we were. I thought my vague memories were childish fantasies but they were real. I remember dressing up and having tea with you. I remember you telling me stories and singing my favorite song over and over. Do you remember, too?" Then leaning close to the frail woman and taking her hand, she started to sing the song they had shared so many years ago.

> *"I'm a poor wayfaring stranger,*
> *travelin' through this lonely land.*
> *I am goin' over Jordan.*
> *I am goin' over home."*

The old woman's body tensed, her eyelids fluttered and she opened her eyes. Her face was still expressionless but in her eyes, Liz saw a brief flash of recognition. Almost imperceptibly, she muttered in a dry, raspy voice, "Elizabeth."

Dropping to her knees, Liz answered, "Yes, Grandma, it's me—Elizabeth. Elizabeth Brinson, your granddaughter. Oh, thank you, God. Thank you." Lowering her head to rest on the woman's chest, she allowed the tears she had held inside for over fifty years to wash away all the pain of the unloved child.

Jan Durham Biography

A native of Savannah, Jan Durham spent most of her adult life in Atlanta after earning her B.S. in Secondary Education from Georgia Southern, but she has never lost her love for her roots in the marshes of coastal Georgia.

She attended Candler School of Theology and after ordination as a clergy member of the United Methodist Church focused on issues of aging and congregational care. She has been a volunteer chaplain with hospice and started an adult day center for families coping with Alzheimer's disease.

She is the author of *After the Example of Christ*, a model for servant ministry by and for older adults, published through the General Board of Discipleship and used in congregations throughout the United Methodist Church. She also co-authored a manual on congregational respite care with the Georgia Department of Aging and the Georgia Alzheimer's Association.

Jan now lives on Skidaway Island on the Georgia coast where the 19th century graves of a woman and her infant son enclosed in a tabby wall inspired her historical novel *Fastened to the Marsh*. She continues her involvement with the Alzheimer's Association and hospice.

She is a member of the Landings Writers' Group and Rosemary Daniell's Zona Rosa Writer's Group. She is currently working on a second novel set on Sapelo Island.

She can be reached at jandurham@Bonaventture.com
www.Bonaventture.com/fastenedtothemarsh/htm

Fastened to the Marsh
Questions for Discussion

1. The title *Fastened to the Marsh* was inspired by lines from Sidney Lanier's "Marshes of Glynn." Watching the marsh-hen build her nest in the marsh grass, the poet is inspired by her trust in nature. He realizes that he too receives strength from nature, in particular the timeless tidal marsh. How do you understand the relationship between the marsh-hen and the characters in the novel?

2. Each of the characters is "fastened to the marsh" as a source of strength and comfort. Where do you find strength and comfort?

3. What is the importance of setting in the novel?

4. Characters in the novel respond to the traumatic events in their lives in a variety of ways. Some view them as God's punishment, others as circumstances to be overcome. How does the maxim, "What cannot be bested must be borne" contribute to the storyline?

5. Do you agree with Elizabeth Mathews' actions toward her granddaughter?

6. "Better to have loved and lost than never to have loved at all." When we love, we risk losing that love. Although the women suffered because they loved, do you think they considered loving worth the risk? Do you?

7. Liz felt rejected as a child and spent her life searching for a sense of belonging. She tried to escape from her heritage; Olivia chose to perpetuate hers. Contrast the life styles of the two women, their choices, and their ultimate satisfaction with their lives.